Rules of Engagement

ALWAYS FAITHFUL

CAITLYN WILLOWS

Always Faithful
ISBN # 978-1-78686-322-5
©Copyright Caitlyn Willows 2017
Cover Art by Posh Gosh ©Copyright August 2017
Interior text design by Claire Siemaszkiewicz
Totally Bound Publishing

ALWAYS
FAITHFUL

Prologue

Staff Sergeant Rowan McKinley studied the steel warehouse from every angle she could see. Since her only viewpoint was from Charlie's battered old truck, that wasn't easy. The security lights being out made it doubly hard. There wasn't another person around or any sign of another vehicle. No activity whatsoever. Everyone and everything was tucked away for the evening, as it should be at midnight.

She glanced at the man beside her. The darkness kept her from seeing his face clearly, but she knew it would be lit with excitement. For lack of a better term, she could almost smell the testosterone in the air. *Or is that beer?* She'd swear he'd been drinking, even if she didn't want to admit that to herself.

It was all Rowan could do to keep from shaking. What in the world had she been thinking to come here? She was a legal specialist, not an MP, not CID and certainly not NCIS. Her stubborn determination to prove herself right had gotten her into this mess — a dangerous mess at that. And if Charlie *had* been drinking, she had been even stupider to get into a vehicle with him.

Rowan wiped her sweaty palms on her camouflage trousers. Her heart pounded so hard she'd swear he could hear it.

Where were her priorities? She had a child to think about. Why should she care if someone was stealing government property? She'd reported her suspicions to anyone and everyone who would listen. Why in the world couldn't she have left it at that? She'd done her duty.

But no... Like a modern-day *Don Quixote*, she'd had to go tilting at windmills. All things considered, her sanity was as questionable as that foolish old coot's.

She studied the hulking white building once more. No guards walking their posts. It looked quiet enough—safe, despite the lack of security lights. It should have put her at ease, but it only set her nerves on edge.

"Charlie, I don't like this. It doesn't seem right. I think we should leave."

He chuckled and gave her a playful slug on the arm. "You're being silly." After drawing his pistol, he slid from the truck and silently made his way to the building. *Easy to be brave when you're a walking giant.*

Rowan frowned when he walked inside. The door wasn't even locked. Now that was odd. *Too easy. A trap?* Possibly. Charlie was too gung-ho or too inebriated to notice—or maybe he embraced the challenge, the danger, the rush.

Rowan glanced around. She was a sitting target.

She searched the floorboard debris of to-go cups for something to use as a weapon. Nothing, not even a floor mat. For one brief second, she considered cranking the engine and getting out of there but dismissed the cowardly plan. She would not leave Charlie. They were safer together.

Curling her fingers around the door handle, she shoved her shoulder against the truck door. It groaned as it opened, announcing her presence to anyone who might have doubted it before.

Crouching low, Rowan ran to the building and ducked inside. Darkness enveloped her. Pitch black. Smothering. Her heartbeat thudded in her ears. Panic clutched at her stomach. In vain, she fought the claustrophobia, the overwhelming fear, the need to battle her way free and the urge to scream out her frustration.

Arms wrapped around her midsection. She stood frozen and lost. She heard scuffling off to her right. There was a blur—a sense rather than sight of movement. Then pain shattered through her head.

Chapter One

Always faithful. *Semper Fi.* Captain Phillip Stuart shook his head at the term. 'Faithful' didn't include forcing yourself on young girls or stealing cash out of a platoon buddy's locker when they were out to sea on a training mission.

What has the Marine Corps come to? Thieves, murderers and rapists? The lot of them should be taken out and shot.

Of course, doing so would put military lawyers out of a job. Heaven forbid the little slime balls didn't get a fair trial. Phillip was eternally grateful he no longer dealt with defense cases.

Shifting slightly on the hard courtroom chair, he straightened his papers and listened to the continuing drone of the defense attorney's voice as she pled her client's case. He didn't know why she bothered. The look on the jurors' faces indicated they had already found him guilty. It didn't matter what extenuating or mitigating matters she threw out. Her client would go to jail for a very long time. He shifted again and let the squeaking wooden chair show his annoyance.

Laura Cushing shot him a glare from where she stood before the members. *Good.* He'd broken her concentration. Not easy to do. She was a tough opponent. But this long, drawn-out trial was stretching all their nerves to the breaking point.

After a few closing words, Laura sat, looking satisfied with herself. She was good. He was better.

Phillip stretched to his full six-four height and flexed his shoulders. With all the stealth of a jaguar stalking its prey, he approached the center of the courtroom.

Intimidate the witness. Impress the members. That was half the battle. A deep breath, a casual glance toward his opponent's table, then…

He attacked, going straight to the heart of the case. He dissected Laura's defense point by point, pulling apart the pieces with the precision of a surgeon. He let his words drift into the minds of those military members seated as the jury. Then, with the same lack of speed, he resumed his seat. The chair groaned under his weight.

Phillip sliced a glance at the defense table. The accused sat there, a fresh-faced young man all of nineteen. His big hands were clasped before him as if in prayer. It set Phillip's teeth on edge. *What right does he have to pray?* Those young girls had begged and prayed before he'd forced himself on them. Had he listened?

Laura snapped to her feet and marched forward to take his place. It was no use. All the golden words she summoned could not save her client. Phillip knew it and so did she. After thirty minutes of deliberation, the members of the jury and the rest of the courtroom had realized it, too.

Phillip listened to the sentence with smug satisfaction. Twenty-five years at Leavenworth. That was what he called justice, although castration might not be a bad idea either.

In the back of the courtroom, one set of parents cried while the others — those of the victims — sighed with relief. The accused — the guilty — let his head drop. It was the only display of emotion he showed. No tears. No regrets. He didn't flinch. Phillip fought the urge to demand to know if the man felt remorse for anyone but himself.

Once the judge had left the courtroom, the prisoner escort came in. Then the young Marine started bawling. Yeah, he had regrets — that he'd been caught. His father refused to look his way while his mother rushed to his side. She wrapped her arms around him in a hug he refused to return.

Rather than watch the guy be hauled away in shackles, Phillip celebrated his victory with a cigar on the back steps of the military justice building. How many times had he reflected on past and future glories in such a way? Lately, though, the battles left his stomach sour, more often than not.

There wasn't much he hadn't heard over his career. Most of it sickened rather than shocked him. Now, prosecuting the rabble of the Marine Corps tired him. Time to reach for the next rung on the ladder.

After graduating law school, he'd thought the way had shone clear, focused, his career path set. He shook his head. His goals had been regimented at the time. They had been all he'd had — a means to forget.

Unfortunately, they were still all he had. Phillip wasn't sure he wanted those same goals anymore.

The door opened behind him. A rush of cool air brushed over his shoulders and back then stopped when the door closed. Phillip knew without looking that it was Laura. He could smell her perfume — an elusive scent that evoked memories of a long-ago time and someone else he wished he could forget.

She dusted off the step and eased down beside him, careful not to snag her hose on the concrete. Resting her forearms on her knees, she stared ahead.

"Congratulations. Another victory for the great and powerful Phillip Stuart."

He chewed on his cigar and absorbed the view of the gray mountains surrounding Camp Pendleton.

"Sarcasm, Laura? How unlike you."

"Cut the crap. That boy didn't deserve twenty-five years in prison and you know it."

"Please save me the she-asked-for-it speech. You didn't have to listen to the sobs each and every time those girls told their stories before trial. Don't tell me it was faked every time. I know better."

She tilted her head his way. "Come on, Phillip. He's only nineteen, still a teenager himself. It was consensual. Daddy caught them and she cried rape. If that girl shed tears, it was only because she got caught. This has been nothing but a witch hunt with an excellent cast of performers. The girl's past conduct showed that."

"Irrelevant. Forensics evidence proved their story."

"It proved they had sex. There was no evidence to support assault of any kind."

"We're not talking about one girl here. We're talking about six. There's no way you're ever going to convince anyone all six of them were lying. Get your bleeding-heart head out of the sand, Laura. We've had this discussion before. It's over. Case closed."

"Obviously, but have you asked yourself this? When you were nineteen, can you honestly say you could resist the charms of a willing sixteen-year-old?"

He leveled a frosty stare her way.

Laura gave an exaggerated wince. "What *was* I thinking? How *dare* I suggest you would be less than perfect?" She slowly shook her head and gave a soft, humorless laugh. "You are the most handsome man I've ever met — Mister Perfect, aristocratic features, golden hair. Poster Marine all the way. But you're dead inside. You have no feelings, no compassion. Your eyes are the coldest gray I've ever seen — like a frozen pond in the dead of winter. I pity the woman who winds up with you."

He blew a puff of smoke into the air. "I take it then that you're saying it's really over between us?"

She gave a small, bitter laugh. "Don't flatter yourself and don't play that game with me. It's been *over* for quite some time now. It was never anything more than an occasional dinner with a friend, as far as I'm concerned."

But the remorse in her eyes told a different story. He had regrets, too. He'd wanted her to be the one to erase the memory of another, to make him love and care and see goodness in the world once more. In the end she, like the few other women he'd dated over the last nine years, fell short of that need. She had been a stand-in, nothing more. Comparing Laura to —

No. Don't go there. It hurt too much. It always did. If he lived to be a hundred, he doubted the pain and bitterness would ever die.

Phillip looked away to give her some shred of dignity. Or was it to hide the guilt seeping to the surface like a festering wound?

Laura pushed to her feet and slipped quietly inside the building.

He ground out his cigar on the cement steps and returned to his office. Victory no longer tasted sweet. Behind his gray metal desk, some stability returned.

His gaze drifted around his office, taking in the mementos of his career with the Marine Corps — his Amphibious Warfare School awards, the jump school medals in their rosewood frame, a souvenir shirt commemorating his time served in the Mediterranean aboard the USS Boxer. If there was an opportunity, he'd taken it. Anything to further his career. Somehow it still wasn't enough. Even though his career was flourishing, he felt an emptiness he could not define.

The small picture of his family shoved into the corner of his desk caught his eye. The four Stuarts stood together at his graduation from Naval Justice School, looking uncomfortable. His father exuding aristocratic disapproval. His mother and sister Claudia smiled uncertainly as the camera caught them in such an atypical family moment.

They'd never understood why he'd had to do it — why he'd turned his back on the Stuart fortune. Phillip hadn't bothered to explain. The year before, Claudia had come to the same realizations he had. Like her brother, it had taken a broken heart to open her eyes.

He turned the picture face down. On second thought, he shoved it into his drawer under a pile of paperwork. With everything else going through his mind, the last thing he needed to resurrect was his relationship with his family — particularly his father.

"Excuse me, sir?" His clerk stuck his head in through the office door. "There's a package for you. It just arrived from the Commanding General at Twentynine Palms. Must be important because they made sure I signed for it."

Phillip tore his gaze from the closed drawer. "Thanks, Corporal."

He shut his mind to his family and accepted the bulky envelope. Once the door closed, he rummaged through the desk for his platinum letter opener, a concession gift from his father upon graduation from law school. Phillip kept hoping someone would steal it.

Then why keep the damn thing? The answer came too quickly. It was a trophy — a reminder of what his father was and what Phillip prayed he would never be.

With a flick of his wrist, he sliced open the envelope. The contents slid out onto the desktop and bold type near the middle of the page leaped out at him.

The accused, Staff Sergeant Rowan A. McKinley, requests your presence as independent military counsel...

Phillip's face drained of color. His gut twisted. Breathing was out of the question.

Odd, when he had been thinking of her only minutes before. But then, when didn't he think of her?

Beautiful, talented Rowan McKinley... The one woman he held up against the others. The one who hadn't bothered to return his heart before she'd walked out of his life.

What the hell is she doing in the Marine Corps? More importantly, what had she done to need the services of a Marine defense attorney?

Time stopped as he grappled for the stack of papers — or maybe it took a giant step back. In either event, Phillip couldn't put two coherent thoughts together. Before he could read on, the door to his office flew open. The tan, inquiring face of his best friend and fellow attorney, Captain Zachary Taylor, poked around the doorjamb.

"I got a call from a friend of mine at the base in Twentynine Palms. There's been a murder involving a staff sergeant, some woman by the name of — "

"McKinley," Phillip muttered. Afraid Zach would see the true depth of his feelings, he kept his gaze locked on the papers. "The case has been offered to me."

Zach lunged for the papers, snatching them out of Phillip's grasp. "Well, aren't you Mr. Popularity. Let's have a look-see."

He scanned the request form, eyes widening. "Why you? You're not a defense counsel. This staff sergeant could have any military attorney at that base or even a civilian lawyer, providing she could afford one."

Zach glanced up before Phillip could mask his feelings. The teasing stopped as Zach's deep brown eyes narrowed with suspicion. He knew Phillip too well. *A definite downfall in having a best friend.*

"What is she to you?"

"What *was* she, you mean." Phillip met Zach's steady gaze with one of his own. "She was once the most important person in my life." His mouth twisted and he whispered, "The bitch."

Zach tossed the papers back to the desk. "That's funny. I've known you for over eight years and you've never mentioned her." He dropped into the chair across from Phillip, resting his feet on the edge of the desk. "Why the big secret? What's the story?"

Phillip sighed and copied his friend's position. Zach's ability to focus on and unearth information was uncanny. Now those relentless abilities were focused in his direction. He forced a deep breath and sketched out his turbulent history with Rowan McKinley.

* * * *

Rowan drew her knees up against her chest and wrapped her arms around them in an effort to control her shaking. Nine hours of confinement in this tiny cell and she still hadn't been allowed to speak with or see anyone — not that they would listen to her, anyway.

Fools.

She took pride in her work. Her record reflected that. Legal administration might not be the blood and guts of the Corps, but it was important. Every separation, every investigative report that crossed her desk was dissected until nothing was left in question. So why would her word be doubted when she suspected foul play in the Lava training area?

Imagining things. That was what Rowan had been told over and over again, despite the five seemingly unrelated incidents that had come across her desk in the last month. Only Charlie would listen and now he was dead.

She was sure the command would see she was right, but the finger of blame was now pointed in her direction.

Rowan rested her head on her knees then winced as the bruised and swollen side of her face protested at the contact. Rocking back and forth on the metal-framed cot, she tried to quell the panic that threatened to overwhelm her. It was so close in the holding cell and she was so alone.

"Stop it!" She pushed the words through clenched teeth. "This isn't going to help you at all."

She flicked her gaze to the camera mounted in the corner of the room on the other side of the cell partition. Its baleful eye watched her every motion, allowing her no privacy. This portion of the room was small, too small. The cell's dimensions barely spanned ten feet across. Even the dim light in the hallway didn't help.

Rowan closed her eyes. *Breathe. Take deep breaths. No hyperventilating.*

Phillip was her only chance at getting out of this. She had to be strong—strong enough to endure the claustrophobia closing in, strong enough to face *him* again.

Phillip. She had forgotten nothing about him. How could she when she lived with his image every day? The way the sun gleamed off his golden head, the ready smile and his eyes.

God, those eyes! They could burn like quicksilver when his temper flared or glow a soft, satiny gray when they made love.

She was probably a fool for contacting him after all these years. But there was no doubt she needed his help and she would accept whatever consequences resulted from having him back in her life. Only Phillip could save her now. That was, if he accepted her request for his services.

The hallway door opened. The roar of the evaporative coolers lessened. A military policeman walked in and glared at her through the bars. "Your request for counsel has been expedited. They're waiting for the captain to either accept or decline the case."

"How long will that take?" Rowan fought in vain to keep the quiver from her voice. "When will I be able to contact my family?"

"You work in legal. You tell me." He lowered his voice. "Frankly, I hope you get what you deserve. He was a friend of mine, murderer."

He slammed the door in his exit, putting pressure back on the cooler. The roar this time was nothing compared to the pulse of blood in her ears.

"Yeah, he was a friend of mine, too," Rowan replied to no one.

She tucked herself into the farthest corner of the cot, her despair as smothering as the walls surrounding her.

Chapter Two

The sound of the Jeep's tires scattering gravel jolted Phillip from his thoughts. Zach roared up to the rented bungalow, jerking his vehicle to a sliding stop in front of the carport.

Phillip gripped the edges of the armrest to keep from being launched head first into the windshield. "You *will* let me know when you bring the ride to a complete stop, won't you?"

"Sorry, old man." Zach grinned. "Just remember to keep your arms and legs inside the car at all times and you'll be fine." His humor faded. "If you decide to —"

Phillip cut off further discussion with a slice of his hand. "I'll let you know."

He swung his legs over the edge and jumped from the Jeep, then drew in a deep breath of ocean-salted air. "I just need to think about this case." He scowled. "And thirty-three is *not* old."

Smiling once more, Zach sketched a mock-salute and tore out of the driveway, leaving Phillip in a small cloud of dust as he dug into his pocket for house keys.

The rent for the small, one-bedroom cottage was high, especially for the ocean view, but the solitude was worth the cost. It overlooked the Pacific from a cliff-side perch. A small rocky pathway was the only access point down to the beach. Everything was quiet except for the rustle of the encircling palms and the faint crash of the sea on the rocks below. In fact, the house was *unusually* silent.

Phillip eased the key in, unlocked the door and slipped into the front hallway without a sound. Cocking his head, he strained his ears against the quiet. A sudden yet faint noise from the kitchen at the back of the cottage brought his head up.

He crept through the living room and paused at the door to the kitchen. It was ajar. Rustling noises reached him from within, punctuated by a *crunch-crunch*. He narrowed his eyes and shoved his shoulder into the door, flinging it wide.

"Oscar!"

The mangled remains of a garbage bag lay in the center of the kitchen, its contents strewn across the linoleum floor from wall to wall. In the center of the mess lay the object of Phillip's ire. The large gray Weimaraner was frozen in place, tongue extended in the act of licking the last morsels of chili out of a discarded tin can.

With a bark of pure joy, Oscar leaped to his feet and jumped at Phillip. His stubby tail wagged furiously and his food-stained muzzle smeared a trail of chili grease all over the front of his master's once-immaculate courtroom uniform.

"Down, Oscar!" Phillip tried to push eighty-five pounds of exuberance off his chest. "Damnation, dog. You are the most ill-behaved beast I've ever had the misfortune to own. I ought to drop you off at the nearest zoo. I'd swear you're as big as an elephant, anyway, and definitely the right color."

He paused in mid-shout, looking into Oscar's love-filled amber eyes. *Useless.* With all the emphasis Phillip placed on rules and order in every part of his life, he had failed miserably with this particular facet. He supposed the unconditional affection Oscar gave was more than enough compensation for his dog's habit of rooting around in every garbage pail he could find. Besides, it was his fault for not taking out the trash before he'd gone to work.

He sighed and gave Oscar's head an affectionate scratch then cleaned up the aftermath of the dog's afternoon snack.

Later that evening, Phillip sat out on top of the carport in a lawn chair, watching a blood-red sun sink into the calm Pacific Ocean. In one hand, he held a snifter of vintage cognac — a gift from his sister that he was sure had set her back more than a few dollars. In the other, the legal paperwork from Twentynine Palms. Oscar lay at the foot of the carport ladder, occasionally issuing a gusty sigh and looking woebegone at having been left below.

Phillip thought of Rowan and the agony she had caused when she'd left him without a word nine years before. He shook his head and winced at the memories.

I was a fool to trust her.

He went over the paperwork for the umpteenth time and weighed the possibilities of the case. What attorney wouldn't drool over a murder case, no matter which side they took?

"What do you think, Oscar? This case is going to be a big one for whomever takes it. It will make them a major player, if you'll pardon the pun." His mouth twisted in a cynical smile at the idea of being promoted to major.

Oscar tilted his head and his stubby tail shook his backside as he gazed up at Phillip.

"What's she doing in the Marine Corps, boy? I don't know how she knew where I was or what I was doing. She's supposed to be a teacher, not a staff sergeant."

But then, hadn't his career choice also changed from those crazy college days? Dreams were one thing. Reality was another.

He took another swallow of cognac, feeling his thoughts drift off to the first time he'd met the lovely Rowan McKinley.

It had been a perfect September day in Washington, D.C., and like a lot of his law school classmates, Phillip had gone down to the park-like expanse of the Mall to lie on the grass, bask in the warm sun and try to get some homework done amid the bustling din of the visiting tourists and sun-worshipping students.

A misguided Frisbee had changed all that. His anger over being smacked square in the face by the flying projectile had faded when he'd caught a glimpse of the long, bare legs of its owner. That memory still managed to steal his breath and arouse him more than he could handle.

He closed his eyes and saw her again.

She had been beautiful, with shining, waist-length hair the color of new copper and tall — taller than most girls he knew, almost six feet, he would later discover. Her long, coltish legs had been lightly tan and had sprinklings of freckles.

His gaze had traveled upward, past her slim hips and gently rounded breasts to her face, elfin in shape with a slightly pointed chin and small, delicate nose. She had anxiously watched him with golden-brown eyes as she'd repeated a question that he had not heard and to this day could not recall. He'd been too mesmerized by her tending to his bleeding cheek with the worn blue bandanna she'd pulled from her slender neck.

It had been the beginning of the wildest, most wonderful and most heartbreaking affair of his life. After nine years, he still agonized over those memories. To let her back into his life now? It was personal suicide. Yet, professionally, it could be the *coup de grace* of his career—that next rung on the ladder, the next challenge he was looking for.

He swallowed the rest of the cognac and climbed down to scratch an ecstatic Oscar behind the ears.

"Well, boy, what do you think? Do I save the only woman I've ever loved or let her rot in jail for walking out on me nine years ago?"

Oscar whined and dragged a wet lick across Phillip's face. With a laugh, he wrestled the dog to the ground, tickling his belly. "You're right, boy. This is just another assignment, not a trip down memory lane."

Oscar jumped to his feet and barked.

"All right, big guy. One good run down the beach, but then I've got some work to do."

* * * *

Rowan tugged the olive-drab blanket around her shoulders, not that she needed it. Desert heat combined with rising humidity made the cell's evaporative cooling worthless. The wool made it worse. Still, she clung to it in the hope that it would provide some measure of security, however small.

Every muscle in her body ached from the killer's attack the night before and the MPs manhandling during her arrest. She tried to shut her eyes against the walls that closed in around her but flashed them open at the slightest sound.

She focused on the roar of the coolers, hoping it would drown out other noise. Then she found herself cursing the blasted thing. She needed to hear, needed to be alert. With night approaching, she wouldn't put it past the guard to try something.

A month ago, she never would have suggested such a thing. Now she knew better. One of their own—a military policeman—was dead. Justice was not an option. Revenge could be. Any action taken against her would be conveniently swept under the carpet. It was a terrible feeling to suspect conspiracy everywhere, yet finding herself behind bars had stolen the last of her optimism.

Rowan's stomach rumbled. Throughout the day, she'd refused meals out of fear of what they might contain. She would not allow hunger pangs to win now. She had to hold out a little longer. Another clenching of her stomach muscles made her wince and she shifted uncomfortably on the lumpy mattress.

Voices in the hallway outside the door drifted to her cell. Rowan raised her head, heart pounding, expecting to see Phillip's tall form. Disappointment plunged her spirits when the door swung open and she saw one of the defense counsels from her own office.

She doubted Captain Connors ever cracked a smile. He was always worrying about all those around him. A father-protector barely in his thirties, here he was rushing to her aid, his serious face interrupted only by the nervous habit of shoving his gold wire-rimmed glasses up the bridge of his nose.

He waited until the escorting MP left. Once the outer door slammed shut, he walked forward and curled his fingers around the bars of her prison.

"I came to see how you were doing."

"I've certainly been better. Have you heard anything from Captain Stuart?"

"Nothing yet, but it's still early," Captain Connors replied. "Look, Staff Sergeant McKinley...Rowan. If it matters, there isn't a soul in the office who believes you did this. If you would just let one of us help you—"

"I want Captain Stuart."

"He's an arrogant, obnoxious son of a bitch."

Captain Stuart perhaps, but not her Phillip. How little they knew of him. Still, people did change with time.

"A son of a bitch who has never lost a case his entire career in either defense or prosecution, sir. If you were going to be tried for murder, wouldn't you want those odds on your side?"

He sighed. "Yeah, I guess I would. Because you are part of our office, a prosecutor has already been appointed from Camp Pendleton—Captain Laura Cushing, a real crackerjack. She's been up against Stuart before and knows his strategy."

"You talk as if you believe he'll take the case."

"A climber like him wouldn't turn it down. It's too high profile, which is also probably why Laura Cushing agreed. Win or lose, any attorney involved will be watched closely, their performance evaluated. That kind of promotion potential is hard to resist."

"Even for you, sir?"

"Especially for me, because I want to help you. We all do."

"I'll keep that in mind if Captain Stuart refuses."

He pushed away from the bars. "Your mother is on her way to see you. I'll let you know when I hear something."

Rowan watched his departure. With her head tilted, she listened for the sound of her mother's approach.

Her mom entered the cellblock alone an hour later. Her status as a civilian did not warrant the courtesy of an escort. She appeared upset and panicked. When she entered the small room and stopped before the barred enclosure, Rowan longed to throw herself into her mother's arms.

Emma McKinley could normally pass for a woman ten to fifteen years younger. Rowan had always hoped she'd inherited those genes. Her mother was trim and took care of herself. She still had the power to turn heads of all ages. But tonight, worry made her look all of her fifty-two years then some.

Stumbling to the bars, she grasped the loving hands that reached for her.

"Oh, Mom—"

"Hush, sweetheart. I came as soon as I could. Why in the world did you have to go snooping? Couldn't you leave well enough alone?" Her gaze took in the livid bruise coloring Rowan's cheek and she winced.

"You haven't been asked to give any statements yet, have you?"

"No, honey, not yet." Mom seemed upset and understandably so. "I still think you should talk with your colonel. Tell him what you told me—your theories about your friend's death."

"I've tried, Mom, but everyone thinks my hypotheses are pretty far-fetched."

Her mother opened her mouth.

Rowan interrupted. "Please, Mom. I know what you're going to say, but you going to the colonel to explain isn't going to help, either. I've been targeted because I know too much about something. If the word gets out that you know what I know, that person or persons could target you, as well."

She reached through the bars to grab her mother's arms. "Please, promise me you'll let me take care of this my way."

Uncertainty written on her face, her mom nodded.

"Good." Rowan forced a smile. "Ian should get back from his camping trip sometime Friday."

"Unless they drive the Cub Scout master crazy before then."

Rowan's fake smile faded. "I want you to get Ian and leave Twentynine Palms right away."

Mom gave a barely perceptible sigh. "Aren't you being a bit ridiculous? For one thing, I need to be here to support you. For another, I have a good job and don't intend to leave it."

"Especially when it could wind up being our only means of support if I get court-martialed out of the Marine Corps and sent to jail?"

"Being realistic never hurt. How many times have you said that yourself?"

Rowan bit back tears. "But, Mom, you don't understand—"

"I understand all too well. I'm not going to run away and hide Ian while you fight this battle alone. You need us both here to support you. Plus, it's time to face up to the past. You knew that when you asked for Phillip's help. When he learns he has an eight-year-old son, you'll be lucky if he doesn't find a way to put you in jail himself."

Rowan let the tears fall. Her mother was right. With or without Phillip, she was damned. She was relying on his professionalism to save her and, in exchange, expected his undying hatred.

"I won't hide Ian for you, Rowan. The boy needs his father. No matter what Phillip may have done, you should have found a way to tell him from the start. You should have—"

"Stormed the walls of Castle Stuart. Yes, I know, but I didn't. What do you intend to do? March Ian to him the instant Phillip appears?" Rowan rubbed at the tears that continued to make tracks down her dirty face.

She saw her mom's golden eyes, so like her own, glimmer with irritation. "I didn't say that, but I certainly can't disguise or hide Ian while Phillip is here. My God, Rowan, the boy is the image of his father—or had you forgotten that?"

Forgotten? Not for an instant. Ian was the constant reminder of the emptiness in her heart.

"Phillip will find out soon enough," her mother said. "If not from someone in your office then surely the minute he gets a look at your record book."

Rowan cursed her own stupidity. How could she have forgotten about her military records? True, Phillip would discover her lie, but it had to be from her first. She had to have the chance to explain things before he read about Ian in her personnel file.

The door opened once more. Rowan turned and offered a weak smile. It was Captain Connors, looking tired and a little rumpled.

"Sir, I thought you had called it a night."

"Just wanted to check on a few things at the office first. A fax was waiting for me. Captain Stuart accepted. He'll be here in time for your confinement hearing tomorrow."

Rowan sagged against the cell bars. "Thank you, sir. There's one more thing I need before he gets here. A favor, sir."

"Sure, what's that?"

"I need you to remove something from my military record book."

Chapter Three

Entering a California Desert Conservation Area.

The faded brown sign flashed past at seventy miles per hour, and on cue, the dry heat slammed into Phillip. He shook his head over the irony of the situation. His car was in the shop because the air conditioner didn't work and he hadn't had time to fix it. *So, what does the government give me to drive? A vehicle with a broken air conditioner. Typical government efficiency.*

Should have left well enough alone.

At least in his '65 Mustang he could have put the top down.

A bead of sweat trickled down his back. At this rate, he'd be drenched by the time he reached Twentynine Palms.

Phillip peeled his arm off the edge of the door. He was lucky to be working on this case at all. His colonel had been reluctant to let two attorneys from his legal office go at the same time. Sending Laura as a prosecutor was one thing. The counsel in Twentynine Palms were too familiar with Rowan, but anyone could defend her.

It had taken an hour of fast-talking to convince his colonel of how important this case was to Phillip's career. Finally, the man had relented. Phillip could go. In the event the colonel might change his mind, Phillip hadn't hesitated to make a hasty departure.

Just thinking about the opportunity brought a rush of adrenaline that made his heart race and his body tense with anticipation. He hadn't felt this way about his work in a long time. This trial would put him over the top. His career would be golden from this time on — *if* he could prove his case. *Rowan's* case.

He also admitted to a certain curiosity. What would Rowan look like after nine years? What kind of person had she become?

He glanced at his watch. In less than two hours, the military magistrate would decide whether or not to transport Rowan to the brig in Miramar to await trial. With a murder charge, there usually wasn't much of a decision to make.

Phillip doubted this Captain Connors was experienced enough to prevent it. From what he could find out, Connors had been out of Naval Justice School less than a year. No wonder Rowan had asked for more experienced counsel.

He thought of Rowan imprisoned — the overwhelming fear she would experience once cooped up — and he refused to allow that to happen. *Nope.* No pretrial confinement for his Rowan.

Phillip stopped himself short. She wasn't *his* Rowan, and hadn't been for a long time. He needed to remember that. Whatever they'd had in the past had to remain there. Objectivity was paramount to victory.

He jammed down on the accelerator and turned onto the exit for Twentynine Palms. The mountain pass beckoned beyond, its rocky landscape dotted with sage and mesquite. City smog and haze melted away, leaving a sky so blue it hurt his eyes.

Plunging into the portal to the high desert, he leaned in to the curves as the little white car chugged with slow determination upward through the pass. At the end of the ridge, the first small desert community greeted him. Had this been a pleasure trip, he would have enjoyed exploring the area's wildlife and hiking trails.

Phillip shook his head. When was the last time he had taken a moment for pure enjoyment? It was always work, his career, getting ahead. He had even fought to keep from being stationed in Twentynine Palms because it lacked the profile he was seeking. Now, seeing the abundance of nature in these pristine surroundings, he wondered if maybe he had made a mistake.

'Are you crazy, Stuart? The heat must have turned your brain to mush. Twentynine Palms? Try the Pentagon. Now there's an assignment.'

A covey of quail — male, female and a long string of chicks — darted across the road, and Phillip smiled. "Cute."

He shook his head over his foolishness and pushed the car up the steep grade that challenged him.

The vehicle sputtered and lurched. Forward momentum slowed to a crawl. An old man in a battered pickup truck zipped past him.

"This is absurd. A snail could move faster than this heap." Phillip smacked the steering wheel with his fist. "Come on, you piece of trash. Move!"

With a sickening feeling of dread, he watched the needle on the temperature gauge swing to hot. Seconds later, an ominous cloud of steam squealed from under the hood.

Phillip eased to the shoulder, jammed the emergency brake into position and flicked on the hazard flashers. He rested his sweaty forehead against the steering wheel.

"I'll bet there isn't a drop of extra water in this vehicle."

In reply, the right front tire popped.

"What else?"

Phillip rummaged through his briefcase and pulled out his cell phone. "At least the battery isn't dead."

He punched on the power and gave a humorless snort. "No signal. Of course."

He jerked open the door. The hinge protested. "Yeah, I know."

After shoving the door closed, he trudged up the road.

* * * *

Rowan rubbed the feeling back into her wrists. Standard procedures called for cuffs, but she was sure her guard had put them on extra tight, expecting her to complain. She wouldn't give him the pleasure. He hovered over her as if waiting for her to make a run for it now that she was unencumbered. Although his constant presence was annoying, Rowan kept the irritation to herself.

"Wait outside," Captain Connors told the guard.

Grudgingly the Marine left, shutting the door behind him.

"The confinement hearing will be in a few minutes. The delay was unexpected. Sorry we couldn't get to it sooner."

"Is Captain Stuart here yet?"

"I was expecting him an hour ago, but he still hasn't shown. Something about car trouble. Not that it matters. You know you can't choose your own counsel for a pretrial confinement hearing."

Rowan wrapped her arms around her midriff. "I know. I just—"

"Would feel better if he were here?"

When she didn't answer, he leaned forward, his forearms braced on his desk.

"At least now I understand why you wanted him to defend you. Now that I've seen your files, tell me this much, attorney to client... Am I to expect a charge of fraternization to be added to the list?"

Rowan forced herself to look him square in the eyes. "No, sir. It happened a long time ago. Just two civilians, not enlisted Marine and officer."

"And you haven't seen him since?"

"Or spoken to him."

Captain Connors sank back in his chair, rubbing his eyes. "I'm growing less fond of Phillip Stuart with every minute that passes. How could a man ignore his child?"

"It's fairly easy when he doesn't know he has one," she replied.

"Good Lord. You've got time bombs all over the place, don't you?"

That was a fact she couldn't deny. "There's no need for him to be bothered with it now. He shouldn't come in contact with Ian."

Connors's face grew stiff. "This is wrong, Rowan. In my opinion, it was wrong from the start. A man should know he's a father."

"What am I supposed to say now, sir? 'Oh, hello, Phillip, long time, no see. Thanks for coming to my rescue. Oh, by the way, we have an eight-year-old son.'

I'll be lucky if he doesn't try to prosecute me himself." She caught herself and realized she'd gone too far, speaking to an officer in such a sarcastic manner.

Connors ignored her outburst and toyed with his pen, rolling it back and forth between his thumb and forefinger. He disapproved. *Fair enough.* But she needed him in her corner.

She swept her wispy bangs away from her forehead. "He won't leave here without knowing. I know how I'll tell him and I know when. I've got it all figured out. Once this is over, I'll tell him, even let him meet Ian if he wants. This has to be done in a controlled manner and at a time of my choosing."

"You mean once you don't need to be in his good graces anymore," Connors said.

"That's a little harsh, sir, but surely you can see the sense in waiting. Why be distracted by personal matters when…"

He lifted an eyebrow, clearly questioning her motives.

Rowan wiped her sweaty palms on her dusty camouflage trousers. "Don't judge. You don't know what happened. I had my reasons. At that moment, they were the right ones. All I ask is that you help buy me some time until this is over."

The captain tossed the pen to his desk. "I'll do what I can. Colonel Scott wants to see you before the hearing. Trust me. You'll have to do some talking to buy his silence."

"You told him?" It sounded more like an accusation of betrayal than a question.

Connors lifted one brow. "How could I not? You know as well as I do that if you want to keep Colonel Scott on your side, you don't keep secrets."

He called for the guard. For a moment, Rowan thought the man would put the metal handcuffs on her again. Instead, he motioned her on. It didn't matter. She was still a prisoner — of her own lies.

* * * *

Phillip paid the cab driver and hauled his bags out of the taxi. He was hot, sweaty, angry and unimpressed with the two long, concrete buildings housing the Staff Judge Advocate's Office. They looked like adobe bombshelters.

Over an hour late.

He stomped toward the front door, ready to shout the structure to the ground if Rowan was on her way to the brig. No receptionist greeted him. No signs directed him. A military clerk passed, ignoring him. Another approached, ready to do the same. Phillip stepped into his path, planting his captain's bars in the man's line of sight.

"I'm looking for Captain Connors." His voice was gritty with dust and barely above a croak.

The Marine drew back, blinked twice then pointed. "He's down the hall, sir, in Military Justice. Want me to get him?"

"No. I'll do it myself."

Phillip's heels rapped a staccato rhythm as he marched a determined line down the hall to glass-partitioned walls. A thin captain with wire-rimmed glasses glanced in his direction. The young Marine beside him backed up a step, eyes wide. The captain's jaw dropped a fraction. He recovered more quickly than the clerk.

"Captain Stuart, I presume?"

"Well, I'm certainly not Dr. Livingstone. Where's Staff Sergeant McKinley?"

"We're getting ready for the hearing."

"Good, then I'm not too late. She is *not* to go into pretrial confinement. She suffers from acute claustrophobia." *I have the scar to prove it.*

"I have everything under control."

"I sincerely hope so, Captain Connors. Because if you don't, I guarantee I'll have her out of the brig tomorrow and we'll do the hearing all over again the right way. Do I make myself clear?"

Connors leveled a cold stare at him.

"Abundantly. I have Staff Sergeant McKinley's record book for your review. If you'll sign here" — he shoved a logbook forward — "you can take it to the empty office down the hall and look through it."

Phillip shoved the book back. *Is the man blind? Has he lost his sense of smell? Couldn't Connors see that I'm melting away like a snow cone in July?*

"I'm not signing anything. Have the clerk make a copy for me. Right now, I need a driver to take me to my room. I'll be back after the hearing."

With a jerk of his head, Connors motioned the clerk into action.

As they walked to the car, the young man shot looks at Phillip from the corner of his eye.

"Something wrong, Corporal?" Phillip snapped.

"No, sir."

"Then quit acting as if I'm about to bite your head off."

"Yes, sir." The corporal locked his gaze forward and kept it there.

They drove up the hill from the Staff Judge Advocate's Office, passing lines of concrete buildings that were all identical in size and shape — long, low and grimly efficient.

The base bustled with activity. The loud pulse of helicopter rotors mingled with the hum of military equipment and automobiles. Phillip watched Marines load gear into trucks and stack boxes of equipment for transportation into the desert. Another training exercise was about to begin. The Marine Corps was all about action.

The driver pulled up in front of yet another concrete building labeled 'Bachelor Officers Quarters/BOQ'.

"This is it, sir. The room should be ready. Want me to check?"

"That won't be necessary. Pick me up in about fifteen minutes." Phillip got out and retrieved his bags from the backseat.

The room was ready as promised. *The first right thing to happen all day.* He thanked the young woman from the front desk when she escorted him there. Once alone, he dropped his bags on the bed and turned the air-conditioning unit up as far as it would go. With arms braced on either side, he let the cool air envelop him.

"God, I could stand here for hours."

But he only had minutes that seemed like seconds.

Phillip pushed away and peeled his sodden uniform from his sticky skin. With any luck, he could return to the office before the hearing was over.

A quick shower, a fresh uniform and he was back at the curb by the time the driver returned.

No side-long glances accompanied their ride to the office this time. A good thing, since he was in no mood to be ogled. Once there, Phillip was shown to the empty office that would be his to use for the duration of the case.

'Spartan' was a good way to describe the small room. Judging from the gym locker and the lingering scent of stale workout clothes, it appeared to double as a changing area. No window existed to clear the air and he made a mental note to at least find an air freshener of some kind.

A copy of Rowan's military record book lay in the center of the desk. He knew he should spend some time reviewing it but nerves wouldn't let him. He had to know how the hearing was progressing.

A prisoner escort stood outside a door at the end of the hallway. As Phillip approached, the guard snapped to attention and made a crisp salute.

"As you were." Phillip nodded toward the door behind him. "How is it going in there?"

"Don't know, sir." He lowered his voice. "As far as I'm concerned, after what she's done, she should be taken into the desert and left to die."

Phillip took a menacing step toward the man. "If I *ever* hear you making any more threats toward my client, you'll be the one on trial. Do I make myself clear?"

The Marine stiffened at the rebuke and nodded, eyes wide.

Phillip moved back. This was taking too long. Just as that thought left his head, the door swung open.

For a moment, he wasn't sure what shocked him more — the fact that her once-long auburn hair was now in a pixie cut or that hideous bruise. He stared at the injury and rage boiled beneath his skin that someone had dared hurt her.

"Have you seen a doctor yet, Staff Sergeant McKinley?" He struggled to keep his voice level and calm. *Lord, she's still beautiful. Still fiery and proud.*

"Medical diagnosed her with a mild concussion," Captain Connors replied for her. "No broken bones. Nothing requiring hospitalization."

"The hearing?"

Rowan cleared her throat. "Base restriction. No brig time at Miramar, sir."

"Then I guess we can get started." He tore his gaze from her face. "Follow me, Staff Sergeant."

"Yes, sir." She fell in step beside him.

"Would you prefer to return to your barracks room to clean up first?" he asked.

"I don't live on base, sir. I have a house out in the country. They'll have to assign me a room for the restriction. I hope it's not too small."

"Try to keep the blinds open as much as possible and you'll be fine."

"Yes, sir."

"Will you stop calling me 'sir'?" he whispered. "You make me feel like my father."

Rowan paused in the doorway of his office and looked at him from under her eyebrows. "Excuse me, *sir*, but I heard you barking orders at Captain Connors when you arrived earlier. You *are* your father."

Chapter Four

Phillip's gaze narrowed to two menacing silver slits. Rowan had seen that expression before and dreaded it, even though it had never been directed at her. Now it was, since she had accused him of being like his father—the very person who had trademarked the Stuart glare in the first place.

She didn't care. He was wrong and no intimidation he could muster, no division of rank, would force her to back down.

"Just what do you mean by that, Staff Sergeant?"

Rowan set her jaw. *Too late to back down now.* "Permission to speak freely, *sir?*" Sarcasm refused to die—her defense against a familiar need for him and the aching pulse of desire that built inside her.

He waved one hand with irritation.

She thought it a pity that rules existed between them now when their relationship had once been no-holds-barred. Or maybe those rules were a blessing, keeping everything in its neat and proper place.

Her breath had caught at the sight of Phillip standing outside the courtroom. Overhearing his voice from out in the hallway earlier was nothing compared to seeing him once more.

Time had chiseled his good looks to perfection, yet those silvery eyes of his were as fiercely penetrating as she remembered. His gaze had enveloped hers, stripping away the years of separation. Her heart had quickened.

Her coworkers peered from their offices as she and Phillip walked down the hall toward his office. Whispered comments followed them. She was a fool to think they wouldn't notice Phillip's resemblance to Ian. It was stronger than she recalled. Her body remembered, though, and ached with a longing only he could inspire.

She flushed with awareness then forced the feeling away. 'Want' had no business here.

Keeping her voice low, she replied, "Running roughshod over everyone who doesn't meet those high Stuart expectations appears to be a family trait."

He adopted that superior air Rowan hated – the one mirroring Donald Stuart, where he peered down his nose at her and flared his nostrils.

"Treating people like porcelain has never been my style, Rowan."

"Browbeating them into submission never used to be part of your style, either. Apparently, it is now." She noticed the growing number of spectators peeking into the hallway. With a jerk of her head, she gestured toward his office. "I think that we should talk in private, sir. We seem to be drawing a crowd."

Rowan stepped inside, expecting him to follow. When she heard the door click shut, she whirled around to face him. If they had been bantam roosters, they would have been circling each other, searching for an opening to attack. "You were saying, *sir*?"

"For heaven's sake."

One giant step in the tiny office brought him before her. Rowan sucked in a breath. It was too close. *Good Lord, it's much too close.* She had no place to go, pressed against the desk. He raised his finger before her eyes. "When we are alone, you are *not* to call me 'sir'. Do you understand me?"

Rowan lifted her chin to a defiant tilt. "Is that an order, Captain?"

"Does it have to be?" Phillip swung around, bracing his hands against the wall. "My God, Rowan, you're my client. I'm here to help you, not argue with you."

Rowan let herself breathe. He was right. This was absurd. She wasn't angry at Phillip or his father but at herself because she was still attracted to him after almost nine long and lonely years.

Chiding herself for such foolishness, Rowan tried to organize her thoughts. "You're right. I'm sorry. I don't know what came over me. I suppose it's just everything that's happened."

His shoulders rose and fell on a sigh. After what seemed an eternity, he faced her once more.

"And just what *has* happened, Rowan?" he asked.

She turned palms up and shook her head. "I hardly know where to begin."

"I can think of one or two million places. I'm still trying to adjust to the fact that you're a Marine staff sergeant. Last I heard, you were going to teach science."

"Last *I* heard, *you* were going to teach physical education and spend your weekends coaching basketball games."

"Well, I guess things didn't work out the way we planned, did they?"

"No, they didn't." Tears stung her eyes but her strength and independence refused to let her cry. Her chest felt tight as she sucked in a breath, within a heartbeat of throwing herself against him and crying until she went dry. If she didn't watch out...

Phillip cleared his throat. "Let's get started." He motioned to the small mauve sofa across from his desk then took his chair.

Rowan tucked her hands under her thighs to hide their shaking. She didn't dare look at him.

"I've got a copy of your record book and the charges here."

She tensed when he flipped open the folder. What if Captain Connors had failed to remove the page containing family information? She'd never known him to do anything legally questionable. Why would he start now? His desire to help her would not extend to withholding personal information. Yet if the page remained, surely Phillip would have said something by now, especially if he felt it was wrong.

"I've only had the chance to glance over everything. As you know, the charge is murder, second degree."

The blood rushed from her head, yet she somehow managed a nod.

"Did you do it?"

She glanced up to find his steady stare boring into her. "How can you ask me that?" Her words sounded raw and anguished, even to her own ears.

"Because it's my job to ask and you are my client." He leaned forward, resting his arms on the desk while he laced his fingers together. "Did you do it?"

"You know me. I couldn't even kill a spider."

"From one wannabe teacher to another—times change and so do people. Answer the damn question."

"No." She met his gaze across the table, daring him to disbelieve her. "I did not kill Sergeant Kemp."

He leaned back. "Good. Now we're getting somewhere. Start at the beginning and tell me everything. Don't worry about leaving anything out. We'll fill in the gaps later."

With a nod, she started, "To be honest with you, I'm not quite sure what I've gotten myself in to."

"Trouble. Murder. Remember?"

Rowan caught a glimmer of humor in his eyes and blessed him for trying to put her at ease.

"Okay, I'll start at the top." She wiped the sweat from her palms, noticed the dirt under her nails and hid them once more.

"There have been a hell of a lot of accidents with the military exercises this summer. One thing after another. Weird things. Helicopters crashing. Airplanes being shot at. Gear and weapons missing. It has all happened in the same general areas—Lava training and the Expeditionary Airfield."

Phillip rested his square chin on the point of his fingers, his gaze assessing, probing. "How do you figure into all of this? You're in the legal department. Administration, for God's sake. Field exercises aren't part of your assigned duties."

"I discovered a common theme to all the accidents when the visiting units came to our office for help. I was the one who typed out the reports. I went to my warrant officer then my colonel—even the units' officers. No one else could see the connection. They thought I was letting my imagination run away with me. They didn't seem to think it was odd that the incidents were all happening in the same places. They called it a coincidence."

"So let me guess. *You* decided to do a little investigating of your own."

He made it sound as though she had sold her body for money. In hindsight, Rowan had to agree it wasn't one of the smartest things she had ever done.

"Did you know the sergeant who was killed?"

"Yes. Charlie Kemp. He's a friend. *Was* a friend," she added. "Has two little boys. Coached Little League this year."

"How did you meet him?"

Rowan stumbled for a response. The correct answer would garner the question of what she was doing at Little League games. As nonchalantly as possible, she shrugged.

"Hmmm, I can't recall. I meet so many people throughout the day. Probably through work."

"Friend, cohort, suspect? Boyfriend? Lover?"

That pissed her off, but she supposed it was a fair question. "Friend and cohort. He was an MP and wanted so much to prove he was good enough to work in the Criminal Investigative Division."

"So he joined your quest."

"And lost his life." Her voice tightened again. This time, she didn't bother to stop the tears. They came for Charlie.

"It's okay," he said. "Take your time. We're in no hurry."

Nodding, Rowan rubbed her cheeks clear and hauled in a breath. "We went to the base airfield at midnight, hoping that if we could figure out who was stealing the gear, we could start tying the other pieces together. A recent string of thefts at the hangars led us to believe we were on the right trail." She sighed. "I think we were set up. When we got to the building that houses the training equipment, we didn't see a soul. It was eerie. At the risk of sounding like a cliché detective story, it was *too* quiet. I wanted to leave. Charlie said I was being silly. He drew his pistol and we went in."

"Were you armed?"

Rowan shook her head. "When I stepped through the door, I caught the blur of a face off to my right. Then someone smacked me on the side of my head and everything went black."

"And when you woke up?"

"I was lying on the ground near Charlie. There were people and MPs everywhere. Someone kicked a pistol out of my hand, handcuffed me and dragged me to my feet. I don't know how the pistol got there."

"The murder weapon."

She nodded. "It's worse than that, Phillip. According to Captain Connors, the pistol was one of the items listed as stolen."

"God, Rowan. What the hell did you get yourself in to?"

She buried her head in her hands. "I don't honestly know. I wish I had minded my own business."

"As I recall, that has never been one of your strong points." He yanked open the desk drawer and plopped a yellow pad of paper and pen onto the desk. "All right, let's go over this again. We need to have the scenario as tight as we can make it. This time, I want specifics. Who did you talk to about this?"

Rowan shook her head. "Anyone who would listen."

"That doesn't exactly narrow the suspects, does it?"

What can I say? She had believed something wasn't right and had been determined to have people listen to her. Phillip had pegged her on that one. She never could mind her own business.

"From the beginning...again."

Rowan drew breath to start. A knock at the door interrupted them.

"Mike Connors. Can I come in?"

Phillip looked up and called him in.

"Sorry to bother you, but there seems to be another problem," the captain said when he cracked open the door. "I'd like a few minutes alone with you. Could you wait outside the door, Staff Sergeant McKinley?"

Rowan didn't wait for Phillip to motion her outside. She got to her feet before he had time to relax. As Captain Connors eased the door closed behind her, she heard Phillip ask, "What's the problem?"

She braced herself against the wall and closed her eyes.

A woman's shriek pierced Rowan's ears. It echoed through the hallway. Rowan whirled around. Something sliced the air beside her ear. She jumped back.

"Whore! Filthy whore!"

Charlie Kemp's widow lunged for Rowan once more, jabbing with the long screwdriver clutched in her hand. The tip caught the edge of Rowan's sleeve and gouged deep into the plasterboard wall behind her. She was pinned and facing a maniac.

Sally Kemp curved her fingers with their tapered nails into claws. "Murderer!"

Rowan blocked the attack with her free arm. Cat-like scores tore into her flesh. She clenched her teeth and jammed her knee deep into the other woman's stomach. Sally gasped, doubled over and crumpled.

With one furious jerk, Rowan freed her arm. The screwdriver clattered to the floor. As Captain Connors came out of the office, he kicked the screwdriver out of the way while she hovered over Sally Kemp.

"You're crazy," Rowan said through clenched teeth. "If you ever raise a hand to me again, I swear to God I'll ki—"

Phillip clamped his hand over her mouth and dragged her into his office. He motioned with his hand for her to stay quiet, then shoved her onto the sofa and shut the door.

"What the hell were you thinking, threatening to kill that woman?" His voice stretched low and furious. "I'm supposed to prove that you're incapable of murdering a fellow Marine, and here you are threatening some civilian?"

"Charlie's widow," she croaked.

"Great." He smacked one fist on the desk. "Even better, threatening the widow."

Fist raised to pop the desk again in frustration, he halted and instead pointed at her arm.

"You're bleeding. She must have gotten you with that screwdriver."

He leaned close to cup her elbow, pulled up the sleeve of her uniform and examined the bloody gash on her skin.

"Rowan," he began then faltered and let go of her arm.

She felt the rivulet of blood trickling down to her wrist and tried to focus her attention on that.

"It's nothing. A scratch." Her head felt stuffed with gauze, light and ready to float away from her body.

"You'll have that looked at." He stuck his head out of the office. Someone get a first-aid kit in here!" He turned to Rowan. "*You* stay here."

Fury boiled in Phillip—not at Rowan's verbal slipup and not at Kemp's widow and her manic attack but at himself for caring about Rowan, allowing himself to feel something more than professional concern. It was that silent trickle of tears down Rowan's cheeks that had stabbed deep into the core of Phillip's soul. He longed to pull her onto his lap, cuddle her close and promise that everything would be all right. Another baser part of him wanted more and he'd hardened. With each minute that ticked by, he throbbed with an intensity that threatened to explode. In the quiet while she tried to compose herself, he daydreamed of flicking open the buttons on her camouflage blouse, stripping her bare and burying himself in the warmth he craved.

Phillip shook the images away and forced his attention back to business. But while his mind cooperated, his body still had other ideas.

He slumped against the wall outside his office, careful to stay away from Rowan's line of sight and he closed his eyes.

He saw the attack in his mind—the woman's wild, distorted features as she'd sliced ferociously at Rowan. Again, a surge of fear twisted his gut. He clenched his hands. Another memory filtered in. The feel of her skin when he'd checked her wound—the smooth, warm touch of hot velvet against his palm, the faint smell of her body, that unique fragrance that was all Rowan. It was intoxicating. He took a quick breath.

A sound to his left attracted his attention. A plump woman wearing civilian clothes was hurrying down the corridor toward him, concern etching her round face. She was carrying a first-aid kit and her gaze swept the hallway, looking for Rowan. Her military identification badge read *Reid, E.*

"She's in there." Phillip jerked his chin toward his office.

The woman stopped and appraised his face for one long, unblinking moment. She seemed to reach a decision and smiled.

"The colonel wants to see you immediately, Captain Stuart," she said with a slight Kentucky drawl. "Don't you worry. I'll take care of Rowan." With that, she stepped around him into the office.

Phillip sighed. *Are my emotions that close to the surface?* Apparently so. He pushed off the wall and started walking in the direction of the colonel's office, already planning Rowan's defense.

Phillip had left the door open only a crack when he'd walked out. Rowan would be willing to bet he would have locked her in if there had been a way to do so without setting off her claustrophobia. She'd have to say she deserved it. Words uttered in anger and haste had nearly doomed her.

By the time Ellen arrived with the first-aid kit, Rowan was shaking from the ordeal. The fingernail scratches throbbed but the screwdriver had left nothing more than a long, shallow gash. It would heal quickly.

The court reporter dabbed at the wound in silence, but Rowan knew that wouldn't last long. Sure enough, the instant Ellen started to wrap her arm, the comments began.

"Ian sure is the image of his father."

Rowan shook her head. The only bad thing about having a best friend was that they had a tendency to lecture.

Ellen tied off the bandage and straightened. "You certainly have given everyone a lot to talk about lately."

"As long as they don't talk to Phillip."

Ellen tsked and turned toward her with a frown.

"Not now, Ellen — and definitely not here. Once Ian is back from camp, help keep him away from the office until I have a chance to tell Phillip."

"You mean he doesn't — ?" When Rowan glared at her, Ellen lowered her voice. "You mean he doesn't even *know* about Ian?"

"Ellen, please. I had my reasons."

"Hmph. I hope they were damn fine ones."

They seemed so at the time. "Not a word, Ellen. Not one word to *anyone*."

"Honey, I don't have to say a word to anyone. Everyone already knows…except the daddy."

She snapped the kit closed, tucked it under her arm and marched from the office.

It was all too much to deal with. Rowan's stomach churned and a headache built behind her eyes. *How can things possibly get any worse?* She leaned back and closed her eyes, wishing she could do the same with her thoughts.

At some point she must have dozed off, because the next thing she heard was Phillip opening the door. By her watch, an hour had passed.

He sat on the edge of the desk, his legs a fraction of an inch from hers. The office was so tiny. Rowan pulled herself upright. Still, the distance was infinitesimal.

"You must be tired."

"A little. I didn't get much sleep last night."

"Hungry?" He tilted his head a little with the question. Ian did that, too. The resemblance hit her hard.

"My stomach's been too upset to eat."

"How's the arm?" He jerked his chin toward it.

"Hurts, but the cuts and scratches are superficial."

"Captain Connors, Colonel Scott and I spent the last hour trying to convince the CO why he shouldn't hold another hearing and have you confined. As it stands, you now have another charge against you and the previous one has been modified."

Rowan shoved herself to her feet. "For what? She attacked me."

His direct gaze never faltered. "The charge is now first-degree murder and adultery."

Her mouth worked but no sound came out. This was a nightmare. In a daze, she plopped back onto the sofa and buried her head in her hands.

"Mrs. Kemp accuses you of having an affair with her husband. Apparently, he made no secret of his attraction to you. He was pretty graphic with his information. A couple of his friends have verified his wife's story."

"It's not true," she managed to say, trying to defend herself against the look of condemnation on his face. "I never, ever slept with Charlie."

"Never flirted? Never held hands? Never kissed?"

She shook her head and forced herself to meet his gaze. "Never anything, Phillip. The idea never even crossed my mind. If he wanted me that way, he kept it a secret. Our relationship was purely professional. We only talked about work."

"Yeah, everyday stuff like conspiracies."

She tucked her head down to hide a rush of tears. One splashed to her knee. "Why don't you let them cuff me now and take me away? They're determined to see me in jail one way or the other. I don't know why I thought you could help me. I don't know why you bothered to come."

"Because you asked me to," he replied.

Rowan heard him sigh, yet she kept her head buried. If he only knew what effect those words had on her lonely soul.

"You were a word away from blowing whatever chance we might have of winning this case, Rowan. I don't care what happens from now on, but you have to hold your temper."

"Yeah, well, so do you."

He gave a humorless chuckle. "I guess I do. Why don't we call it a day? Go to your room, get some rest and we'll start again in the morning. I can probably win the adultery issue on the grounds of hearsay. Adultery is very hard to prove. As for the rest? Well, we'll tear into some of those reports tomorrow. Okay?"

Rowan blinked her vision clear and stood. "All right. Thanks." She paused. "And Phillip?"

"Yes?"

"Thank you for coming to defend me." She turned and walked out of the door.

Business-like and professional. That was how Rowan preferred to keep things. That was the way their relationship had to be now. Professional, no matter what sexual attraction she felt for him.

Still, she couldn't help but notice he wore no wedding ring, not that it mattered where they were concerned. Even if he did manage to forgive her for lying about Ian, even if she could forget how Donald Stuart's plans for Phillip had torn them apart, she was a staff sergeant and he was a captain. It was a criminal offense for them to fraternize. The future held no more hope for them than the past had.

Chapter Five

"How are things going?" Zach asked Phillip as they talked on the phone. Zach was obviously fishing for more information about the case.

What could he say? That he'd wanted to crush Rowan in his arms at the first sight of her? That he'd wanted to strip her naked and make her his again? That he'd wanted to hold her close each time her eyes had flooded with unshed tears?

"They're going fine."

Zach snorted. "Fine? You expect me to be satisfied with *fine*?"

"I do. Look, I need a favor. Get my car from the shop and bring it up. The government vehicle died on me. I'm getting another one from the motor pool for now but I won't be able to use it off-base. I think I'd rather stay here at Twentynine Palms over the weekend instead of going home. Maybe I can turn up some more information."

"No problem. I'll follow Laura up on Friday and hitch a ride back with her. She's prosecuting the case, you know." His voice held a hint of amusement.

"You know that I know, Zach. Why bring it up?"

"The irony of it, I suppose. Interesting chain of events, huh? Ex-girlfriend prosecuting ex-girlfriend. Better hope Laura doesn't find out."

"If she does, I'm sure she'll maintain a professional distance," Phillip replied.

"Like you're doing?"

Phillip rubbed the ache from his neck. "Zach, please, just bring the car."

"Will do."

"By the way, I forgot to warn you. Oscar got into the leftover chili last night. His stomach might be a little upset."

"A little? That's an understatement. He's got enough gas for ten men. Thanks for the warning, but I don't know what's worse — Oscar with an upset stomach or Oscar whining because he can't sleep with me. I've never seen a bigger baby. Gotta go. See you Friday."

Phillip was sorry he'd ended the conversation so soon. At least talking with Zach, no matter how annoying, kept his mind off other things.

Because you asked me to. Phillip was amazed at how easily the words had come and how true they were. Rowan had called on him for help, knowing only that he would put faith in such a fanciful tale. Odd as the whole thing sounded and although everything pointed to her guilt, he believed her.

He had imagined this moment for years — the day he'd meet Rowan again. All the hurtful words, each vengeful scenario he'd played in his mind, every demand for answers had disappeared the instant he'd seen her. She'd hurt him with her long-ago desertion and the feeling had remained. Now that pain was overshadowed by the rage that had filled him when he'd seen the bruise marring her ivory cheek.

With a wry smile, he recalled her battle in the hallway — like an Amazon warrior. She could give a fair account of herself when backed into a corner. It was probably obvious to whoever had attacked her at the airfield, since they hadn't the courage to face her head on. That meant her attacker knew her well.

It was possible that leaving her alive was a mistake, but he wasn't so sure. The whole thing smelled of a setup, even the story of her affair with Kemp.

Phillip had been surprised at the spurt of jealousy that had overcome him when he'd thought she'd been sleeping with Charlie Kemp. Her insistence that she had not led to other questions. If not Charlie Kemp, then who had been with Rowan all these years? There had to have been someone — maybe a lot of someones. Nobody could remain celibate for nine years — at least not a woman of Rowan's passionate nature.

All those questions were best left unspoken. It really wasn't any of his business.

Yet his gaze had wandered again and again to her finger. No ring. No tan mark. No husband. Right? Did she have a boyfriend? If so, why wasn't the jerk here to support her when she needed it the most?

Phillip flipped through the pages of Rowan's military record book. The record of emergency data listing family members was missing. A Leave and Earning Statement showed extra pay for living in town, but he already knew that. Tax status was single with one exemption, just like a thousand other Marines.

"We're getting ready to close up shop here," Connors said from the doorway. "You need a ride back to the BOQ?"

"No, thanks. I'll walk. There's a page missing from Staff Sergeant McKinley's record. The record of emergency data."

Phillip looked up in time to see the man shrug. "Clerk probably missed it. Why?"

Because I want to know if she's married. "I thought someone should notify her family about how the hearing went."

"I called Emma right away. She'll be here as soon as she gets off work."

Phillip wrinkled his forehead in confusion. "Work? Rowan's mother works here? In California?"

"She manages a small bookstore in town. You probably drove past it on your way in."

He nodded, remembering the cab passing through Twentynine Palms, passing shops decorated with colorful murals depicting local desert history. He'd been so worried about being late for the hearing that most of the scenery had passed by in a blur.

"I don't understand," he said, more to himself than to Captain Connors. "Emma lives with Rowan? Where's James?"

"I don't know any James." Connors looked puzzled.

"Her husband. Emma's husband."

"Oh, I believe he passed away before Ian—excuse me, it's been a long day—before *Rowan* joined the Marine Corps."

Phillip felt as if someone had punched him in the gut. James *dead*? They had been so close. James McKinley's stories of his tour in Vietnam as a young Marine had inspired Phillip to choose the Corps as his profession.

Why hadn't Rowan called him? Losing contact with James in the breakup with Rowan had been hard enough — and now to discover the man was dead. His heart tightened with grief.

"Do you know how — ?"

But Connors was already gone. Phillip pushed away from the desk.

He had to talk to Rowan.

A welcome desert breeze greeted him when he stepped outside, bringing with it the scent of sage. A rumbling off in the distance called to him. He glanced to the mountains nearby where a thundercloud dusted the tops with rain. Nature's cleansing of the world's impurities. *If only everything in life could be so simple.*

* * * *

Rowan was standing on the third-floor landing of the enlisted barracks watching the desert storm drift over the mountains when she first saw Phillip walking down the road toward her building. It was hard not to notice him, dressed as he was in a red pullover shirt and khaki cargo shorts. He still had the best-looking legs of any man she'd ever known. He possessed that special gait of all Stuart men, the one that spelled arrogant confidence. It was part of their DNA. Ian had it too — in full measure.

She hoped he was out for a late afternoon walk. The direction of his gaze told her differently. He was looking right at her. There couldn't have been a worse time for him to visit.

From the other direction, Rowan saw her mother's car coming down the road. It was inevitable, the two of them meeting, but it should have been on her terms, in the office setting she'd envisioned. A nice, neat and orderly conversation, not this spur of the moment meeting.

Phillip reached her first. Her mother was still dealing with the myriad of stop signs along the way. With any luck, Rowan would have Phillip gone before her mother got here.

Who am I kidding? The only luck she'd had lately was bad. Every plan she made fizzled before she had the chance to institute it. *Why should this be any different?* Still, a little more notice would have been nice.

Resigned to the inevitable confrontation and determined to roll with it, Rowan waited for Phillip to reach her on the third floor.

"To what do I owe the honor of this visit?" She leaned back and rested her elbows against the rail. "Am I being charged with yet another crime? No, wait. Don't tell me. I'm now being implicated in an international espionage plot. Perhaps the drug lab in the back of my van has been discovered?" She managed a nervous grin.

There was no humor in his eyes. "Damn it, Rowan, why didn't you tell me about your father?"

Rowan didn't know whether to laugh or cry. She was prepared to argue with Phillip, not dredge up painful memories of her beloved father.

"I *did*, Phillip. I called the moment it happened and every day until the funeral. Your father took the messages. When you never showed up or even called, I figured you didn't care."

His face twisted. "How could you think that? I loved James."

"What else was I supposed to think? You never returned the call—any of the calls," she replied.

His answer was strained. "I never got the messages, Rowan. My father never gave them to me." The grief in his eyes was real. "How? When?"

It was all Rowan could do to keep from wrapping her arms around him. He seemed so hurt and had every right to be—as did she. If Donald had lied about her calling, then it could very well mean he'd lied about everything else he'd told Rowan.

Of course, he'd lied. Why give him the benefit of the doubt? She should have seen it then, but Donald had been clever. He'd seen her vulnerability and had struck a wedge between her and Phillip—the perfect opportunity to rid the Stuart family of an unwanted interloper so obviously not cut from the same social cloth.

"Dad had a heart attack a couple of weeks after you left. The doctors performed a quadruple bypass but he never regained consciousness. A month later, he was gone."

He bowed his head. "I'm sorry, Rowan. I'm so sorry. Is that why you broke it off when I called that time?"

Among other things. "I thought you didn't care."

He gave a humorless chuckle. "Well, the old bastard finally managed to do it, didn't he? My father tore us apart."

"Looks that way," she said. "How did you find out about Dad's death?"

"Connors told me."

"Phillip, we really need to sit down and talk about this."

The slam of a car door drew their attention down to the parking lot.

"Emma's as beautiful as I remember. I understand she's managing a bookstore in town," Phillip said with a slight smile.

Rowan shoved away from the rail. "Well, Captain Connors *was* informative. Did he tell you my bra size, too?"

Smirking, Phillip arched an eyebrow and glanced her way. "Does he know it?"

"Do you?"

He gave her a lazy smile that sent chills down her spine. "Thirty-six B."

Rowan couldn't help it. She laughed. For added measure, she gave him a playful shove.

Her mother paused at the sight of them standing together, then hurried forward to wrap Rowan in a one-armed embrace while she dropped the overnight bag to the landing.

"I'm so happy you're not being sent away," she whispered softly against Rowan's cheek. "I don't think I could bear the thought of you being locked away in the brig."

After gathering her composure, she turned. "Phillip." She smiled then extended her hands to him. "I mean…Captain Stuart."

Phillip slipped his hands into hers then pulled her forward into a tight hug. "Hello, Emma. Now don't get formal on me. How have you been?"

"You know me." She kissed his cheek. "As long as I have my daughter nearby, I'm a happy woman."

"I am so sorry to hear about James. I've only just learned."

Emma held him at arm's length. "I should have realized. That damn father of yours. I should have trusted my instincts. To be honest with you, there was too much going on at the time for me to do more than survive." She squeezed his forearms. "Kind of what we're trying to do right now. So, tell me. Can you help my little girl?"

"I'm going to do my damnedest, Emma." He hugged her once more. "Have you eaten? Let's go grab a pizza. I saw a place around the corner from the legal offices."

Rowan poked her head between the two. "I don't think that's a good idea. I'm sure Mom has other things to do. Don't you, Mom?"

Her mother ignored her. "Actually, no dear. I don't." She smiled up at Phillip. "I'd love a pizza. Sweetheart, go clean up and change while Phillip and I catch up on news."

The last thing Rowan wanted to do was leave the two of them alone, but they had banded together, summarily dismissing her. She had to trust her mother to leave the subject of Ian for her to deal with as she planned. Or would that also be taken neatly out of her hands by fate?

Rowan's stomach churned. She'd deal with that if it happened and prayed she would at least have some control over the situation.

As she ducked back into her room, their conversation drifted her way.

"The California desert is certainly a big change from your old home in Virginia," Phillip said.

"It's not so bad," Emma replied. "Of course, I do miss my dream job back there and the base doesn't have opportunities for a professional reference librarian. But I'm happy. What about you?"

The question took Phillip by surprise. There was no lying to this woman. She knew what you thought before you thought it. She'd always made him feel as if she could see inside his soul. The only days of happiness he had ever known had been with the McKinley family. Nothing in the last nine years had changed that. No wonder his life felt so empty. This was what had been missing—the warmth and love that Rowan's family gave unconditionally.

He forced a smile and knew it didn't reach his eyes. "I've been managing, Emma."

"Sounds almost routine," she told him.

She'd nailed it on that one. That was exactly what his life had become—a constant struggle up the ladder. Success was all he cared about. All other emotions were shoved away. The hell of it was, now that he had seen Rowan again, they were rushing back at him with the force of a cannon ball.

"Tell me everything."

He rubbed his nose and attempted to hide a smile. "That might take a while."

"I have all night."

She always did have the time for someone in need of a confidante.

They were still talking when Rowan returned. Without thinking, he let his gaze wander over what the standard Marine camouflage uniform had concealed.

Her cotton tank top clung to her curves, outlining in perfect detail the swell of her breasts—which, to his disappointment, were covered with a bra. Then there were her legs—long, delicately tan, slightly freckled and exposed. Always athletic, her muscles were leaner, more defined—sleek, not bulky. He imagined her running by his side, her pace perfectly matched with his.

He forced his attention to her face. That was also a mistake. Out of old habit, he reached out and brushed an errant strand of her still-damp hair back into place.

Rowan jerked back as if electrically shocked. Her lips opened, unconsciously beckoning. The temptation was enough to kill him.

"Come on, you two." Emma steered them toward the stairwell. "I'm starving."

So was he — and not for food.

* * * *

Rowan couldn't eat to save her life. On the patio at the little restaurant she sipped a Diet Coke and toyed with a slice of pepperoni pizza while the two of them chattered away.

The headache she'd hoped was gone had returned with a vengeance. Anxiety churned her stomach. *What if Mom slips up and mentions Ian?* She never could keep a secret, and this was a whopper. The two of them tossed words between them like tennis players volleying balls over a net. Their sudden silence jolted Rowan back into awareness.

She looked up to find them staring at her. "I'm sorry. Did you say something to me? My mind was elsewhere."

"Your mom wanted to know if you cared to tell her any more of what was going on," Phillip said.

Not really. But she's going to find out soon enough anyway. In hushed tones, Rowan explained everything.

Phillip turned attorney once more. She could see that in the concentrated lines on his face and the piercing gleam of his shrewd eyes. She wondered if this had been planned. He would think her relaxed and off-guard. *Wrong.* She was tenser than ever. Her mind went blank as she stumbled over her words. With each fumble, Phillip interjected a comment or question, turning each sentence inside out. By the time she was done, Rowan was physically and emotionally drained.

Mom squeezed her hand. "Always have to stick your nose in where it—"

"Emma, please don't."

Phillip's voice was soft but the tone brooked no argument. Rowan appreciated his consideration.

"We've already been through that. Rowan, you're going to have to do better with your story. If you can't tell your mother without faltering, how do you expect to tell the court?"

So much for his consideration. "Why do I feel like you set me up?"

He shrugged a shoulder. "Not setup. I saw an opportunity and took it. You need to use every practical opportunity to rehearse your story. If you think *I'm* bad, wait until the prosecution has a go at you. If she even suspects a hint of weakness, she'll exploit it."

"You must be hell on wheels in the courtroom, Phillip Stuart."

A smile lit his features. "Isn't that why you asked for me?"

With a nod, she conceded the point.

The ride back to her room was quiet. Rowan expected Phillip and her mother to drop her off and go. Instead, he came with her and waved her mother on.

"Thanks, Emma. I'll walk from here. I want to see Rowan to her room and talk to her a bit more about the case."

Mom smiled and reached out of the window to grasp his hand. "I'm so glad you're here. We need you, more so than you might realize."

Phillip leaned down and kissed her cheek in response.

Rowan waited until her mother drove out of the parking lot. "I think I can find my way from here."

"Indulge me, will you?" He motioned to the stairs, then followed her.

Rowan fumbled for her keys as they approached the door. If she could just get inside... Being alone with Phillip made her feel dangerous things. Every instinct drew her unerringly toward him and her fingertips tingled with the urge to caress the angular planes of his face.

Phillip slipped the keys from her fingers and opened the door for her, shoving it wide. "Are you going to be — ?"

Glass exploded behind them, cutting off his words.

Phillip grabbed her and dived into the room, covering her body with his. Bullets sprayed overhead. A lamp shattered. The wall locker splintered.

She clung to him, lips sealed tight against the urge to scream.

Doors slammed and footsteps pounded on the landing. The shooting stopped. He rose to his knees and wrapped her shaking body to his.

"It's okay, Rowan. It's going to be okay."

She nodded against his chest.

Thunder cracked overhead. In the last hour, the storm had moved over them—an appropriate metaphor. It was nothing compared to the turmoil surrounding her. Someone was trying to kill her. This time, there sure as hell could be no doubt.

Chapter Six

Phillip drummed his fingers against the doorframe. Military police and agents from both the Criminal Investigative Division and Naval Criminal Investigative Service were crawling all over the barracks. None of them had been able to turn up a clue.

He would have accused them of not looking had it not been for the efficiency of the lean civilian agent in charge. Jess Alderman snapped the lackadaisical troops into action, shooting off orders with the rapid-fire action of a machine gun. His thatch of silver-white hair stood out among the short military haircuts, an easy target for Phillip to concentrate on while he waited with mounting impatience.

He followed Alderman's every move, as if by doing so he could direct the investigation. Although Phillip felt satisfied the man was doing all he could, there were still other matters that nagged at him.

Alderman shot out a few more orders then returned to the room where Phillip stood guard over Rowan. The news was grim. That was apparent from the stern set of his mouth and the splintered toothpick that jutted from between clenched teeth.

Good, at least someone else is unhappy.

"How's she doing?" Alderman's voice was a gravelly rumble that matched his weathered face.

How do you think she's doing? "She's managing quite well for someone who's just been shot at." Phillip's voice dripped sarcasm. He didn't care.

Alderman tucked a small spiral note pad into his shirt pocket. "It looks like the shooter was positioned on the roof of the bowling alley."

Phillip glanced in that direction. Wherever someone stood, they would have a clear shot at Rowan's third floor barracks room.

"No one saw much. Marines were either inside taking shelter from the approaching storm or outside watching it. Whoever it was, he was careful not to leave any evidence behind."

"Especially since he had so much time to clean up after himself."

Alderman remained quiet for a few seconds as if carefully considering his next words. Phillip got the impression this was common for him. It would have to be in his line of work.

"All I can do is apologize for the delay, Captain Stuart. It will be reported to the Provost Marshal. As I explained, for some unknown reason, at the same time Staff Sergeant McKinley was being shot at, the alarms went off at the armory. All of PMO's attention was focused on the resulting base shut-down."

"It was thirty minutes, Mr. Alderman. Thirty minutes."

Alderman's eyes narrowed. "If you would like to make a formal complaint, I can arrange for you to do so."

"What would be the point? Under the circumstances, I'm beginning to think that no one would care and nothing would be done."

He set his jaw. "I assure you that this will be investigated as thoroughly as any other incident on this base."

Phillip snorted. "Then we're all in big trouble" — he jerked his thumb toward Rowan, who sat behind him on the remains of a chair, clutching a Styrofoam cup of water — "unless you intend to hire Staff Sergeant McKinley to help you with the investigation. Seems to me she's done more to uncover information around here than anyone else. Of course, no one has bothered to give an ounce of credence to anything she's said. Now someone's trying to shut her up permanently."

Alderman glanced over Phillip's shoulder at Rowan. Phillip dared the man to say something derogatory about her, anything to give him an excuse to lose his temper.

"I'm not that familiar with her situation," he finally said. "Malcolm Collins is the agent in charge of that case. I'm sure you'd like to read his report as soon as possible. Come by my office in the morning. Malcolm should be there and we can talk. In the meantime, we can place Staff Sergeant McKinley in protective custody — "

"Lock her up?" Tamping down his irritation, Phillip took a deep breath. "Until I know who I can trust, I trust no one. Staff Sergeant McKinley's safety and welfare will be my personal concern."

Again Alderman's gaze drifted to Rowan, then back. He flicked the remains of his toothpick over the edge of the balcony. "I'll be glad to provide an escort for you."

"That would certainly make it convenient for us to be located later." A stupid thing to say. On a base this size, it would be child's play to find them.

"If I didn't know better, Captain, I'd say you were accusing an MP of this attempt on her life."

Phillip didn't know whether to laugh or shout. *Is Alderman really that dense?* "What else is there to think? Military policemen on this base think she murdered their coworker. An attempt is made on her life at the same time the armory alarms go off. The MPs take their sweet time getting here. Coincidence? I call it conspiracy. I think it's about time that someone besides Staff Sergeant McKinley had the balls to check it out."

He turned to Rowan. "Grab your bag. We're leaving."

Easy to ask, hard to do. As long as she sat in this one spot and concentrated on the cup clutched between her hands, Rowan could control the body-shaking tremors that engulfed her. But to stand, much less move? He might as well have asked for the moon, but somehow through sheer force of will she rose.

He held out his hand. "Give me your keys. I don't think you're in any condition to drive."

Drive? Rowan stiffened in panic. Her van was a little boy's haven. Matchbox cars, action figures, travel games and an Etch a Sketch were tucked into the nooks for easy access in any traveling situation. For Ian, that could be anything from a trip to the store to a trip across country.

"Can't we walk?" she asked without thinking.

Phillip's brows shot up. "With some madman out there shooting at you?" He pulled Rowan to her feet and walked her toward the stairwell.

"But I'm almost out of gas." The excuse was so feeble it didn't even elicit a response.

"Keys." He thrust out his hand, palm up.

Rowan fumbled through her purse but her fingers were shaking too badly to be of much use. She was aware of Phillip looming over her.

"Want me to look?"

Her fingers closed around the key ring. "I have them."

"Good. Let's go." He started down the stairwell.

Drifting in his wake, mind a-whirl, Rowan knew she had to stop him. She grabbed Phillip's arm before they reached the foot of the stairs and gasped, "My uniforms and clothes. They're in the room. Could you run back and get them? I'll meet you at my van."

Exasperation swept over him. "You wait right here. Don't go anywhere."

The instant he disappeared up the stairs, Rowan sprinted for the parking lot, not caring how many heads turned her way. A glance over her shoulder confirmed he was still occupied. After throwing open the side door of the Caravan, she crawled inside.

It wasn't as bad as she'd thought—mostly because she had asked Ian to clean his things out before he'd left for his Scout trip. Still, she might as well have had one of those little yellow signs that blared 'Child On Board'.

Grabbing the blanket that she kept tucked away for emergencies, Rowan piled every scrap of childhood evidence into the center and shoved the incriminating bundle under the last seat.

"Lose something?"

At the sound of Jess Alderman's roughened voice, Rowan jerked around.

"I don't suppose you would consider a consensual search of the vehicle." He chewed slowly on a fresh toothpick and eyed her thoughtfully.

"There's nothing to search for, Mr. Alderman."

He glanced to the backseat. "Then what's the rush?"

"A little housekeeping, that's all. I wouldn't want my defense counsel to get a bad impression of me." Rowan tilted her chin, daring him to challenge her excuse.

He grinned. "No, you certainly don't want that. From what I hear, you'll need all the help you can get."

After a mock salute, he walked away, but not soon enough for Rowan to get back to the building without being detected. She caught Phillip's thunderous approach from the corner of her eye and refused to look his way. Instead, she opened the van's front door and slipped into the driver's seat.

"I see you still don't listen worth a damn." Phillip heaved her bag into the van then slid the side door closed with a sharp tug.

Even though she was expecting the noise, Rowan jumped when the door slammed. He wrenched open the passenger door and paused.

"I was feeling closed in and needed to get out of there." Anxiety made her voice tight and high. *Please don't let him look under the seat.*

"Hmm."

A noncommittal response. He was distracted by something near the passenger's side door. What was he staring at? A toy? Ian's shoe? What?

"Would you like me to drive?" he mumbled.

Anything to divert attention away from the incriminating bundle under the back bench. Rowan relinquished the wheel and scooted over to the other seat. She busied herself by fastening her seat belt then realized Phillip still hadn't moved.

"What's wrong?"

His frown deepened. "You have a melted crayon stuck against the side of the seat."

Damn it, Ian. How many times have I told you? "I was baby-sitting for my friend Ellen over the weekend. One of her kids must have left it."

"Hmm."

Another nonresponse. What was he thinking? Had he guessed? She should tell him now and get it over with.

"Phillip, I—"

He held up his hand for silence. "Please, just give me the keys."

Grateful for the reprieve, she dropped the key ring into his open palm.

Neither of them uttered a word during the short drive. Even when she realized that their destination was his room, Rowan kept her mouth shut. He knew as well as she did that female visitors were prohibited. Surely he wouldn't jeopardize their already precarious situation by adding an infraction of the rules, but that looked exactly like what he intended to do.

She must have made some noise of protest because he faced her after he'd shut off the engine.

"There's not much choice for your accommodations tonight unless you want to go back to the detention cell. Although judging from your current popularity, that might not be a bad idea. At least it's under security watch."

Before she could defend herself, he continued, "Your stubbornness got you into this mess, Rowan. You need to stop trying to be so damned independent. If you're going to pull more foolish stunts like wandering around by yourself, please let me know so I can get out of the line of fire. You may have a death wish, but I certainly don't."

She hiked her chin up a notch. "I don't have a death wish, Phillip."

"Good. Then let's call it a night. It's been a hell of a day and I strongly suspect tomorrow won't be any better."

Rowan wanted to rail against his condescending tone. *The smug jerk. Who does he think he's fooling?* If their situations were reversed, if it were he who had suspected foul play, gung-ho Phillip would have done the same things she had. At least the old Phillip would have.

Weariness seeped into her bones as she followed him to the room. No one challenged her presence. In fact, they didn't pass a soul. By the time he ushered her inside, it was all she could do to put one foot before the other.

After a passing glance at the ugly artwork on the wall, she collapsed onto the tiny sofa and tucked her arm under her head for a pillow.

"You can't sleep there," she heard Phillip mutter. "You need to get some sleep and it's too small. Move to the bed. I'll catch a few minutes of rest on the couch."

She was conscious of making some sound of acknowledgment or maybe she nodded, but the effort to move seemed too much for now.

Phillip grabbed his duffel bag and ducked into the adjoining bathroom, the only private area left—the only place where he could let down his defenses for a few minutes.

He clutched the edge of the sink to stop his hands from shaking. Deep breathing and splashing cold water on his face helped to revive his senses. A cold shower would have done more, but Phillip was afraid the running water would mask any noise of an intruder. He had to remain alert. Two life-threatening incidents in less than twelve hours… He could almost feel his hair turning gray.

It wasn't that he had never been shot at before. He'd been in war zones, and there had even been a time when he had prayed that a bullet would pierce his heart and take away the pain of losing Rowan. Not now. This time it was personal. This time he wanted to live, for Rowan's sake.

She was on to something. Phillip would have to give her that much. Whatever she had uncovered, it was big enough to kill for. That meant there had to be evidence somewhere. His problem was trying to find it in time. Tomorrow would be a busy day.

Somewhat composed, he returned to the main room. Rowan was sleeping soundly, although he couldn't see how since she was curled up into a little ball in order to fit on the sofa. He was tempted to carry her to the bed then dismissed that idea. If she slept, she had to be comfortable enough. Still, he tucked a pillow beneath her head and tossed a sheet over her.

Stretching out on his stomach on the bed, he watched the rise and fall of her shoulders as she breathed. He saw her soft nape and vividly recalled the taste of it on his tongue. The memory of their long-ago lovemaking hardened him. He wrenched his gaze away and shifted to a more comfortable position.

They had yet to speak of the past. It was probably just as well. What good would it do when there were no tomorrows for them? She'd run out on him when he'd needed her most, when his life had been turned around and upside down by his father's scheming.

So much for the rosy future. The present was all that mattered and maybe, just maybe, they might be able to salvage a casual friendship from the whole mess. Anything more than that and they could both kiss their military careers goodbye.

Rationalizing didn't help. His body still ached to hold her close. Common sense told him he was being stupid. The two warred throughout the night, making sleep elusive. Dreams haunted him in those rare snatches of time when sleep did come. The slightest sound pumped adrenaline through his veins while he waited for an attack that never materialized.

By dawn, he had given up the fight for sleep. He sat up on the edge of the bed to watch the minutes tick off before the alarm rang. Then he noticed the white paper lying inside the door. Careful not to wake Rowan, he walked over to it. The words scrawled in black marker were readable without having to pick it up.

People who ask too many questions get killed.

"What is it?" Rowan asked, her voice groggy with sleep.

"Just your basic generic threat. I doubt that we'll find any fingerprints on it, but just in case…" Phillip picked it up by one corner and dropped it into his briefcase. "Get cleaned up and we'll grab some breakfast before we head to your office."

"I don't think I could eat anything." She rubbed the sleep from her eyes. "I'm still a little stressed over last night's excitement." Her light dusting of freckles stood out sharply against her pale face.

"Well, I'm starving. You didn't eat much last night. You've got to be a little hungry. Come on."

"I'll clean up and change into my uniform at the office."

"Fair enough."

Rowan looked ill. The bruise on her face stood out against the pallor of her delicate skin. He sympathized. His stomach was in knots. It didn't matter how generic the threat. It was still ugly and frightening.

They walked out into the dry desert morning, a radiant pink sunrise mocking the horror of the night before. Each breath felt like hot oven air and the sun hadn't even climbed over the horizon.

He checked over his shoulder while they walked toward her van. Except for the early formations of Marines running, no one was in sight, but that didn't mean they were safe.

"Somehow I'm not surprised." Rowan's weary voice bordered on tears.

Phillip followed her gaze. Every tire on her van was slashed. "Son of a... I'm calling the MPs."

She laughed without humor. "Why bother?"

"I'm not about to let this go, Rowan."

She looked up at him with cynical golden-brown eyes. "You just don't get it, do you? All the MPs care about is getting even. One of their guys is dead. They're out for their own type of justice and the facts be damned. In addition to that, somebody else doesn't like my investigating and is threatening me. I'm tired, Phillip — tired of everything."

She pivoted on her heel and started down the street.

"Where are you going?" he shouted at her retreating back.

"To work, while I still have a job."

Rowan kept up a steady pace, knowing Phillip would be right behind her.

The stakes had grown in the last twenty-four hours and she prayed they did not include her mother and Ian. So far, the threats and physical violence had been directed at her. But as Phillip's investigation into her case continued, she expected whomever was responsible would become more desperate. Nothing would be considered too sacred to keep her silent. Why else would she have been framed for Kemp's murder?

"Will you slow down?" he snapped from behind her. "It looks like I'm chasing you."

Rowan kept walking. "I want to call Mom. I need to know that she's all right." *I need to know if Ian is all right.* "My cell phone was confiscated by PMO."

He snagged her arm and pulled her to a stop. "If you really want to worry her by telling her what's been going on, I have a cell phone in my briefcase."

Her shoulders sagged, defeated by his logic once more. "Of course I don't want to worry her. I need to know that she's all right. I'll call from my office."

They walked on in silence.

Someone would have to report this latest indignity to Colonel Scott. She'd let that someone be Phillip. Alone in her office, she picked up the telephone. Her mother answered on the second ring.

"I wanted to see how you were doing this morning, Mom."

"A lot better than you — or so it sounds. Is everything all right?"

"Everything's fine. I was wondering if you had any word from Ian? Is he having a good time?"

Her mother laughed. "Sweetheart, he's camping. How can he call?"

"I know. I love you, Mom. Have a good day."

"You too, sweetheart. And, Rowan?" Her voice was warm and steady.

"Yes, Mom?"

"It's going to be all right."

"I know, Mom," she choked out, then slipped the phone into its cradle.

Tears she'd previously held back with an iron will were allowed to drift unrestrained down her cheeks. Rowan didn't know how long she cried, only that when the knock came at her door she wasn't cried out. Dashing her hand across her cheeks, she invited the person in.

Captain Connors poked his head though the door. "Captain Stuart wants to see you in his office."

Rowan gave a quick nod. "I'll be right there. By the way, I want to thank you for removing that page from my record book."

"I wasn't going to, but frankly, his attitude pissed me off."

Rowan managed a smile. "He tends to have that effect on most people."

He shrugged. "Something like that. He's not a nice person, Staff Sergeant. Better keep that in mind."

There was no sense arguing with him. "I will." She sucked in a breath to calm her nerves and walked down the hall to Phillip's office.

She hesitated at the door to the office when she heard Phillip on the phone to someone named Zach. He needed his help with the case. There was also mention of a woman and Rowan felt an unfamiliar jab of jealousy. She was about to step away when Phillip spied her. With a distracted smile, he motioned her inside and continued speaking.

"I'll see you in a couple of days then. Give Oscar a hug from his dad."

Oscar. Phillip had a child. *A son.* Strange how badly that hurt.

"I talked to Colonel Scott. Your preliminary hearing is being moved up to Monday," he told her as he hung up.

Rowan nodded. Her military arraignment. The hearing that decided if she would be tried for murder.

"So, you know what that means."

She shook her head.

"The prosecutor is on her way up. We've got a lot of investigating to do in the next few days."

"Do you know anything about her? What is her reputation as a prosecutor?"

Phillip busied himself putting her arraignment papers away in his leather briefcase. "As I mentioned before, she's good — good at her job, I mean. Aggressive. I know that from past experience." He faced her. "She's good but I'm better. When my friend Zach arrives from Camp Pendleton, we will have some more legal help with this case. He has some excellent ideas. Would you like to hear them?"

Rowan already knew more than she cared to. No matter how impossible a future was between them, it still wrenched her heart that another woman shared his life and had given him a son.

Chapter Seven

"I understand you had quite a morning."

Phillip looked up from the base map he was studying when Jess Alderman walked in. It was about time someone came to get him after he'd cooled his heels in the waiting room of the Naval Criminal Investigation Service for well over an hour. What little patience he had remaining was kept in place by an iron will that was rapidly rusting.

"That certainly is an understatement."

"I spoke with CID. There were no fingerprints on the paper, except for yours in the corner — also, no evidence near the van."

"There's a surprise."

Phillip didn't care how sarcastic he sounded. It was all too convenient, too pat — too professional for a bunch of military policemen enraged over the death of a colleague. It had to be someone else. Perhaps the criminal was extremely clever — or else someone somewhere was covering up evidence.

Alderman swung the door open wide. "You can wait in my office. Malcolm is tied up right now on the phone, probably with the same civilian contractor who was pitching a fit over the theft of some tank-targeting equipment from the firing ranges."

Phillip followed him down the hall. "Seems like an odd thing to steal." He heard a voice rise in argument as they passed one room and he raised his eyebrows.

Alderman jerked his thumb toward the closed door. "Collins. With nothing but hundreds of miles of desert in any direction, we're pretty accessible. Thieves will take anything that's not nailed down and often those things that are, if they can get away with it. If there's money in it, they'll take it—copper, electronics, explosives that didn't detonate. With a base this size, mostly uninhabited, there isn't much we can do about security. A while back thieves broke into a maintenance shed out on one of the ranges and took thousands of dollars' worth of tools. Just waited until the military shooting exercise was over, drove up the back way and cleaned it out."

"Let me guess," Phillip said. "Same civilian contractor."

He nodded. "He's furious. The multiple thefts are going to wreak havoc with contract negotiations. He comes in here yelling at us about security, but there isn't much action to take at the moment and we didn't find much evidence. All we could do was notify pawn shops in the neighboring towns. Coffee?"

Phillip declined. He'd had enough to float a ship. "Tools are one thing, but targets? How much money could they be worth?"

"A small fortune." Alderman poured himself a small cauldron of coffee and eased into a vinyl chair opposite where Phillip now sat. "It's not the target they want. It's what's attached to it — the box for pyrotechnics that sits at the base of each one. High-grade aluminum. Heavy as the dickens and worth a pretty penny."

"How much are we talking about?"

"Five hundred to a thousand dollars per stolen device. We know that the thieves steal hundreds of them every time they make a hit, so each successful robbery brings them a big chunk of change."

"Let me guess." Phillip rested his forearms on his knees. "The turnover is good because the aluminum bases have to be replaced for the next series of training missions."

Alderman nodded. "Right. The Marines can't stop training while we check each pawnshop for the missing targets. The government has to buy replacements, so the thieves wait for the chance to steal them again. It's not a bad living if you can get away with it."

"Which is apparently what they've been doing. Have you staked out the place?"

He shrugged. "Tried once. No luck. With our limited manpower and resources, there isn't much more we can do."

Somehow Phillip was beginning to think that was their stand on everything. His disgust must have shown because Alderman leaned forward.

"This main part of the base is small, but you have to remember there are also nine hundred and thirty-two square miles of desert out there and that doesn't include the camp areas. There are just a handful of us. What else can we do to cover a military base this size?"

Phillip leveled a steady stare back his way. "Apparently, as with everything else I've seen so far, nothing."

Alderman tilted his chair back, all rapport washed away by Phillip's insult. "That's hardly a fair statement. You're judging us on an isolated incident."

"Attempted murder, vandalism, threats, murder, theft of government property... That's one hell of an incident, Mr. Alderman."

He slugged down some coffee and gave a lazy grin. "Most of it was solved with the arrest of your client, from what I understand."

Phillip didn't buy Alderman's good-old-boy routine for a moment. The man was sharp as a razor. "Awfully convenient, don't you think?"

Alderman danced his thumb over the rim of his mug. "Criminals are bound to slip up at some time."

Phillip cocked his head to one side. "Maybe. I only hope this one will slip up in time to save Staff Sergeant McKinley."

Alderman tipped his chair back, seemingly digesting the words. "I know you have to defend your client to the utmost, but have you considered that she could have planted that note under your door last night?"

"Now that would have been a good trick. She slept the night through. I know because I watched her."

"Too bad you weren't watching to see who left the note."

Phillip's jaw twitched. The man had cut right to the core of his guilt. *If only I had been more alert.*

Alderman took a swig of coffee. "All I'm saying is, don't be too zealous until you read the investigation report."

"Something which appears as though it will take an act of God to achieve."

He grinned. "I'll see what I can do." He set the chair to rights and left the office.

Phillip rubbed his temples in a slow circle. Why did he get the impression they had played a mental game of chess? Trouble was that he wasn't sure who'd won the match. But one thing was certain. He was going to have to fight for every piece of evidence in this case. If Alderman thought another delaying tactic was going to make him give up, he was dead wrong. Phillip would sit here until he got the investigation report he'd come for or until they physically removed him from the building.

Minutes ticked by again. He made a note of it. If push came to shove, Phillip could shove pretty hard. A few well-placed phone calls would do the trick.

"Good morning, Captain Stuart. Sorry to have kept you waiting." A balding man of slender build eased into the room, one hand extended in greeting while the other absently massaged his midsection. Each breath he took was an effort.

Phillip stood and accepted the handshake without hesitation, but that was as cordial as he intended to get.

"Malcolm Collins. I'm the investigating officer assigned to the Kemp murder case. Sorry I'm late. I was tending to an important personal matter."

Personal? I've been biding my time waiting for Collins to handle personal business? "Well, this is pretty damned important, too. I've been waiting for well over an hour. When I make an appointment, I expect it to be kept."

Alderman eased into the room behind Collins.

"What's more important than a murder investigation?" Phillip asked.

Collins whirled around. "Just get off my case. I've got you on one side and my wife and her smart-assed attorney screaming at me to sign divorce papers on the other. Child support is killing me. I don't know if I'm ever going to see my kids again and the bitch has the nerve to scream for spousal support. She's got everything else. I'm surprised she's not asking for the clothes off my back."

In the dead silence that followed, a red flush covered Collins' face. He ran a finger around the inside of his collar, trying to loosen his necktie while he composed himself. While coughing into his hand, he stared at a spot on the far wall.

"Sorry. I've been pretty busy. We're a little short-handed around here. This divorce is killing me in more ways than one."

"I understand." At least he'd had the decency to admit his mistake. Phillip felt a small measure of sympathy for him. The subject was best left to die. "I'd like to look at those reports now, Mr. Collins."

"Got them right here." Collins reached into an enormous file folder and dragged out a thick sheaf of papers, wincing from the effort.

"Is there a problem, Mr. Collins?"

"I was doing some work on my roof over the weekend and fell off the ladder. Just bruised some ribs." He held up the papers once more. "I would have made you a copy, but our machine is down."

"I'm sure you'll have one for me by the end of the day. In the meantime, if there's a private place where I can read through this, I would appreciate it."

"Sure. No problem. Plenty of empty offices around here."

He led Phillip down the hall then left him on his own. Still, Phillip couldn't shake the feeling he was being watched. After settling at the desk, he started on the document.

A lot of the information was missing. Autopsy report on the deceased. Forensics evidence. Bullet trajectory. Photographs of the crime scene. Ballistics report of the weapon. That would all come later. The evidence already there bothered him.

As he already knew, the pistol was found in Rowan's hand. Tests showed trace metal there as well, indicating she had fired the weapon. To make matters worse, the weapon was one of the ones listed as having been stolen weeks earlier from the base armory.

Collins' notes suggested that Rowan and Kemp were having an affair. Statements from the deceased's wife and a few of his friends supported the motive for the murder—jealousy because Kemp refused to leave his wife for Rowan.

Kemp had received two bullet wounds. One was superficial to the leg—the second, a fatal shot to the head. A rough sketch of the crime scene showed the position of Kemp's body and where Rowan had been found. There was even a supposition on the investigator's part. She had shot him in the leg, the two had struggled, Kemp had struck her on the head, she had shot him a second time—the fatal shot—then passed out.

Phillip studied the sketch. There was one heck of a distance between the two. Of course, it was hard to tell from a drawing. He needed to get a look at the scene of the crime and wondered if that would be as difficult a process as getting a peek at this initial investigation report.

Page by page he evaluated the material, noting those items he felt needed more clarification. By the time he finished, it was well beyond lunch.

"Done?" Alderman asked when Phillip finally left the room.

He slid the file onto the edge of the agent's desk. "For now. Where's Mr. Collins? I'd like to see the crime scene. I presume it was sealed."

"It was. I'll get Malcolm and we can leave right now if you'd like. Need a lift or do you have a vehicle?"

"I'll follow you out there." He hoped the new government vehicle checked out to him would last the trip.

* * * *

'Out there' was the most desolate landscape Phillip had ever seen. Sand. Miles and miles of sand, broken only by a sparse creosote bush here and there. Even the multi-colored mountains in the distance couldn't ease the barrenness of the place. Infinite heat drew moisture from his skin. If this car died on him, the only sign he had been on the planet would be his bleached bones buried in the hot desert. He tried not to dwell on the possibility.

After thirty minutes of driving, they reached the airfield. There were the obligatory military buildings — the warehouses, the office spaces, even an attempt at civilization with small stores and eateries for visiting troops. Other than those signs of life, all that awaited them was never-ending, scorching desert.

They stopped before a large metal building. Yellow crime tape stretched over the doorway. As soon as they left their cars, a Marine lieutenant trotted toward Alderman.

"I hope you've come to tell me we can go inside now. The commanding officer's barking left and right about it. It's really holding up our unit's work." He waved his arm toward Collins. "Your partner here doesn't seem to understand."

Alderman shook his head. "Sorry, not until everyone is satisfied that all the evidence has been collected. Your CO will have to be patient."

Collins clapped the man on the back. "I'm sure he wants to see justice done as much as the next person. Have him call us if he has any questions."

Leaving the disgruntled lieutenant staring after them, they ducked under the tape and walked into the building's dim interior.

Phillip expected some measure of relief from the oppressive heat, but the sun had turned the equipment building into an oversized oven, creating a wall of heat that slammed into him with the force of a hammer.

"Over there." Collins pointed ahead.

Phillip and Alderman followed him to a taped outline on the concrete floor behind a row of fifty-five-gallon drums. Dried blood patches remained to mark Kemp's head wound.

"Where did you find Staff Sergeant McKinley?" Phillip asked.

Collins pointed to chalk marks ten feet away. They were the only clue that someone had lain there. He glanced back toward the doorway. Another discrepancy glared back at him. Rowan had said she'd been struck the minute she'd entered, yet they'd found her unconscious some fifty feet away from the door, deep inside the building.

"Still think she's innocent?" Collins asked, his tone mocking.

Phillip's gaze flicked up to him. Collins stood, arms crossed with a cocky smirk on his thin face. Off to one side, Alderman stared at his colleague with undisguised dislike.

"Aside from the fact that it's my job to believe she's innocent, Mr. Collins, I do."

Collins brought his hand to his mouth and slowly rubbed his lips. "Why, when the evidence is overwhelmingly against her?"

Phillip raised an eyebrow. "Body language, Mr. Collins. It tells a lot about whether a person is lying or telling the truth."

"And she has quite a body to look at, doesn't she?" Collins said with a sly grin.

"What the hell is that supposed to mean?" Phillip snapped.

Alderman stepped between the two. "That was uncalled for, Malcolm." His voice deepened to a threatening rumble.

Collins gave a short, barking laugh. "Sorry. This case is so cut-and-dried. I'm a little frustrated that the good captain can't see that. As short-staffed as we are, I hate to have to spend time on wild goose chases. That's all."

"Then go on back to the office. I'll ride back with Captain Stuart when he's finished looking around."

Collins shot Phillip an annoyed glance then left. Once he was out of range, Alderman faced Phillip.

"I apologize for my coworker. I can only put it down to job stress and his divorce problems."

"Spare me the excuses, Mr. Alderman. Why the sudden concern?" Phillip demanded to know. "What did you see that changed your mind?"

Alderman ran his fingers through his snow-white hair. "Only about a hundred different things. Well, maybe that's a bit of exaggeration."

"But enough to raise questions."

He nodded slowly. "A lot of questions."

"So you think she's innocent, too."

Alderman chuckled. "I'm not going that far, but I will agree something isn't right."

Phillip didn't care what the man thought as long as he finally had someone willing to investigate this more thoroughly. "Such as?"

Alderman squatted down before the outline. "Kemp was supposedly shot in the leg first, then they struggled. Why isn't the blood more dispersed? There should be spots of blood all over the place if they struggled. There's no blood pooled from where his thigh rested on the concrete floor. None at all.

"Then let's look at where they found McKinley—face down ten feet from the body. Face down, unconscious. Given that she supposedly passed out after struggling with Kemp, as far as I know, there are no bruises that indicate where she fell on the concrete. Her skin shows the mark from a direct blow to the face but not an impact bruise from hitting the floor. Also, where's the blood from her head wound?"

"I'm sure she bled"—Phillip said—"wherever it was she fell."

Alderman's knees popped as he stood. "So, you think she was moved?"

Phillip lifted an eyebrow. "If you go by her statement…yes. As far as I'm concerned, her statement is the only thing consistent with this whole investigation."

"I'd have to agree with you."

It's about time someone did. "Then get a forensics team you can trust out here to go over this place with a fine-toothed comb."

* * * *

There weren't enough hours in the day. It was as simple as that. The team of six men worked with a painstaking accuracy that left no doubt in Phillip's mind they were being thorough. The forensics agents were already working under a handicap. The murder had occurred three nights before and had been tainted by everyone who'd entered the building thereafter. Fortunately, it looked as though the crime scene had remained intact.

They found Rowan's original location—right inside the front door. As Alderman had predicted, there was a faint, telltale sign of spittle and a smear of blood from where her cheek had hit the floor. Scuff marks from her boots marked where she had been dragged before she had apparently been carried to her final destination.

Chances were good that once the experts sifted through all the evidence, there might be enough to clear her. Then they needed to find the murderer in order to prove to everyone, beyond a shadow of a doubt, that Rowan was innocent.

"That's about all we can do for now, Jess," the lead team member said. "Anything else?"

"One more thing. I need someone to follow the captain and me back to the legal office." He cocked his head Phillip's way. "Unless Staff Sergeant McKinley's clothing from that night has already been taken as evidence."

Judging from the way she'd looked when he'd first seen her, Phillip would have to say no. He shook his head. It galled him that Collins had treated the case in so cavalier a manner, and on the return trip to base mainside, he said as much to Alderman.

The older man shrugged. "I know it isn't a valid excuse, but again, all I can offer is job stress. There are just three of us now. He's been a little on edge for several months. His wife leaving really tore him up. He's been battling with her ever since. Every time he gives her what she asks for, she asks for more. She uses those girls as weapons."

"Then why in the world would he be assigned a murder investigation?"

Again the shrug. "He was the agent on call that night. Simple as that. I suppose I should have reviewed everything more carefully from the start, but I never expected him... Well, I guess he thought it was just cut-and-dry, as I said before. All I can do now is to try to correct things as best I can."

He rested his elbow on the edge of the door and stared at the passing landscape. "It's later than I thought. Do you suppose Staff Sergeant McKinley is all right?"

"I called Captain Connors. He's watching out for her."

He wasn't the only one.

Phillip saw Laura's car before they turned into the parking lot. It was right beside Rowan's van, which now sported four new tires. Phillip experienced that instant, gut-wrenching worry that all men get when one old girlfriend meets another. He prayed that neither would discover the relationship. He cursed Zach for putting that idea in his head in the first place.

All three were waiting in Phillip's office. Connors and Laura chatted away as if they were old friends. Rowan was tucked into the corner of the loveseat, reading a book. As if pulled by a single cord, all three looked up when Phillip walked in with Alderman.

"How did it go?" Connors asked.

"Interesting." A vague answer, but the only one he intended to give while Laura was there. She was, after all, the prosecuting counsel. The fact she was so near his client without him present was also alarming. Phillip didn't entirely trust Connors to keep their interests guarded.

He turned toward Laura. "You're here early."

"With the hearing going on Monday, I thought I'd better come up and get started. Do you intend to share what you've found?"

"Do you have a discovery request?"

She looked at him for a half second then burst out with a laugh. "Okay, I'll play the game."

"We're going to watch the autopsy tomorrow if you'd like to join us."

She screwed up her face in disgust. "No, thank you. I don't even like to see the pictures. I suppose you'd like to be alone with your client?"

Phillip held the door for her.

She smiled. "You'll have that discovery request in the morning."

"I have no doubt." He shut the door on her exit then locked his gaze on Rowan. "Where's the uniform you were wearing the night of the shooting?"

"It's right here in my gym bag." She whipped open the zipper and held the garment up for verification. "I was taking it back to wash tonight."

Alderman cracked open the paper sack he had tucked under his arm. "Nope. Put it in here. All of it. Uniform, underwear, boots—unless you're wearing them."

"No. I didn't have the time to polish them last night."

"Good for you," he said with a broad smile and held the sack open for her.

Phillip watched her confusion as she placed each item in the sack. At the sight of the boots, he wanted to cheer. The rubber heels and leather backs were scuffed where she had been dragged.

"I don't understand," she said when the last item was tucked away. "Other than being dusty, there's nothing on them — no blood, no dirt, not a smudge."

Alderman folded the top and stapled it closed. "That's what we're hoping. If you're ready to call it a night, I'll escort the two of you back to the room."

Rowan tossed her bag back to the floor beside her. "That won't be necessary. I'll be staying in the office from now on. When some of the guys from my department found out what happened last night, several of them volunteered to stay here in shifts and keep an eye on me. They went out for burgers and should be back soon."

"No." Phillip spoke without thinking. The thought of her being alone with a bunch of guys he didn't know made his stomach twist.

"Excuse me?" She used that tone that usually heralded trouble. There was going to be a fight and she was digging in deep.

Phillip braced his hands on his waist. There had to be a quick solution to pull his foot from his mouth. "You've already got an adultery charge hanging over your head. How will it appear if you stay here alone with a bunch of male Marines?"

"Coworkers and friends, *Captain*," she replied, with a tilt of her chin.

"Men, *Staff Sergeant*."

Captain Connors cleared his throat and they turned toward him.

"How do you think it looks for her to continue to stay with you? She's got friends who care about her and want to help. Let them. I'll be here, too."

Phillip conceded the point with reluctance.

"I'm sure your wife will appreciate it too." Rowan shot Phillip a sidelong glance through narrowed eyes.

He drew back, blinking in surprise. "My wife? I don't have a wife. Who told you that?"

"I... You were talking to your friend about... I heard you talk about a woman."

He jerked his thumb toward the door. "Laura. Captain Cushing. I wanted her to know the hearing was moved up."

"But Oscar...your boy," she stammered.

Phillip stared for what seemed an eternity before bursting into roars of laughter. "My dog."

"Your—?"

"Dog. Wanna see a picture?" Without waiting for a reply, he sat beside her and pulled out his phone.

Connors groaned and rolled his eyes. "I think I hear the lieutenant bringing our dinner. I'll leave you two with the puppy pictures. Back in a few minutes. I swear it's worse than looking at pictures of someone's kids."

Phillip ignored him and shoved the cell into Rowan's hands.

"A Weimaraner." Her eyes brightened with tears as he smiled. "Isn't he adorable? How old?"

"Eighteen months. He was six months there." He scrolled to another photo—his favorite. The one playing ball at the beach, ears blowing in the breeze. "This was last month."

Rowan's smile widened, though she felt like crying. He doted on the dog. She could imagine what he'd be like with his child. The years stolen from them tore at her heart. They'd never get them back. The loss of that time with Phillip made her almost physically ill with regret.

But what about the future? What would he truly feel once he discovered he had an eight-year-old son? Would he indulge Ian as he did Oscar or would he refuse to be a part of the boy's life? She couldn't hurt Ian by presenting him with a father who wouldn't acknowledge him. But wasn't she hurting him more by allowing him to hero-worship a man he'd never met?

That was her fault. She should have nipped it in the bud when it had first happened. But she couldn't take that adulation away from him and instead helped feed it. Now they'd both pay.

Blinking her vision clear, she pointed to the picture. "He sure loves you, doesn't he? What are you two doing here?"

He draped his arm over the back of the sofa and leaned closer. "Playing ball. He's trying to take it from me. Zach took the picture."

"Got any more?"

"Naw. Zach made me delete most of them. He said it didn't make a good romantic impression on the ladies."

"Oh, I disagree. It's a great icebreaker."

"You think?"

"I sure do." She handed him back the phone and shot a smile his way. "What woman could resist?" she finished in a whisper, voice trailing off with uncertainty.

Her lips were a fraction of an inch from his. If he only knew how tempting. If he only knew how much she wanted to close that infinitesimal distance. Her heart hammered against her ribs. It was wrong—a step neither of them should take for a hundred different reasons, all of which didn't matter at that moment. She wanted to taste his mouth. Phillip tilted his head, ready to slide his lips over hers.

Footsteps in the hallway yanked them to their senses.

"Well" — he slipped the phone back in his pocket and stood with brisk movements — "that's Oscar. Sounds like your guards are here so I'll let you call it a night. I'll have Captain Connors make arrangements with the hospital for you to have your body thoroughly checked for bruising. I'll be back on Friday."

Rowan willed herself to breathe again once he had gone. Her heart soared with joy. He wasn't married. He was free — and he still wanted her. The look in his eyes had told her and she knew it well.

"Don't, Rowan," Captain Connors softly told her from the doorway.

She glanced up at him, her cheeks flushed from a combination of embarrassment and desire. With shaking hands, she accepted the hamburger and fries he handed her way. "I don't know what you mean."

"Yes, you do." He walked in and shut the door. "I recognize the look. You know it can only lead to disaster for you both. I've managed to convince the colonel there's no fraternization going on between the two of you. Please don't make me a liar."

Rowan nodded and bit into her burger, but the misery choking her made it almost impossible to swallow.

Chapter Eight

Laura tensed beside Phillip as they walked into the coroner's examining room. He was surprised she had risen to his taunt of *coward* and come along. If the paleness in her cheeks gave any indication, she regretted it now. He felt a twinge of guilt about baiting her. She could never resist a challenge and he could never resist throwing one in her path.

"Oh, God." She clutched a facemask to her mouth. "It's a real, live dead body."

Jess Alderman chuckled but kept any teasing remarks he had to himself. Mike Connors simply placed his hand against Laura's back to steady her, even though beads of sweat were forming on his pale brow.

Jess and Mike… Phillip smiled. In the ninety-minute drive, all formalities had faded. Even though the words were never spoken because of Laura's presence, they were embarking on a single mission — to save Rowan. That unity somehow managed to make them easy friends as they traded stories about past cases.

"Why did I ever allow you to goad me into coming here?" Laura groaned.

"You want the evidence firsthand, don't you?" he said with a grin. "You don't want to have to wait for the official report. That could take weeks."

"It's freezing in here." She dusted warmth into her arms then hugged them against her chest. "I fail to see... Oh, my God."

Her face took on a greenish tinge as the coroner faced them, one bloodied hand extended their way. As if in afterthought, he pulled it back.

"Sorry. Reflex. Come in. We're about to get started. Everyone gather around for a good look."

The men did so. Laura hovered in the background for a second or two then crept forward.

"Homicide or suicide?" the coroner asked.

"You tell us," Laura mumbled from behind her mask.

Phillip silently applauded. She was willing to be objective, no matter what circumstantial evidence she had seen so far.

With a nod to his assistant, the coroner began. All his observations were recorded on tape. The microphone dangled from a cord centered above Kemp's body. A forensic photographer snapped pictures.

"The deceased appears to be a healthy male."

A little too healthy, in Phillip's opinion. If it had been true that Rowan slept with the man, Phillip might have been tempted to pick up a scalpel and —

"Height, six-foot-four. Weight, two hundred fifty pounds."

The man could have easily overpowered a fine-boned woman like Rowan. Phillip scribbled the annotation on his notepad. Yes, a bodybuilder and in superb health,

Kemp had been in outstanding physical condition, even for the Marine Corps.

"Two gunshot wounds are on the body. One on the upper right thigh, leaving no exit wound. The other is on the head, upper right temple, exit wound behind and below the left ear. Gunpowder marks are near the head wound."

That was the first piece of evidence that corroborated the report. Kemp had been shot at close range, not ten feet away where Rowan was found.

"Numerous abrasions and contusions mark the body."

The coroner listed the locations while the photographer clicked away shot after shot. The more mundane aspects followed — measurements, skin discolorations. Phillip heard Laura mumble something about it not being so bad after all. Then the coroner opened the body.

She gagged and dashed from the room. When the first organ was lifted out, Mike joined her.

The photographer snickered. "Rookies."

The coroner worked on, ignoring the distraction, but Phillip swore he saw the man's eyes crinkle with humor.

Cold-hearted bas —

Phillip stopped himself. Hadn't his reaction been the same when Laura had first said she didn't want to come here with them? This morning he had teased, cajoled then just about bullied her into going by citing professional responsibility. It was no one's fault but his own if Laura's heaving stomach drew smiles from the autopsy team.

Very compassionate of you, Phillip.

He'd make it up to her after this case was over. Maybe they'd go to dinner, even do a little something else later. That would certainly ease his constant ache for Rowan.

Phillip cursed himself. *Now, who's the bastard?* It was over between him and Laura and had been for some time now. She didn't deserve to be used.

Is that what you've become, Phillip Stuart? A user of people? Like Donald?

Evaluating his life over the last several years, he found that it certainly seemed that way. True, he had friendships, but he wasn't above stepping on people if it had furthered his goals. His initial relationship with Laura had served one purpose. He'd needed a woman and she'd been there. There had been no thought to her feelings in the matter, save the fulfillment of her physical needs. He'd cold-heartedly slept with her night after night, satisfying his need for physical release, then just as heartlessly had ended the affair.

Rowan was right. He *was* his father — the very image of the man he most despised. The realization made him queasy. Then the coroner cut into Kemp's stomach.

A vile gas seeped into the room, engulfing them in its stench. Phillip gagged, clamped his hand over his mouth and dashed out, the photographer close behind him.

Despite his roiling stomach, Phillip couldn't help but throw out the jibe, "Rookie," before he and the photographer slid onto the bench in the hallway. Laura and Mike were nowhere to be seen.

The man dropped his head between his knees. Sucking in a breath of fresh air, Phillip closed his eyes and leaned his head against the wall, willing himself not to lose his breakfast.

After a second or two, the photographer gave a weak chuckle. "That's what I get for being cocky."

"What the hell was in that guy's stomach?" Phillip asked.

Before the other man could answer, Phillip caught a whiff of cinnamon. He dared a peek and found Jess holding a toothpick out to him, blue eyes twinkling with unsuppressed amusement.

"I usually switch to cinnamon when I come to these things."

Phillip accepted it with a nod of thanks, but his stomach was still too uneasy to do anything more. "Does it help?"

Jess shrugged. "Doesn't hurt." He held one out to the photographer. "The examiner asked me to tell you that he wants you back in there or you'll have to get yourself a replacement."

The man snatched the wood away and shoved it into his mouth then squared his shoulders and marched back in.

"Braver man than me," Phillip said.

Jess gave him a light jab in the arm. "You came all this way to get the information firsthand. You're not going to let a putrid smell stop you now?"

"Guess not." He poked the toothpick between his lips and forced himself to his feet.

Metal clinking into metal greeted them when they walked in. The stench still lingered. Phillip swallowed the urge to puke and edged closer.

"Welcome back, gentlemen." The coroner pointed to a small metal bowl with his forceps. "Got a little present for you."

Phillip sidled up, wanting to look but afraid of what he would see. A bullet winked up at him.

"I found that in his stomach," the coroner said. "The bullet traveled up his thigh, bounced off the hip bone and through the intestines before stopping there."

"Is that why he smelled so bad when you opened him up?"

"Partly, and the fact that he had a killer dinner of liver smothered with onions and garlic, all washed down with beer. Whoever shot this guy could probably smell him coming."

"Was he drunk?"

The coroner snorted. "Definitely. Blood alcohol content shows he was well over the limit."

"Would have certainly affected his judgment," Jess said. "Might even cause him to think his own cohort was the enemy and knock her out."

Phillip caught another whiff of the deceased and rolled the toothpick to the other side of his mouth. "Maybe. I'd have a heck of a time proving that one. Seems a stretch."

Jess shoved a fresh toothpick between his teeth. "Won't be harder than anything else."

If Kemp attacked Rowan, the question still remains – who shot Kemp? "Any chance the wounds were self-inflicted?"

The coroner plopped Kemp's liver on a scale and noted its weight into the recording microphone. "None. Nothing supports it. This guy definitely fought with someone before he died and gave a good account of himself. Just look at all the bruises he's got." He motioned to the arms and torso. "You can even see the imprint of the other guy's knuckles."

"Guy? Not girl?" Phillip asked.

The coroner laughed. "Not unless she has man hands. The average woman could never have taken this man on face-to-face and given him this type of pounding. Look at the size of him. He's built like Herman Munster." He spread his arms wide. "In addition, look at the size of the bruises left by the assailant's knuckles. The hands that caused those marks were large, powerful. A man's hands, in my opinion."

A smile tugged at the corners of Phillip's mouth.

"Looking at the trajectory of the bullet, it's likely that Kemp was knocked down first then shot."

Phillip nodded. Rowan could have shot Kemp with no problem, but she lacked the brute strength necessary to knock him to the ground before shooting him. In addition, her knuckles were unmarked, unbruised. The force she would have needed to pound those marks into Kemp would have left her knuckles bloody and raw.

"So the angle of the bullet and the splatter of brain matter conclusively show that Kemp was on the ground when he was shot?" Jess' voice demanded absolutes. "He wasn't shot from a distance?"

The coroner nodded. "Powder burns are on his temple," he said simply. "I'd say Kemp was struggling with someone who had a gun. He was knocked to the ground and shot point-blank, simple as that."

Jess pointed to Kemp's leg. "What about that? Before or after death."

"Definitely after. There's no swelling or bleeding. Why do you suppose someone would want to shoot a man who was quite obviously already dead?"

"I can think of one good reason." Phillip tossed the gnawed toothpick into the nearest trashcan then left the room and its grisly contents.

* * * *

The ride back to Twentynine Palms was quiet. In the back seat, Phillip and Jess stared out of their respective windows. Still battling queasiness, Mike drove while Laura sat beside him, ramrod straight.

"There's a rest stop," she suddenly said. "I need you to pull over."

Mike careened into the exit. Before he could come to a complete stop, she was out of the car and running for the ladies' room.

Mike twisted around to look at them. "What did you find out?"

Taking turns tag-teaming the information, Phillip and Jess talked as quickly as possible.

Mike massaged the back of his neck. "So, nothing conclusive either way. She might have shot him, but it's unlikely she beat him up beforehand. Now what?"

"When did you arrange to have Rowan examined?" Phillip asked.

"Couldn't get her in for an appointment at the base hospital until tomorrow morning."

Phillip muttered a curse. *Are we ever going to get a break? Why is everything so damned difficult?*

"They're booked, Phillip. No way to get her in earlier." Mike gripped the steering wheel. "Malcolm should have had her examined more fully the night of the murder."

There were a lot of things Malcolm should have done. "If you ask me, Collins should be fired." He waited for Jess to come to his colleague's defense. Silence echoed from the other side of the seat.

"If we have to wait until morning then we have to wait. It's not like I don't have enough to occupy my time until then."

Like the Lava investigation reports regarding the equipment thefts. The ones that had piqued Rowan's concern in the first place. An enormous pile of those memos, bulletins and reports waited for him in his room.

"Sounds like an all-nighter to me." At the sight of Laura making her way back to the car, Mike paused and pushed open the door for her. "If you bring your work down to the office, I'll help."

Not a bad idea. Just as quickly, Phillip dismissed it. He needed to concentrate. Just knowing Rowan was in the same building would be too much of a distraction. He would want to be with her, to keep an eye out for her safety, protect her at all times.

Phillip realized he was jealous. He wanted to watch and see who she shared her smile with, to question any look another man gave her. He wanted to pound his fist into the face of any Marine who got close enough to smell the sweet, tempting fragrance of her perfume. Staying in the same building would not be a good idea.

"No, thanks, Mike. At least one of us should get some sleep."

* * * *

"A common thread. A hint. A clue. Something!"

The urge to hurl the reports against the wall was too great. Phillip could understand Rowan's frustration, the reason she'd become involved. Unless that sector of the base had suddenly become the desert's version of the Bermuda Triangle, something highly illegal was going on in the Lava training area.

In the last month, a fighter jet had crashed there — the apparent cause an errant bullet from the ongoing military training exercise. The trouble with the theory was that the jet had been in a no-fire zone. Fortunately, the pilot had ejected.

Not so fortunate had been the helicopter crew flying over that same area a few days later. That time, the investigators had determined the cause to be a ruptured fuel line. Two men had lost their lives in the crash and the military exercises had screeched to a halt for three days while the investigation had taken place.

But that hadn't stopped the rash of bad luck at Lava. Recovery teams and their parent units had all begun reporting losses of equipment — a computer here, tools there, the pistol that had wound up in Rowan's hands. Once the training exercises had started up again, there had been two reports of skittish pilots firing on the employees of a mining company adjacent to the base.

Phillip dissected the reports, searching for something — anything — to help him break the case. There had to be something somewhere in the reports that explained the death of Charlie Kemp, to explain why Rowan was being set up to take the blame for his murder. He found one common element — the general location of the incidents. Hoping a fresh approach in the morning would net him some results, Phillip set everything aside and returned to his room for a few hours' sleep.

He felt Rowan's absence the second he walked inside. Common sense told him housekeeping had changed the linens and tidied up, erasing any scent she might have left behind. His heart and body said otherwise. A hard, unrelenting ache tightened his gut and swelled his cock to the breaking point. Phillip stripped his clothes off in his haste to reach the shower, not caring where they landed. He gripped his erection with one hand and reached for the faucet with the other. The sudden blast of cold water aggravated him rather than calmed things down. He braced himself in the corner, jerking off while he waited for the shower to warm. Orgasm tore through him, bringing Phillip to his ass. Hard breaths shuddered through him as emptiness replaced his lust.

After fumbling for the soap, he washed, forcing Rowan's case to the forefront of his mind and keeping it there. Other memories refused to be denied his attention. Phillip eventually crawled into bed, praying sleep would take him. When it did, dreams took over. He gave up a little before sunrise and returned to his search for answers.

By the time noon approached, he was no further along than he'd been the day before and he was grouchy on top of it.

"By the look on your face, I'd say you had a rough night."

Phillip glanced up at the sound of Jess' voice. He closed his eyes and rubbed the bridge of his nose. "You could say that. I don't understand what could be so important that someone would take the risk of causing all these accidents rather than be discovered."

"UFOs?"

He would have laughed if he had been more awake. Instead, Phillip flashed Jess a look from one eye that said, *Spare me, please.*

Chuckling, Jess slid to the sofa. "Where have all the incidents occurred?"

Phillip flipped the base map around and pointed. The intense expression on Jess' face jolted him. "What? What is it?"

The answer was slow in coming. Finally, Jess frowned and pushed the map back to him. "That's the same damn area where those target devices are always being stolen."

It was too simple. "Someone wants to protect their livelihood as a scrap dealer enough to kill?"

"Maybe not that so much as their identity." Jess narrowed his eyes.

"You mean someone who has a lot to lose."

Jess nodded. "Someone who has access to the Lava area. Someone in the military. Maybe someone with enough rank that they would want to protect themselves and their career at any cost."

Mike ducked into the room, shutting the door behind him, his normally serious face alight with excitement. "I got a call from the doctor. Other than a bruise on her hip, shoulder from when she fell and the mark on her face from where she was struck once, there isn't any other mark on Staff Sergeant McKinley to indicate she was in a fight. Plus, there's no way her fists ever came into contact with Kemp hard enough to make those bruises the coroner showed us."

Phillip tossed his pen to the desk. "That takes care of that. Gentlemen, I'd say we have enough to get the charges dropped."

Jess leaned forward. "Don't be too hasty."

Is the man crazy? "It's circumstantial. All of it. Sloppy circumstantial evidence at that. No judge would put Rowan away with this much reasonable doubt."

"And no one knows that but the three of us," Jess replied. "Look. We have a dangerous situation here, a dangerous person. Kemp lost his life trying to uncover this. Staff Sergeant McKinley put her reputation and career on the line, as well. Are you going to let that go to waste?"

"Well, I'm certainly not going to let her be court-martialed for it." Phillip's voice bordered on a snarl. He forced the anger down.

"I'm not saying you should. I'm saying, let the hearing on Monday go without presenting this evidence." Jess' eyes glittered like two chips of blue ice.

Mike braced himself against the wall and crossed his arms over his chest. "What will that accomplish?"

"Maybe it will give the person responsible some breathing room to hang himself. He'll think he's successfully framed Rowan for his crime and become lackadaisical. Then we nail him."

"And if not?"

"Then by the time the court-martial goes, Phillip will have doubled the evidence to clear her beyond anyone's doubts — ballistics reports, the autopsy report, forensic evaluation from the crime scene…"

Phillip massaged the ache in his forehead. "I don't know. It sounds like we're using her as bait."

"Then talk to her. Ask her. I'd be willing to bet she'd agree," Jess said.

That was the problem. He knew she'd agree. Phillip was the one who didn't want to take the risk. He looked at Mike.

Mike shrugged and adjusted his glasses. "Wouldn't hurt. I don't think she's back from the doctor yet. Probably went to grab a bite of lunch."

Reluctantly, Phillip found himself nodding. "I'll talk to her after lunch then. If she agrees, that's how we'll proceed."

"All right then." Mike swung open the door. "You look like you need to burn off some stress. Want to join us in a little basketball?"

"Be right there."

* * * *

Humiliated. It didn't matter that the examination had been done for her benefit. Rowan had still felt violated when she'd been forced to strip down. Having photographs taken of her body had added to her discomfort. Yes, the doctor had remained sympathetic and courteous, but still…

She pulled her van to a stop at the office. As usual, the men were engaged in their noon ritual of basketball. The sand between the two legal services buildings had been packed down into a rough basketball court. Not NBA regulation, but still popular with the Marines. To her surprise, Phillip was in the thick of things.

He was as good at athletics as she remembered, sinking shot after shot with precision and flair. Adding to his skill was the glorious wonder of watching his sleek body in motion, something the other women in the office had definitely noticed as well.

Rowan wandered to the shaded bench where Ellen and another woman sat, ogling the men—one in particular. Their appreciation of the male physique could run a little bawdy at times, and judging from the giggles, she knew now was no exception. However, this time silence descended when she approached.

She said nothing but simply squeezed onto the end of the stone bench to watch the action. A beep from a car horn turned all heads toward the adjacent parking lot.

A tan, darkly attractive man in a cherry red Mustang waved. Phillip shouted back and the car door opened. In a flash of gray fur and floppy ears, Oscar the dog zoomed toward his daddy.

Phillip had little time to prepare. The minute he squatted down to Oscar's level, the dog pounced, knocking him flat in the sand and smothering Phillip's face with doggie kisses. The basketball game halted while players laughed at Phillip and the wiggling mountain of gray fur pinning him down.

Rowan gave her first genuine smile in a week.

Another horn sounded from the parking lot, followed by a voice that normally brought joy to Rowan's heart.

"Mom!"

The blood drained from Rowan's face as she lurched to her feet. Rather than take Ian home, the Cubmaster had brought him to her. Another plan ruined. Somehow, she had to salvage the situation.

She forced her legs to move. Phillip mustn't see Ian. But Ian, in his delight at seeing his mother and longing to share every tidbit of his adventure, had already started to run her way.

If she could get him into the building before — *Too late*.

Distracted from his joyous reunion with Phillip, Oscar whipped around toward the noise and made a galloping beeline for Ian.

Dog and boy met in the center of the makeshift basketball court. Ian shrieked with delight as Oscar transferred his tongue-licking to the boy's hands and face. The silence surrounding them was deafening. Everyone seemed to be waiting to see what she said and Phillip did. Her well-known secret was seconds away from implosion.

Phillip chuckled and rose to his feet. Nothing like the love of a dog, no matter how exuberant. Judging from the boy's laughter, he thought so too. Oscar loved children.

He dusted the sand from his clothes. Laughing, he walked over to retrieve Oscar before the boy drowned under all those kisses. "I think you've made a new friend."

Phillip froze at the first glimpse of that small face — a mirror-image of his own. His knees buckled from the shock. He forced himself to stand upright.

"What the...?"

His jaw worked but no more words came out. It was a mistake, wasn't it? A crazy coincidence. *No.* This child was his son. His son! But how in the world — ?

"Mom, whose dog is this?"

The boy, alight with pleasure from Oscar's enthusiastic welcome, looked directly at Rowan. A frown wrinkled the space between his eyebrows as he focused on her bruised face. "What happened?"

Rowan strode forward and welcomed her son with a hug and a kiss. "I had a little accident. I'm all right now."

"I'll bet you cried." Ian touched her face with the pads of his fingers.

"Yes, I did. It hurt a lot."

He tossed a hug around her then planted a kiss to her cheek. "Are you all better now?"

Rowan hugged him back while she blinked away tears. "Much better. Thank you."

She glanced over his shoulder at Phillip. Taking a deep breath, she stood and faced him, putting the boy in front of her. "Sweetheart, there's someone here I want you to meet. This is Phillip Stuart, your father."

Phillip refused to look at her. He kept his gaze riveted to the son he'd never known he had. All these years she'd lied.

Silence surrounded them. The office staff stood frozen with shocked fascination. They had to have seen the resemblance, had to have known. But had they conspired to help Rowan keep her horrid secret or think that by his presence Phillip already knew? Then he remembered the missing page from her record book.

Confusion turned to rage. *The bitch. The lying, cold-hearted bitch*. With hands clenched at his sides, Phillip took a rigid step toward Rowan.

Mike hooked his elbow. "Not here. Not now."

Phillip let this common sense direct him and peered down at the boy, who was gazing up at him with a mixture of wide-eyed awe and undisguised hero worship. He didn't even know the child's name.

"Ian, why don't you and your dad take Oscar inside and give him some water," Mike said. "He seems pretty thirsty from his long trip through the desert. There are some plastic bowls in the supply closet."

Ian. At least she'd done something right, using a name they'd chosen for their first-born son. That tiny pleasure did little to ease the agony of her deception.

Eyes and smile still wide, Ian nodded, slipped his hand through Oscar's collar and tugged him inside.

Rowan caught Phillip's arm before he could follow. "Phillip, please. Be gentle with him. He's just a little boy. He doesn't understand."

"That makes two of us."

"He worships you and has since he was three. He's convinced you're a crime fighter and you've been on a secret mission. Please don't hurt him."

He jerked free of her hold. "What kind of a person do you think I am?"

Rowan gasped at the pain in his eyes. "Phillip, please."

"A crime fighter?"

"I was afraid—"

"Right about now you should be. And if you think I'd actually hurt a child, you can damn well go to hell. That's where you deserve to be, anyway, for keeping me from my son all these years."

He shoved past her and marched into the building.

Chapter Nine

Phillip couldn't string two coherent thoughts together. Fortunately, he didn't have to. Ian did all the talking.

The child sat on the floor near Phillip's feet and scratched Oscar's neck. He watched the boy with a sense of amazement. *A son. My son.* Ian babbled on about his trip, probably to cover his nervousness. Phillip remembered he had done the same thing as a child.

How could she do this to me?

The question screamed to be answered. Just thinking about it made Phillip's heart twist with an indescribable pain. Losing Rowan all those years ago had been nothing compared to this.

He feathered his fingers across Ian's shoulder, trying in vain to quell their shaking. Seeing the child explained Rowan's association with Kemp through Little League, her need to have a van, the crayon melted against the side of the seat of the vehicle.

My son. She had stolen his son from him, denied him the joy of watching him grow in her belly, of seeing him born, holding him as a baby, being a part of his life, of truly being a father. And she would have continued to do so if she hadn't gotten herself into trouble. She would have continued to lie, knowing full well where to find him, never giving him the opportunity to know his son.

With each thought, Phillip's eyes teared. Another alien event. He didn't cry. Men didn't cry, but that was exactly what he wanted to do. Cry. Shout. Rage. Take Rowan's pretty little neck and —

"Is your undercover job done now?"

"My what? Oh, yes. All finished."

"Mom said you were very brave. Don't worry. She never told me about your job. I guessed, then she had to tell me."

At least she had told Ian something, no matter how ridiculous, and didn't let Ian think badly of him or pretend he was dead. "Yes, it's all very secret."

"I understand. You can trust me. I'm real good at keeping secrets."

Obviously a trait he learned from his mother.

"Can you come home and live with me and Mom now?"

"We'll have to see about that. But I'm back in your life to stay and we'll be able to spend lots of time together."

"That's good. Your dog, too?"

"*Our* dog."

"Great. I've always wanted to have a dog but we move a lot. Mom said she would worry about a dog if we had to go overseas and couldn't take him. She said it wasn't fair to leave a member of the family behind, 'cause that's what we might have to do."

Ian was right. Moving overseas with a pet was a problem and Phillip was a little ashamed of himself for not having considered the issue before. What would happen to Oscar if he got orders to Okinawa or Korea? Again, he'd thought only of himself and the fun of owning a pet, not the pet's welfare if he received orders to a far-off Marine base.

It was like Rowan to plan for the future. He had never known her to be less than precise. With some sick realization, he wondered if his father had been right about her all along. Was his share in the Stuart fortune too big a temptation? Would Rowan have done anything to get a piece of it? Perhaps get pregnant to keep him at her side? His disinheritance from the family fortune had been about the time she had deserted him and their relationship.

Phillip shook his head. *No.* As angry as he was, he couldn't believe that. He had been as responsible for Ian's conception as she — too lazy to make a trip to the drug store. A Stuart grandchild would have been blessed with everything and anything money could buy, whether or not Phillip inherited. It made no sense. *None* of this made any sense.

Was this all a part of some need for revenge because he hadn't contacted her when he'd enrolled in Officers' Candidate School all those years before? Or because he'd failed to appear for James' funeral — even though he'd never gotten the message in the first place? At the time, he'd thought their relationship stronger than that.

Yet, if revenge had been her motive, why hadn't she bothered to turn the child against him? A child's hatred was the most potent weapon a mother could wield. The more he thought about it, the more questions he created.

"What's our dog's name?"

Phillip smiled. At last a question he could answer without much thought. "Oscar."

"What kind of dog is he? I've never seen a silver dog before."

"He's a Weimaraner. They're originally from Germany, bred to hunt and retrieve." Phillip rubbed one of Oscar's silky ears. "The only things Oscar retrieves now are cans out of my garbage pail."

"I think he likes me."

"I know he does, and I do, too."

As if to reply, Oscar flicked his tongue across Ian's face then gave Phillip a lopsided puppy grin when Ian giggled in response.

How old is Ian? Eight, of course. If Phillip really thought about it, he could probably figure out the exact time he was conceived.

Tall for his age, lean. He was tan, his reddish-blond hair almost golden from days in the sun. All boy, judging from his appearance after the camping trip. He was filthy.

Phillip ruffled the boy's hair. "You could use a bath."

Ian's blue eyes brightened. "So could you."

Glancing down at his sweat-soaked workout gear, Phillip had to laugh. "You're right about that. Let's go to my room and clean up."

"I don't have any clean clothes."

Of course he didn't. He'd just come back from camping.

"We could go to my house," Ian suggested.

Rowan wouldn't like that in the least and Phillip knew it. He narrowed his eyes. *Why should I care what she likes?*

"Good idea. Let's get your backpack and the house key from your mom." He grabbed a clean change of clothes from his locker and grinned down at the boy. His son.

Ian sprang forward and tossed his arms around Phillip's waist. "I'm so happy you're finally home. I love you."

Those damnable tears popped into his eyes and he wrapped a tight hug around his boy. He had never expected to hear those words from a child, at least not anytime soon. Yet he found a void in his life suddenly filled.

"I love you, Ian." No hesitation. No question. He loved Ian with a fierce joy that made him tremble with its force.

Ian hopped back, a broad, impish smile cutting his features — a smile very much like Rowan's. Their child.

Phillip bit back the urge to smash his fist against the wall. *Damn her.*

"Let's go." Ian hopped to the door. "I can't wait for you to see my room. Come on, Oscar."

Oscar tagged faithfully by Ian's side, letting Phillip follow in their wake.

Rowan felt like throwing up. In the fifteen-minute eternity since Phillip and Ian had walked into the other building, she'd cried gallons of tears. They showed no sign of letting up any time soon.

The unraveling of her secret had caused a sensation in the office. Not that everyone hadn't already been aware of the relationship that obviously existed between her son and her newly acquired defense counsel, but most had never guessed Phillip hadn't had a clue about Ian.

She'd heard the gasps of shock at that pivotal moment. Whispered comments had followed. Then there had been the looks—questioning, accusing and condemning.

"Here they come."

At Ellen's words, Rowan leaped to her feet and peeked out of the window. Phillip and Ian were coming from his office in the other building. They crossed the basketball court between the structures and walked in the door to Legal Services.

"He looks like he's calmed down."

Fat lot Ellen knew. Phillip's smile was for Ian, but the ice-cold fury in his eyes was reserved for her.

He slowed his pace to match Ian's stride while Oscar trotted faithfully alongside his new playmate. As they neared her office, Ian dropped Phillip's hand and skipped ahead.

"Mom, me and Dad need the key to the house. We're gonna take a bath and I'm gonna show him my room."

She swallowed the lump in her throat. "Sweetheart, I don't think…"

Phillip walked very close to Rowan and kept his voice pitched low, so as not to alarm Ian in any way. "Give me the key, Rowan."

His tone left no room for argument. Resigned to the hole she'd dug for herself, she retrieved the key and placed it in Phillip's outstretched hand. He snapped his fingers over it.

"Phillip, I—"

He cut her off with one swift slice of his hand. "Don't." He turned to Ian. "Why don't you get Oscar settled in the car?"

Ian smiled. "Okay. Where's my—?"

Before he could ask the question, Ellen handed him his backpack and scooted him out of the door.

Once he was out of earshot, Phillip whipped around to Rowan, all pretense of civility gone. "I'll deal with you later. You can count on that. And let me give a little warning. If you even so much as think of leaving this base to follow us, I'll have you back in that detention cell so fast it will make your head spin."

He pivoted on his heel and marched away. Rowan took a step and would have run after him had Ellen not held her back.

"Not now, sweetie. It's going to be bad, no matter how you look at it. At least you have a hope that when he's ready to have a piece of your hide, it'll be in private."

Rowan moved to the door, watching Ian and Phillip cross the now-empty court and walk to the parking lot. *So much the same.*

Ian's eyes widened at the Mustang's white leather interior. "Wow, those seats are cool." His voice carried across the short distance.

"They sure are." Phillip's voice carried as well. He flashed her a dark glare. She braced herself for what he might say next.

"But I have one rule. No crayons in my car." He helped Ian into the backseat then slipped into the driver's seat.

It was all Rowan could do to keep from following, but she knew Phillip well enough to know he did not give threats lightly. One foot off this base and she'd be behind bars.

She watched them drive away. The license plate caught her gaze, bringing more tears. *Lil Red.*

It had been nothing more than a shambles held together by rust and will when they'd found it all those years ago. A hint of the original red color had remained and Rowan had dubbed it 'the little red car'. She had been by Phillip's side when he'd ordered the personalized tags, with him when Donald had raged at the rusted heap leaking oil on his pristine brick driveway, had sat enthralled while Phillip had planned each step of restoration then she'd actually crawled under the car and helped him with the work.

Now look at it. Another reminder of the years lost. No, the years stolen. She had to find a way to make Phillip understand that.

Ellen squeezed a hug around her shoulders. "It was inevitable. Too many people knew. Someone was bound to slip up sooner or later. Maybe you should call your mom."

Rowan shook her head. The last thing she needed at the moment was an I-told-you-so lecture.

* * * *

Phillip hoped he would be able to find his way back to base after negotiating all the turns and back roads it took to get to Rowan's house. According to Ian, they lived in the boonies — a charming phrase for 'out in the middle of nowhere'.

He should have guessed as much. With Rowan's uneasiness about closed-in places, living in town or on base wouldn't hold much appeal. As it was, he was surprised at how many houses there actually were out of town.

"There it is." Ian pointed excitedly at a turnoff. "Where the trees are."

Philip jolted off the pavement onto a dirt road and winced at the cloud of dust and pings of rocks as they bounced off the undercarriage of the Mustang.

So much for a clean car, not to mention the paint job.

Rowan's two-story house was on a rise about a mile down the road. Even from this distance, Phillip saw light glinting off the windows of the small two-story, which surely offered a one-hundred-eighty-degree view. An abundance of trees and other greenery provided a welcome break from the stark landscape and shade from the desert sun but not enough encroachment to make Rowan feel shut in.

A twinge of guilt hit him at the memory of his threat to have her locked up. It had been a dirty tactic. In retrospect, he couldn't say that he really would have carried it out.

Who was he fooling? He'd meant it. She deserved to suffer after the lies she'd told. He longed to see her disabled by panic and fear, to crawl on her hands and knees and beg him...*beg* him to have her released. His revenge would be in saying no. The small fantasy gave him a modicum of satisfaction.

Pulling to a stop before the house scattered the birds, ground squirrels and jackrabbits lounging in the welcome shade near the front entrance. Ian shoved open the door before Phillip could stop him. In less time than it took to blink, Oscar was out of the car, hell-bent on chasing down the closest offenders, barking madly.

"Oscar, no!"

The dog charged on, plowing through rows of carefully manicured pansies, marigolds and geraniums. A bed of irises became casualties of his zeal. With each pound of the dog's big paws, flower after flower was ripped from its bed. Finally, free of the obstacles of civilization, Oscar tore off across open landscape.

Chasing him was out of the question. Phillip knew that from experience. Oscar would come back when he was done romping, successful or not.

He surveyed the damage left in his wake. Emma's garden was destroyed.

"Your grandmother is going to kill me when she sees what Oscar did to her garden."

"That's not Grandma's garden. It's mom's." Ian pointed to the house on the next acreage. "Grandma lives there. The people died and it was for sale, so she bought it." He lowered his tone to that of a conspirator. "Mom says she thinks Grandma might have a boyfriend. We see a car there from time to time."

It was hard to imagine Rowan gardening and harder still to think of Emma with anyone but James. He had to forcibly recall that James was dead and had been for... "Did you know your Grandpa McKinley?"

Ian shook his head. "He died before I was born."

That would explain why James hadn't called to tell him about Ian. He never would have stood for this nonsense had he been alive. It still didn't excuse Emma — and certainly not Rowan.

"Shouldn't we go after Oscar?" Ian asked.

"He'll come back when he's ready." *And not a minute sooner.* "What we do need to do is try to fix your mom's garden."

No sense in setting a bad example for his son. The very air Rowan breathed might infuriate him, but he still had to show the boy a good example.

Ian retrieved a hand trowel and shovel from a shed behind the house while Phillip tried his best to right the broken stems on the irises. It was hopeless, but at least the bulbs were intact and would grow back. He'd try to save what he could of the broken flowers for a vase. Oscar was simply going to have to learn that this was not acceptable. The trouble was catching him in the act before he took off. Phillip sighed. Time for dog obedience school — again.

As if sensing Phillip's thoughts, Oscar trotted back to the house, tongue dragging, a cockeyed grin on his face. With no hesitation, he plopped down in the cool dirt of the rejuvenated flowerbed and rolled.

"Oscar, no!"

The dog looked at Phillip as if he were crazy. Ian grabbed his collar and tugged him to his feet. "Come on, Oscar. Let's get a drink of water."

Visions of dirty paws on a carpet panicked Phillip. Before he could stop him, Ian had the door open. Oscar slipped through it like he owned the place. Phillip sprinted after them, expecting disaster. Oscar sprawled onto the cool tile inside the door then watched adoringly as Ian came back from the kitchen with a bowl of water.

Tension eased from Phillip's shoulders. The house was decorated for living, not for show — unlike his own white-carpeted childhood home.

Practicality and comfort were visible everywhere he looked, from the tiled floors at the entryway to the brown Berber carpet in the living room beyond. Even Rowan's furniture was designed to hide the rigors of childhood.

To his right, a staircase led to the upper level. Light poured down from above, inviting him to take a peek.

"That's Mom's," Ian said. "You can take a bath up there if you want. I always use the one down here."

Phillip smiled. "That's okay. I'll wait until you're done."

"Okay, you can put your stuff here in Grandma's old room." Ian pointed down the hall. "And here's mine, if you want to look around." He tossed his backpack in then darted into an adjoining bathroom.

Phillip wandered around the house, studying the knickknacks, the books on the shelves, the magazines on the coffee table. He felt lost, out of place — and why shouldn't he? He was never meant to be here. An intruder.

A small glass bird on a high shelf caught his eye and he smiled involuntarily. *She still has it.*

Rowan had seen the golden wren for sale at a small Georgetown antique store. It had been their first date and Phillip had noticed her lingering over an object in a corner of the shop. He remembered the delight in her eyes when she'd cupped the fragile ornament in her palms — much too expensive for her limited budget. He'd gone back to the store the next day and purchased it for her.

Phillip ran his finger over the bird's outstretched wing tip. His feelings for Rowan during those first days of their relationship came flooding back — the excitement, the agony of each look, each touch.

He sighed. Then she'd cut herself out of his life, leaving a gaping wound in his heart. She had also taken away his unborn son. Phillip sighed again and scanned the rest of the shelves.

The photo albums on the bottom shelf of the oak bookcase caught his eye. He recognized a few of them from his and Rowan's time together. At least that hadn't changed about her.

She was meticulous in recording each facet of her life — photos, ticket stubs, brochures. Every event, every experience in her life could be found in those albums.

In college he had laughed at her obsession. Now he treasured it. In those volumes lay the key to the years he had missed with Ian.

With his index finger, he started to pull off the album most likely to contain Ian's history, the one beside the last volume he was familiar with. Then he paused. He wanted to savor each memory, to curl up with Ian for a detailed explanation. He couldn't very well do so until they were both cleaned up.

Phillip glanced at the stairway leading to Rowan's room. *It's only a shower. What does it matter?* He'd already lost eight years of his son's life. He didn't want to waste one second more. After snatching up his change of clothes, he took the stairs two at a time, determined to beat Ian back to the living room.

He wasn't prepared for the sight of Rowan's room and the emotions it evoked. He told himself that it was a room — nothing more, nothing less. Decorated in muted tones of peaches and cream, the windows opened on two sides to encompass the surrounding desert landscape. It was a haven. A sanctuary. A place for lovers.

A glance toward her king-size bed turned his stomach into knots. How many men had lain with her in that bed? How many had tasted her sweetness? Had she ever once called out his name in those moments of passion? Ever thought of him? Ever longed for him as he had her?

The answer was clear — no, not if she could deny him his child. Oddly, he recalled once more his father warning him of such a thing. It galled him to think his old man may have been right all along.

"I'll be damned if I'll ever let him know that."

There was no sense mooning over the past. It had been over between the two of them long ago, especially for her. He moved on to the adjoining bathroom. Another shock hit him.

A garden tub greeted him the minute he stepped into the room—big enough for two, set in an alcove surrounded by beautiful potted plants. It was an oasis in the middle of the desert. Their tub. A long-ago dream for their future together. Sweet regret mixed with bitterness.

"Why, Rowan? I don't understand."

At that point, he didn't want to. After slinging his tote bag to the tile floor, he stripped down and stepped into the adjacent shower stall.

Don't look or think or feel. Just shower and get the hell out of here.

Memories still invaded, twisting his heart and making him ache for what was and could never be again.

"Damn. Damn. Damn." He twisted the cold water on full blast and let it shock his system back to normal. It didn't help. In fact, he was beginning to wonder if he was ever going to be normal again.

He grabbed the soap, worked up a good lather on his washcloth and rubbed it against his chest. The scent of lavender enveloped him. Perfumed soap. He was washing with perfumed soap—just what he needed to make his day complete. Hopefully, no one would notice if he rinsed until he was a prune.

* * * *

"This is when we went to Legoland." Ian pointed to the picture then delved into a rambling dissertation on all they had seen and done. "And this is when me and Mom went hiking in Joshua Tree National Park." There was a beautiful shot of the two of them on top of a giant boulder.

"You climbed up there?"

"Yeah. It wasn't really very hard." Ian paused to consider a moment. "Well, Mom helped me over the really high rocks. We go hiking a lot."

"What about Grandma?" The unasked question— Who took the picture?

"Oh, Grandma doesn't go. She hates hiking."

"Then, who took the picture?" Another unasked question— What *man* took the picture?

"Ellen did. She hates hiking, too, but Timmy wanted to go, so she went with us. Timmy is my best friend. We're in Cub Scouts together."

A car pulled to a stop before the house. "Grandma's here." Ian jumped down and raced for the door. He tugged it open before Emma could reach it. "Grandma, come look. My dad's home!"

Her eyes brightened with Ian's excitement as she hugged him. "I heard. Mom called me."

Oscar trotted up for attention.

She laughed and scratched him behind the ears. "What a pretty boy you are."

Oscar was in love. He immediately dropped to the tile floor and offered his belly for scratching.

Traitor.

"That's Oscar. He's mine and my dad's dog." He grabbed her hand and tugged her farther into the room. "Come on, Grandma. Mom has to work this weekend.

Dad made us dinner. We're having spaghetti and meatballs. I helped."

"It smells delicious." Her gaze fell on Phillip and her smile faltered. "Phillip."

"Emma." He set aside the album. "Dinner's about ready. Would you like a salad?"

"That would be nice. Thank you."

Polite and correct. What else could they say with Ian present? It made for an awkward meal. He watched the time tick by until it was bedtime for Ian then exercised another parental right which had been denied him. He read a story and tucked him in.

"I love you, Dad. I'm glad you're here with us now," Ian said with a sleepy smile.

"Me, too. I love you, Ian. Have a good sleep." A final tuck, hug and kiss then he eased the door shut and marched down the hall to confront Emma.

She raised a hand before he could draw breath to begin. "This is between the two of you. Leave me out of it."

"That's not good enough, Emma. I thought we were closer than that. You and James were like parents to me. You know that. How could you — ?"

"James was dead, Phillip. It was all I could do to survive that. Each day was another day barely getting by, another day without the love of my life, another day of tears and misery. As I said, this is between you and Rowan. I'm the grandmother, not the referee."

"I don't understand, Emma. I loved her! How could she — ?"

Emma shook her head. "Stop, Phillip. There's more to this mess than any one of us knows. You need to talk it out from start to finish with Rowan and hear her side of the story."

"Fine. I'll take it up with Rowan." He brushed by her to leave but got no farther than three steps when he saw Zach waiting for him in the living room with Mike Connors.

"What the hell do you two want?"

"Thought you could use a beer," Zach said.

"Leave me alone." He tried to push between them.

Zach snagged his arm. "I said…we thought you could use a beer."

Phillip jerked free. "Sounds like I'm going to have one whether I want it or not."

"Hey, this is me. Come on. I know how you feel."

"You have no idea how I feel," Phillip ground out through bared teeth.

Zach held his place. "True, but I have a good imagination, always very important for an attorney." He grinned and raised one eyebrow in the patented Zach smile. "How about that beer? It'll calm you down. I'll buy."

"You don't have enough money to calm me down."

"Humor me then."

"Or the two of you will wrestle me down to the nearest bar?"

Mike stood. "Something like that." He clapped a hand onto Phillip's back. "Let's go. You can kill her later."

Phillip arched an eyebrow. "Or you? You knew about this and didn't tell me. In fact, it wouldn't surprise me if you were the one who removed the information from my copy of her record book." His eyes narrowed.

Mike shrugged. "I don't have a clue what you're talking about. If something was missing… Well, that's what you get for not making your own copies of your client's files." He was sarcastic, a pointed reminder of Phillip's earlier rudeness.

"Very funny, but I'm not laughing." Phillip curled his hand into a fist. He wanted to smash something. Mike's face was a tempting target.

He forced himself to relax. This wasn't Mike's fault. It was no one's business but his and Rowan's. Maybe the two idiots were right. Maybe a quick drink would calm him down. Everything was coming to a boil—events, his emotions. It was knocking him off-guard and out of control.

"All right. Let's go. I don't want to be out all night. I still have some unfinished business to take care of."

Zach swung open the door. "Just a beer or two." A wicked look danced across his face. "I've got to tell you, Phillip. You're the best smelling date I've had in a long time."

Phillip shot him a glare and folded himself into the backseat of Mike's battered old blue Celica. The backseats were definitely not made to accommodate tall passengers.

They took him to a small bar in the center of town where the only music was the constant click of pool balls and the murmur of the customers. There, in a corner booth, two beers turned into three, then four, then Phillip lost count. Before he realized it, he was pouring out his guts.

Zach and his incessant drive to know all somehow managed to pry loose the entire story. As much as Phillip had wanted to keep this inside, the words flowed—not just the ones about hurt, betrayal and revenge but also the desire, the need, the love still burning beneath his hatred. His friends listened with little comment, and in the dark recesses of his mind, Phillip knew they wouldn't judge him.

"Unwinding from your hectic week?"

Bleary-eyed, Phillip glanced up at the man standing in front of their table. He was familiar.

Who is this guy?

Then it clicked. Malcolm Collins, the NCIS agent who had botched the evidence gathering in Rowan's case.

"Mind if I join you?" He sat without waiting for a reply.

Phillip watched Zach and Mike exchange a look before Mike said, "As a matter of fact, we do. We were having a private conversation."

Collins smiled. "Just one beer. I'm expecting some friends any minute." He motioned to the waitress then turned that sly smile of his back their way. "Interesting day, huh?"

Phillip stared a hole through the man and offered no response. The slight didn't faze Collins.

"Still think your client's innocent, counselor?"

Mike leaned forward. "First of all, Malcolm, you know as well as I do that you don't ever talk about cases in public. Secondly, these personal events have nothing to do with Rowan McKinley's innocence or guilt."

"Don't they?" The waitress brought his drink and Malcolm slugged it down. "Seems pretty clear to me. The only thing I haven't found out is who her accomplice is."

"What the hell is *that* supposed to mean?" Phillip's voice echoed in his ears. Had he shouted? Apparently not, since a glance around didn't reveal any eavesdroppers.

"Well, counselor, it seems pretty clear that the recent attempt on Staff Sergeant McKinley's life wasn't an attempt on her life but on yours."

"What?" The word came out in chorus from the three of them.

Collins rested his elbows on the table and pressed forward. "Check out this scenario... She killed one man. What's another? She knows she's guilty. She knows she's going to jail until hell freezes over. She has a kid she obviously doesn't want the father to know about. She's determined that the father not get his hands on the kid after she's locked up, so she concocts this scheme to get him here as her defense counsel then sets up a hit."

Phillip stared at the man for less time than it took to blink then tossed back a belly-shaking laugh.

"You should be writing fiction, Malcolm," Mike said.

"Should I?" he asked with a smirk. "Have any of you asked yourselves how well you really know Rowan McKinley? This gentleman doesn't know her at all." He indicated Zach, then pointed at Mike. "You've only known her about a year. As for her intrepid counselor here, we know how well he knows her, but people change and that was a long time ago."

Nine years, to be exact. Phillip's laughter faded. He hated Collins for sowing even the smallest seed of doubt. Rowan had lied about Ian, but lying about murder entered a whole new ball game. She couldn't. She wouldn't. *Would she?*

Collins polished off his drink. "Thanks for the company. I see my friends now. Have a pleasant evening, gentlemen."

"What a bunch of crap," Zach said after the agent left not only them but the bar as well.

"I'll say," Mike grumbled. "He stuck us with paying for his drink."

"Guess that divorce is taking more out of him than we thought." Phillip tossed down the rest of his beer and set the bottle in the center of the table. "I need to go back to Rowan's house and get my car. Someone else is going to have to drive me from there back to the base." He fought a wave of dizziness. "I need to talk to Rowan."

"Not a problem." Zach slid out from behind the booth. "I'll make sure you get to her, but you have to promise me something."

"What's that?"

"No matter what happens tonight, you won't lose your temper."

When Phillip hesitated, Zach leaned forward. "Promise."

"All right, all right. Let's get out of this place."

The combination of beer, the cool dryness of the nighttime desert air and the rocking motion of the car made Phillip drowsy. He fought sleep with every mile, determined to stay alert enough to have it out with Rowan. He rehearsed words, played out scenarios. She was nothing more than a witness on the stand — a witness whose composure he was determined to break.

He jerked upright when Mike turned off the engine. Sleep had claimed him after all. Rubbing his eyes clear, he reached for the door handle then froze. Rowan's van was parked beside his car.

"What the...?"

Mike kept the electric locks in place. "The battalion commander removed her restriction this afternoon."

"He can't do that without—"

"He can do whatever he wants," Mike said. "He's a lieutenant colonel."

"Fine. Open the damned door."

Zach draped his arm over the front seat and swiveled to pin Phillip with a direct stare. For once, his tone was dead serious. "You promised. Remember?"

"That's before I found out that I was being deliberately led around by the nose while Rowan was released. Now open the door. I have a right to an explanation."

"Is anything she says tonight going to make a difference to you now? It happened. It's over. It's in the past and you can't change that. Accept your son and the life you can have together now and go on."

"Open...the...door!"

"Your word as an officer and a gentleman?"

Phillip flopped back in the seat. It was no use. Zach was about a million times more stubborn than any other individual he knew. It was either make the promise or stay here and rot. He felt too drunk and tired to spend the night in the back of a Matchbox car.

"Fine," he said through clenched teeth. "I promise."

Until I get inside that house.

Chapter Ten

Through the living room window, Rowan watched Phillip unfold himself from the backseat of Captain Connors' car. He'd been drinking and it showed. Each step was cautious, as if he thought the ground would collapse beneath him. It was so unlike his normally confident stride where he owned the world and the world knew it. If her current circumstances hadn't been so dire, the sight would have been funny.

She wanted this done, but there would be no sense trying to talk to him tonight. He'd be unreasonable. Anything they did manage to discuss, he'd not remember come morning.

Hugging herself against disappointment, she turned to her mother and Jess Alderman. "I'm going to bed."

Her mother shook her head. "You can't avoid talking to him forever. Why don't you get it over with?"

"I would if those two hadn't taken him out to drink."

Jess coughed into his fist. "You're the one who wanted him gone by the time you got home."

"I didn't want a confrontation in front of Ian, but I also didn't want him snockered. He won't listen to a word I say. And if he does, I'll doubt he'll remember it in the morning. I'll talk to him tomorrow."

"When he's hungover and defenseless," Jess muttered.

Her mother chuckled.

Rowan whirled around to face them. "I'm glad this amuses the two of you."

"You have no one to blame but yourself," her mom replied.

Not exactly. There was someone else to blame. Unfortunately, at that time, Rowan had been too young and too easily intimidated. The years since then had taken care of the rest.

The front door swung open before she could escape upstairs. She saw Oscar leap to his feet, tail wagging. It stopped in mid-swing when his master's anger became apparent.

Phillip jabbed a wobbly finger in her direction. "You!"

"I refuse to speak with you when you've been drinking." Rowan strode past him as he staggered in the entryway. She grabbed the banister and scooted onto the first step.

"Apparently you refuse to speak with me whenever it pleases you." He stomped after her. "Like nine years ago!"

"Keep your voice down," she snapped over her shoulder. "You'll wake Ian." Without another glance, she turned and started upstairs.

The staircase shuddered behind her. "Damn it, Rowan, don't walk away when I'm talking to you."

She took the stairs two at a time, anxious to put as much distance between them as possible. It wasn't enough. His legs were longer, his determination powered by alcohol. As she closed her fingers over the doorknob, he was just a few steps behind.

"I said *wait!*"

He closed fingers of steel over her wrist. He spun her around. There was a growl from behind them that built to a snarl. Before either of them could react, eighty-five pounds of fur and muscle leaped at Phillip, knocking him forward through the doorway and pinning him to the floor with Rowan beneath.

"Oscar!"

His reprimand only earned another growl. Over Phillip's shoulder, Rowan watched wide-eyed as the dog bared his teeth. Two paws and the balance of his weight pressed down on Phillip's back.

Footsteps thundered up the stairs. Zach stopped inside the doorway. "Good God!"

Phillip propped his elbows on either side of Rowan's head to ease his weight from her. It was no use.

"Maybe he's trying to protect her from you," Zach suggested.

"That's ridiculous," Phillip snapped. "He's not her dog. He's mine. He's supposed to be on my side."

But that was exactly what Oscar was doing. With each growl, Phillip's anger grew, which only escalated the dog's anguish. It was obvious that Oscar was torn between his love for Phillip and his desire to protect Rowan.

Zach crossed his arms and leaned against the wall. "Looks and sounds like someone else wants you to keep your promise. You'd better find a way to calm down or you'll both be there all night."

Phillip's lips drew out to a thin line. He glared down at her.

"I can't believe you turned my dog against me."

"I didn't," she snapped back. "If you weren't behaving like a buffoon…"

Oscar's amber-eyed gaze dropped to her. Her eyes widened. The dog meant business.

Phillip lifted the corner of his mouth in a ghost of a smile. "Well, looks like I'm not the only one being told to behave. Question is, how do we get out of this predicament?"

"He's your dog. You do something." Rowan wiggled in a vain attempt to find a more comfortable position. Phillip's weight was growing heavy.

Too late, she realized her mistake. One press of her belly to his groin brought another heat flaring to life. Her heart hammered in response. She was barely aware of her breath quickening, so intent was she on the deliciously familiar sensation rippling along her skin.

It would be so easy to surrender, to slip her arms around his neck, to drape her legs around him.

The anger in his face softened. Lust replaced it. His gaze caressed her face, settling on her lips. *If he kissed me now…*

Still holding her captive with his hooded gaze, Phillip traced circles against the outsides of her breasts with his thumbs, stealing her breath and shooting darts of pleasure throughout her body. Rowan closed her eyes on a soft gasp. His breath was hot against her neck, his lips a half heartbeat from nipping that extra tender spot under her ear. Her heart raced with anticipation.

Oscar shoved his nose between them and assaulted them with an intensive, indiscriminate series of dog kisses. Phillip sputtered and rolled away.

"Oscar…" Another licking followed. Phillip wiped the back of his hand across his cheek.

All was forgiven as far as the dog was concerned, but Rowan was too rattled to move. She flipped over and crawled to her knees then edged to her bed and leaned against it for support.

Zach snagged the dog's collar. "Come on, you overgrown mongrel. I think they've learned their lesson."

Phillip shoved himself to his feet, swaying slightly. "I'll be by in the morning for Ian. We'll be spending the weekend together at Disneyland. Do you have any problem with that?"

His voice dared her to challenge him.

Rowan shook her head. "He'll be ready to go." It came out as a croak. She was surprised it came out at all. From the corner of her eye she watched Phillip leave, shutting the door behind him.

After pulling herself onto the bed, Rowan drew her knees to her chest. She ached everywhere their bodies had touched and especially where they had not. *This is never going to work.* The wanting had been bad enough when they were on congenial terms. Now the undercurrent of old wounds was forcing them together in a state of heightened emotions.

Rowan didn't think she was strong enough to resist — didn't know if she wanted to. Visions of muscled thighs and a rock-hard stomach passed through her mind. What was a career compared with the passion they'd once had?

Had. That was the operative word. It was in the past, washed away by the years in between. Any reaction he had to her nearness tonight was nothing more than second-nature. After all, he was just a man—a very passionate man.

And she was just a woman—a woman who had made more than her share of mistakes and been forced to live with them. A woman now, no longer a girl bullied by a narrow-minded, selfish old man. She banged the bed frame with her fist, yet her frustration remained.

Damn the beer. She should rush right down those stairs and tell Phillip everything. He was calmer now. Surely he'd listen. A smile tugged at her lips. Oscar and Zach would see that he did.

She hurried to the window. His car was already gone. Perhaps it was just as well. It would give him time to cool down and sober up. Give them both the time to take a giant step back from what they had almost let happen just now. She'd catch him in the morning before he left with Ian.

There was a scratch at her door. Rowan opened it and Oscar slinked into her room, whining. With the most apologetic look she guessed he could muster, he draped himself along the floor beside her bed.

Rowan stretched out next to him and rubbed his chest. "I know how you feel, boy."

After a few minutes, she slipped into her nightshirt, crawled into bed and turned out the light. Another long, sleepless night was going to keep her up. She just knew it.

She glanced down beside the bed. Two plaintive eyes reflected silver in the moonlight. Patting the edge of the mattress, she smiled and said, "Come on up. You've earned it."

The bed sagged with Oscar's weight as he snuggled next to her.

"Do you mind telling me exactly what we're doing?" Zach asked.

Phillip watched the light in Rowan's bedroom go out. He'd be damned if he knew what he was doing. All he had wanted was for Zach to stop the car off the dirt road in a turn-around a few hundred yards from the house and let him think for a minute or two. The cool desert air helped clear his head and focus his thoughts. Zach had stayed quiet until now.

"I was wondering if leaving Jess and Mike there for surveillance will be enough protection for Rowan, Ian and Emma." A lie, but maybe it would be enough to keep Zach off his back.

"They'll be fine."

Phillip's head spun with images of Rowan beneath him, rubbing against him. He'd been hard with want the instant it had happened. Thinking about it only made the ache worse. There was no doubt about it. If not for Oscar, the two of them would be making love right now and damn the consequences.

"Snap out of it," Zach said. "You're treading on dangerous ground and you know it."

He knew it all right, but he didn't want to admit it to himself, much less Zach.

"You were ready to fuck her. If that stupid dog of yours hadn't butted in, you would have."

Phillip scratched at the stubble along his cheek. His alcoholic haze was quickly fading, leaving the start of a throbbing headache. "Oscar's not stupid."

"After what I saw tonight, I may have to agree with you. In fact, I'd say he's a lot smarter than either of you. I've never seen you look at a woman like that. You wanted her. You still want her and you still love her, no matter what she's done now or in the past. You admitted that in the bar tonight."

"Wrong. I despise her." Another lie. Angry, yes. Angrier than he'd ever been before. But despise? Never.

"Just as extreme an emotion as love. You hate what she did, but you're so crazy in love with her that you can't even think straight. My God, Phillip, we're talking professional suicide here. She's an enlisted Marine. She's *your* client."

Phillip watched a gray Ford pickup cruise past them. Zach was on a roll. There was no stopping the lecture. "She's Ian's mother. I can't avoid her. We have a child to raise."

"Then raise him—separately. Stay as far away from Rowan McKinley as you can or you can both kiss your military careers good-bye. And you might as well ask yourself another question."

He was worse than a parent. Phillip sighed. "What's that?"

"How in the hell can you objectively defend this woman?"

Phillip had already been asking himself that question. The way he felt right now, thinking about Ian and the time they had been denied... A part of him wanted Rowan to hang, to spend each and every day of the rest of her life in prison. At the same time, he wanted to hold her slender body in his arms and make love to her on that king-size bed until they both collapsed from exhaustion. Rage, lust, hurt, exhilaration—it was a heady combination.

Zach snorted. "The command is going to have a field day over this. You know it won't take long for our colonel to find out about Ian. He probably already has.

You should have seen the look on Laura's face when she saw that kid. She's going to demand you be released from the trial — and you should be."

The pickup slipped by once more. The headlights momentarily blinded them. Phillip welcomed the distraction.

"I'll take care of Laura," he said.

"And who's going to take care of *you*?" The question came with the force of a knife thrust.

A hot glare from Phillip wasn't enough to make Zach stand down. Nothing could when he was lecturing.

"Do you want me to defend her?"

Phillip sucked in a breath, hoping it would clear the growing ache in his head. It only made him dizzy. "I'm a professional, Zach. I'll defend her."

"Objectively? To the utmost of your ability? No matter what she may have done?"

"No matter what." Phillip stared at the house, all dark now. "Zach, you don't think she would really have me killed, do you?"

"Malcolm's big theory sounds far-fetched to me," he replied. "Even if she was guilty, why bother to have you killed? You never would have known anything about the boy if she hadn't asked you here. If she had gone to prison, her mother would have raised Ian and you would have been none the wiser."

"Then why would Collins suggest it?"

Zach shrugged. "He's probably angry because you brought his botched investigative efforts to light and he wants to get even. From what Mike told me, Collins didn't do one thing right with that crime scene."

"I don't know. I don't trust the guy. Maybe I should have Jess or Mike check him out."

"Phillip, we don't know these people. Who's to say you can really trust them?"

"Right now I have to trust them with Rowan's and Ian's lives. Are you saying I shouldn't?"

They stared at each other for what seemed an eternity before Zach slipped the car into gear and drove back to Rowan's house.

* * * *

Rowan woke to find Ian snuggled against her. With all the room the king-size bed offered, she was allocated a two-foot wide space for herself. Reaching over to scoot him aside, she was greeted with a sleepy-eyed grin.

"Well, good morning." She wrapped her arms around him and gave him a big hug. "How long have you been here?"

Ian stretched. "I don't know. Dad and Oscar took up all of my bed, so I came up here."

Phillip came back?

"I'm starving."

He was always starving. "Pancakes and bacon?"

"Now I'm extra-starving."

Rowan laughed and swung her legs over the side. "Then I'd better get busy."

She stopped long enough in the bathroom to clean up and get dressed. By the time she trotted downstairs, Ian was curled in the chair watching cartoons.

The smell of coffee lured her onward. Rowan expected to see her mother in the kitchen with breakfast underway. Instead, she found Phillip's friend Zach and Captain Connors sharing sections of the newspaper, cups of coffee steaming in their hands.

"Is my mother still asleep?"

Neither bothered to look up, but the lawyer friend answered, "She and Jess went to her house last night when we came back. She felt everyone would be more comfortable with a little more room. Jess didn't want her alone over there, just in case."

Rowan nodded and extended her hand. "You probably already know this, but I'm Rowan McKinley."

He looked up with a warm smile and slipped his hand into hers. "Zach Taylor. I have the dubious honor of being Phillip's best friend." He grinned, flashing a set of dimples.

"Then I would say you have your hands full."

"Phillip would tell you it goes both ways."

Rowan laughed softly. A flash of silver outside the kitchen window caught her eye. "I see Oscar's up."

Captain Connors craned his neck for a look. "Been chasing birds and squirrels and having a great time."

"No matter how inept he is at it," Zach added.

"Well, we'll see if the smell of breakfast cooking will tempt him back inside before I no longer have a flower garden. How about it, Captains?

Connors glanced her way. "Only if we can leave the formalities back at the office. Agreed?"

Rowan smiled and nodded. It made sense, especially if they were going to continue to be in close quarters. Then she paused.

"Zach, why did you come back with Phillip? I thought you were both going to return to the Officers' Quarters."

He smiled, a devastating combination of dark eyes and square jaw. "Simple, really. We couldn't find our way to the main road in the dark."

Rowan and Mike laughed.

The first whiff of frying bacon brought all the laggards to the kitchen—Oscar, Ian...and Phillip. Rowan tensed when he walked in. He wore a T-shirt and running shorts that were as rumpled from sleep as his hair. Without a glance or a word to her, he brushed by and helped himself to a mug of coffee.

"Can I have some coffee, too?" Ian hoisted himself onto the countertop.

"Get down." The gentle reprimand was simultaneous from both parents.

He hopped to the floor without question. "Can I?"

"Just a little," Phillip replied.

Rowan almost protested until she saw him fill a cup with a splash of coffee, then topped it off with lots of milk and two teaspoons of sugar. He lifted an eyebrow, asking her approval. Rowan gave a single nod.

Phillip handed the cup over to Ian. "There you go, bud. A cup of coffee fit for a man."

"Thanks, Dad."

"Once breakfast is over, how would you like to go with me to Disneyland?"

"Oh, boy! Mom, too?"

Sensing Phillip's hesitancy, Rowan turned with a smile she didn't exactly feel. "I think your dad wanted it to be a guy thing, just the two of you. Besides, someone has to stay home with Oscar. And I have to clean house and do yard work. Why don't you get your suitcase and put in enough clothes for two days? I'll check it after breakfast."

He ran off to his room, coffee forgotten.

Phillip leaned against the counter. "Thank you for that."

Rowan turned back to her bowl of batter. "Not a problem... Phillip, before you go, I think you and I need to talk."

"There's nothing to talk about. There's nothing you can say that will make a difference. Everything is in the past. You did what you did and that's that." His voice was low and harsh.

She spun around. "That's not fair."

"I could spend hours telling you about what's not fair. But again, it wouldn't make a hell of a lot of difference at this point. The fact is that I have a son and I intend to be the best damn father I can, now that I know about him. You can save any explanation you've got for him when he gets older and asks where his father really was for the first eight years of his life, not that stupid story you let him believe."

"Phillip, I tried to tell him the truth, but he turned it into something he could understand."

He shook his head, halting her. "I don't want to hear your lame excuses. How many times do I have to make that clear? Now, if you will pardon me, I have to get ready to take my son to Disneyland."

He tossed down his coffee and set the mug aside with a thud so hard Rowan was afraid it would break. She held back the pain and frustration with an iron will she didn't know she possessed.

The mask stayed in place until she waved goodbye to them an hour later. Once Phillip's car was well down the road, she let her shoulders sag. An arm slipped around her and she turned to Zach's understanding gaze.

"He'll have to cool down sometime." Zach gave her a comforting squeeze. "But you know, if it will help, I'm here to listen."

Rowan sat and rested her chin in her hands. The words came, slowly at first, then like a flood as the dam of emotions burst. Her long-kept secret was finally out in the open.

She looked up. Both Zach and Mike stared at her in open-mouthed surprise. "That's why I have to get him to listen and try to make him understand why I never told him about Ian."

"Good God, Rowan, Phillip is going to go ballistic when he hears this," Zach said in a rush of breath. "He has to know. You have to talk to him."

She nodded and started to clear the table, anything to keep her mind focused. "You saw. He won't give me the time of day. He's so angry and upset, and I really can't blame him." She picked up the empty coffee mugs. "He needs to hear the whole story, start to finish—why I left him the way I did."

Mike jumped up to help. "You can snag him tomorrow night when he gets back with Ian. We'll make sure he gives you his full attention."

A simple plan—or so it seemed. But so had all the others been before they had blown up in her face. She was beginning to wonder what good it did to plan when life threw obstacles into her path on a whim.

Rowan occupied her time with household chores, enlisting her two bodyguards for tasks too heavy to accomplish on her own. It helped to exhaust her body and mind while she counted down the hours until Phillip's return.

But when that moment came, Phillip derailed their plan before it could be put into effect. By the time Rowan realized that he had no intention of remaining, Ian was inside the house and Phillip already driving back down the road to the base. She stared at the dust trail in dismay.

"You want me to go after him?" Mike asked.

Rowan shook her head. "No. He can't avoid me forever." She set her jaw, determined to make him listen.

* * * *

Rowan paced a groove in the hallway outside the defense offices. Phillip obviously wasn't coming. He was going to let her flounder. Why else wouldn't he have shown up?

It was noon already. Her arraignment was in one hour. He couldn't have chosen a more appropriate revenge. She would be in prison for the rest of her life, Ian would be his and she could just about guarantee that Phillip would never let her see her son again.

Inside Phillip's office, Zach glanced at his watch for what must have been the hundredth time. Rowan could almost count the minutes each time he did. It was a mystery to him as well. She could see that in the furrows along his brow, even if he didn't say so.

"I hate to say this, but with everything else that's happened, do you suppose someone made sure Phillip didn't get here?"

Rowan froze when she heard him ask that of Mike and Jess. The thought hadn't occurred to her. *What if something has happened to Phillip?* Never mind her circumstances, Ian would be devastated.

"We don't have much of a choice," Mike said. "I'm the one most familiar with the case. I'll have to go in as her counsel."

Before the last word could die away, the outside door swung open and Phillip strode in, dressed crisply in his green court uniform, briefcase clutched in his hand.

"Sorry, I'm late. I had some business to attend to." He motioned Rowan into his office and shut the door behind them.

Rowan fidgeted. The room was small enough, but with five people crammed in there, she found it a little unnerving.

"Let's get started. We have a lot to cover before —"

A sharp rap on the door interrupted him. With an impatient flick of his wrist, Phillip yanked it open.

Laura Cushing started but held her ground. "I need a word with you."

"You can have as many words as you'd like, counselor." Phillip leaned out of the way to let her in.

After a moment or two of hesitation, she crossed the threshold and shoved the door shut behind her. "Very well, Captain. I would have liked to discuss this with you privately, but since you are again being uncooperative, I thought it only fair to warn you that I intend to demand that you be released from this case. This will give you the opportunity to withdraw gracefully as counsel so someone else can step in."

A ghost of a smile flitted across Phillip's face, almost too quickly for the others to catch.

"Who's going to step in for you?"

She was puzzled.

"If you demand I be released, I intend to do the same with you. Surely you can see the folly of one old girlfriend prosecuting another — or do you really want the court to know you and I had an affair?"

The words sliced into Rowan's heart. It was foolish to think that either of them had pined for the other over the last nine years. She certainly hadn't been celibate. But to hear the words, to see the other woman... It cut her to the quick and she wondered if Phillip had made his bald statement with that purpose in mind.

Laura spared Rowan a glance then squared her shoulders. "All right, Captain Stuart. Have it your way. I can be objective and professional if you're sure you can be."

Phillip swung open the door. "I can take care of my own business. Thank you so much for caring, but your concerns are not really necessary anymore."

Laura flushed, obviously embarrassed and uncomfortable. Without another word, she left the office. Rowan felt a twinge of sympathy for the woman. Until now, she'd never realized Phillip could be ruthlessly cruel—a trait no doubt inherited from his father.

His voice enclosed them once more. "All right, Rowan. This is what we've got to work with. The choice is yours. I meant to discuss this with you on Friday, but... Well, I'm sure we all know what happened on Friday."

He laid out the evidence to date in simple terms. She could walk away scot-free today or go in for the long haul and, with luck, bring down the murderer. It seemed the choice was hers, but she couldn't concentrate, couldn't make a decision.

"So, what's it going to be? Which way do you want me to go?" Phillip asked.

Rowan clenched and unclenched her hands. She wanted this done with, her life and reputation restored. Yet, here was the opportunity to finish what she had started, this time with a team to help her—and Phillip.

"What about the danger to Ian and my mother?"

"Not to mention you," Zach added.

Jess popped a toothpick between his teeth. Rowan wasn't sure if that meant the whole plan made him nervous or that it earned his seal of approval.

"There is a risk," he said in his gravelly drawl. "You know that. We're doing everything we can to protect all of you. But if this guy thinks you're going to take the fall for his crime, maybe he'll start to get careless and tip his hand. Either way, it'll also give us more time to investigate. In the meantime, we're gathering more and more forensic evidence to ensure that you're cleared of all charges."

Rowan glanced around the room, hoping someone would tell her what to do. No one met her gaze. The decision was solely hers. She drew in a deep breath to calm her nerves.

"I want to catch this guy."

Phillip snapped to his feet. "Excellent. Then let's set a few snares and see what we come up with."

Sally Kemp was the first person Rowan saw when they walked into the courtroom. She sat in the far row of chairs, back against the wall, hate blazing from her pale eyes. Near the front of the room at the prosecutor's table, Laura Cushing shuffled papers and ignored them. At the court reporter desk in front of the judge's bench, Ellen gave Rowan a nod that said 'hang in there' then the proceedings began.

This was the first step toward trial. Arraignment…the Article 32 hearing. If the evidence presented upheld the charges, the case would go to trial. By holding back the evidence of Rowan's innocence, Phillip was guaranteeing that would happen.

The Hearing Officer assessed them.

"Is there anyone here who would like to recuse themselves?" he asked.

Phillip glanced up. "No need. We're all professionals here."

"Let's get started then."

Even knowing what she and Phillip had planned didn't make it any easier for Rowan to sit there and listen to it. For each piece of evidence the prosecutor presented, he gave no argument.

Malcolm Collins took the stand and threw out his pathetic evaluation of the crime scene. The smoking gun issue was brought up. On the surface, it all appeared bad for her. She prayed that Phillip, Jess and Mike hadn't erred in the evidence they had tucked away.

Phillip's one and only true act of defense was to request that the charge of adultery be dropped on the grounds of hearsay. Prosecution presented no opposition.

By the time the hearing was over, two hours had passed. Rowan had a headache that wouldn't quit, her stomach churned and her nerves were shot. Crowded once more into Phillip's office with the men, Rowan listened to the debrief and the men's plans but could offer no insight of her own.

"I guess that takes care of that business for now. On to other important matters." Phillip sat at his desk, hauled a sheaf of papers from his briefcase and tossed them to Zach.

"I need you to serve these on Rowan."

Zach glanced at the documents. "Phillip, you can't—"

"Do it."

Rowan's heart fluttered like a frightened bird caught by a tomcat. Phillip's cool, professional demeanor was gone, replaced again by the livid anger. It showed in the cold set of his face and the stiff tilt to his head.

Reluctantly, Zach handed her the papers. Rowan took them with shaking fingers. She was afraid to look, afraid not to.

"The custody hearing's tomorrow morning at eight-thirty. Make sure you're there." Phillip shoved to his feet and stalked from the room.

Through a haze of fear, Rowan examined the forms. Phillip was suing for custody of Ian. Clamping her hand to her mouth, she dashed for the ladies' room.

Chapter Eleven

"I'm surprised you aren't out having a victory cigar. You remember. Your usual celebration after serving someone a crushing blow?"

Phillip didn't bother to turn around when Zach stalked up behind him. He stared at the activity in the parking lot and the constant flow of vehicles in and out. "What are you talking about?"

"You know exactly what I mean. That was a rotten thing to do to Rowan. How could you possibly think of taking Ian away from her?" His voice held the unmistakable sound of reprimand.

"I didn't. Better check your facts before you go jumping to conclusions next time, counselor. It's joint custody with a healthy child support payment each month to help her out."

"Why—?"

Phillip held up his hand then motioned with a tilt of his head. "Check it out. That gray pickup in the parking lot."

"So?"

"I think it's the same one that passed us the other night when we were parked down the road from Rowan's house. It was also in the area last night when Ian and I got back. I dropped him off as quickly as I could but it was gone by the time I got to the main road to take a better look."

Zach edged closer. "You're waiting to see who it belongs to?"

"Yes, I thought I'd —"

A woman's cry from within the building cut him off.

"Someone help! Kemp's wife is trying to kill Rowan!"

Phillip raced inside with Zach mere footsteps behind.

"Bathroom," the woman shouted, pointing.

They burst into the room. The door slammed against the wall, shattering plasterboard. Sally Kemp didn't budge. One mad-eyed glare at them was all it took for her to tighten the purse strap she had around Rowan's pale throat.

Rowan clawed at Sally's fingers but the bloody gouges didn't pierce the other woman's rage. Rowan jammed her elbow in the woman's ribs but Sally didn't move. Rowan was tall and in top physical condition, but Sally's grief and fury lent her the strength of a madwoman.

Phillip clamped his hand over Sally's wrist and squeezed until she cried out and fell back. Rowan slumped to the floor, gasping for breath. After pushing Sally toward Zach, he drew Rowan to the loveseat in the women's changing area while his friend.

"I thought cutting your tires would be enough," the woman shouted as she was placed into restraints. "I should have slit your throat when I had the chance. Even that wouldn't be payment enough for murdering my husband." She began crying, a series of incoherent sobs that escalated into hysterical, shrieking wails.

Rowan rubbed at her neck. After staggering to her feet and shoving past Phillip, she paused, clearly enraged, in front of Sally Kemp. "I didn't sleep with your husband, you delusional maniac! You want to point fingers? You point them somewhere else."

"Take Mrs. Kemp out of here," Phillip ordered. "Call the psych team from the hospital. Maybe they'll admit her right away. Tell them it's a priority."

"Sir, I imagine they'll take her down to the hospital in Pendleton pretty quick." The police escort secured her from Zack then hauled Sally Kemp outside. She fought them each step of the way until they finally had to hog-tie her and carry her to their vehicle.

"Maybe they'll make her a permanent resident, too," Rowan shouted after them.

Phillip caught her elbow. "That's enough."

She jerked free, eyes huge in her pale face. "How could you do this to me? How could you even think of taking Ian?"

Phillip pulled back and drew himself to his full height. "You'd better reread the custody papers more carefully. I could never take Ian from you the way you took him from me."

Rowan returned to the loveseat and picked up the documents. Her hands shook as she flipped through them.

"Joint custody and a thousand dollars a month in child support, plus a division in child care costs, if that ever became necessary," he told her.

"Phillip, I—"

"How could you think I would hurt you or Ian in that way? He isn't a yo-yo, Rowan. He's a little boy who needs both of his parents. I told you that I intended to be a father. I wasn't lying."

With each word, he edged closer until her fragrance wrapped itself around him. Phillip noted Rowan's pallor and the darkening of yet another series of bruises around her neck. First her face, then her arm, now her neck… His Rowan was a mess. *My Rowan?*

Zach cleared his throat, drawing their attention to the small audience gathered in the hallway, listening with avid interest. It seemed that once again they were providing entertainment for the office. They drew apart and the spectators dispersed, urged on by Zach's persistent glares.

Phillip cleared his throat. "Zach, please take Rowan home. You can follow her in my car. I'll get a ride and meet you there later this evening."

When Zach opened his mouth to protest, Phillip cut him off. "I'll explain later when I catch up with you."

* * * *

Rowan and her mother sat out on the back porch sipping their tea and watching the setting sun streak the desert hills with purple and rose shadows. Some of her most precious childhood memories were of tea parties with her mom when she had been a little girl. As she'd grown, plastic cups had changed to porcelain then to mugs, and life's problems had dissolved with the childhood routine. But she wasn't a child anymore, and all the tea in the world couldn't fix this issue.

Blowing across her steaming mug, Rowan tried to think about what she would do if the Marine Corps found her guilty of murder—what she would do if

Phillip failed her and her family. Yes, the evidence should clear her, but what if something went wrong?

"When are you going to let go?" Her mother's softly spoken question broke the evening's hush, sounding unnaturally loud.

"What do you mean?"

"You've always been a great one for planning, even when you were a child." Her voice was fond with remembrance. "But it's time to let someone else worry about your life for a change."

"I'm not sure what you're saying." Rowan took a hasty gulp of too-hot tea and winced.

"What I'm saying, dear, is that you need to trust Phillip. Stop brooding over what-ifs and let the man do what he does best. That *is* why you requested him in the first place, isn't it?"

Stung, Rowan retorted, "I trusted Phillip nine years ago, and see where that got me."

Her mom gave her a reproachful look. "That's not kind and is most certainly untrue — and you know it." Adding a spoonful of honey to her tea, she stirred. "As a matter of fact, it's partly because of Phillip that you're where you are today."

She shook her head. "Naturally, I wouldn't have Ian without him. But as for my career in the Corps, that's my doing, not his."

"Dear, you know as well as I that had things progressed with Phillip, joining the Marine Corps would never have been an option for you." After taking a long sip of tea, her mother went on. "When your father died, you were forced into a role of responsibility beyond your years."

Rowan made a noise of denial but her mother kept talking.

"You took charge and organized our lives. When I was ready, you helped me get back to work and learn to live with my grief."

"Mom, you would have pulled through on your own. You're a strong woman."

"Perhaps. It was such a shock, though. I really couldn't function for a long time after your father's death. For you, not having Phillip to depend on made you stronger. I swear I don't know how you did it, knowing how your heart was aching for him *and* your father."

Reaching out and squeezing her mother's hand, Rowan thought back to those tumultuous years and sighed. "We made it together, all of us."

"We did because you chose a difficult path and made it work against all odds. Now it's time to think about yourself."

"All I do is think about myself, Mom." Rowan finished off her tea and set the mug down on the glass-topped patio table between them. "I think about how stupid I was to follow Charlie into that building in the middle of the night and how I should have known better."

"That's not what I meant and you know it."

Rowan saw the quick, darting shadows of Pipistrelle bats diving for insects attracted to the glow of their garage light. "I'm like those moths the bats are after, drawn by my curiosity to a dangerous situation then consumed for my folly."

"You did what you thought was right. Stop blaming yourself and work with Phillip to find the answer to this horrible puzzle. Stop fighting him."

Rowan sighed. "Phillip wants joint custody of Ian, Mom."

"I know. He told me today when I came to pick you up from the office."

Rowan's laugh was self-reproving. "I shouldn't be surprised that he was so generous with his terms. It's just that I feel as if he's coming into my life and taking control of more than my legal problems. Everything is coming apart and I don't know which way to go from here."

"Feelings can do that to a person."

"I don't have time for feelings now, Mom. The only thing I have time to worry about is what you and Ian will do if I get sent to Leavenworth for fifty years. I guess Ian won't be a problem. Phillip will watch out for him. I'll have to sell the house — unless Phillip wants it. No, I'll sell it. You'll need a power of attorney. I hate to think of you all by yourself. My God, we don't even have health insurance. I've depended on the military to provide —"

"Enough!" Her mother smacked her mug down onto the patio table with a sharp crack. Standing, she stared down at Rowan, hands braced on hips.

"There are things in life you cannot plan. Love is one of them. Rowan, if you can't seize each moment and live your life to the fullest, you will wake up one day and the only thing that you will have to hold on to will be regret."

With that, her mother walked back to her own house with a guard, leaving Rowan curled up in her chair, tracing the rim of her cold mug with one finger.

Rowan glanced up into the night. A shooting star blazed across the darkness, followed by another.

Make a wish, quick! Even that childhood tradition failed to lift her spirits. Wishes were for dreamers and she'd quit dreaming years ago.

* * * *

Phillip had spent an hour pleading with Laura to drop him off in the desert then hours more waiting for his prey to show up. He trusted her to help him more than he trusted anyone else right about now. It had finally paid off. He watched the gray pickup truck roll to a stop on a side road not far from Rowan's house. Whoever it was had a clear view of both Rowan's and Emma's houses but hopefully not Phillip's hiding place deep in the creosote bushes.

He drew the binoculars up for a closer look, but the darkness obscured the driver except for the telltale ember of a cigarette. Phillip inched forward, afraid to turn on his flashlight for fear of discovery. The Marine Corps had taught him outdoor survival but skulking through nighttime desert underbrush had not been part of that training. He only hoped there wasn't a rattlesnake lurking in his vicinity.

A coyote yipped out a call, answered by the pack. The eerie howls set his pulse racing. Phillip forced himself to stay calm. It was only a coyote—a dog. Right? A wild dog out at night looking for an easy meal, probably hoping he'd find a man stupid enough to be crawling through the desert at midnight.

One step…two. Before he realized it, Phillip was within ten feet of the vehicle. He hunkered down onto his haunches and lifted the binoculars. *Malcolm Collins.*

Phillip smiled to himself. So, the weasel was doing a little snooping on his own, but why?

What are you after, Malcolm? Better yet, what are you trying to hide?

The thought came so quickly that it surprised Phillip. Of course Collins could have something to hide. Why else would he have botched Kemp's murder investigation?

Great theory. Now where's the proof?

Phillip decided not to instigate a confrontation. If they were able to gather evidence that somehow incriminated Malcolm Collins, it wouldn't do to tip their hands too soon.

The last light in Rowan's house blinked out. Seconds later, Collins cranked the motor to life and eased down the road, back in the direction of town.

"Tomorrow," Phillip murmured and straightened to his feet. The uneven layers of sand beneath him didn't cooperate. He slid, teetered for balance then toppled backward into a large patch of cactus.

* * * *

Rowan didn't know which woke her first, Oscar's bark or the knocking. She was on her feet and downstairs in time to hear Zach say, "Good God, Phillip, what happened? Have you been shot?"

Phillip's response was puzzling. "Shut up and help me."

She could barely see their forms in the dim light of the darkened doorway. In wide-eyed horror, Rowan watched Phillip slump belly-first to the floor. He could barely move. A thousand questions slammed through her. *Who shot him? How badly is he hurt?*

Zach flipped on the light. Her shock and fear melted away and she burst into peals of laughter. Zach's rich bellows soon joined hers. Clumps of cholla cactus spines dotted Phillip's back and buttocks, piercing him through his dark cotton shorts and shirt.

"Will one of you please quit laughing and pull them out?" he snapped.

Still giggling, Rowan went into the kitchen and retrieved a paper sack and a pair of needle-nose pliers.

Zach sat on the floor and leaned against the wall to watch the extraction. "What happened? Someone shoot you with a cactus-loaded shotgun?"

Rowan tried to stop grinning and failed. It was a novel experience to be able to assist Phillip for a change. She relished the moment.

"I fell," he grumbled.

Zach smothered a snort. "You sure did. What were you doing out in the desert in the middle of the night? You could have been hurt."

He jerked his head up. "I was hurt."

Pliers raised, Rowan pulled back, amusement tickling her from head to toe. "And the answer to the question is?"

Using his arms as a cushion, he laid his head down. "Where's Mike? He's supposed to be watching the house."

"He has to sit duty at the base tonight." Rowan started with the spines that were easiest to reach, those barely hanging on. "The question? Don't move, please. These are very difficult to pull out."

Phillip winced. "There's been a truck hanging around here lately. I wanted to see who it was."

Zach tucked his legs under himself meditation-style. "And?"

"Malcolm Collins."

She paused, pliers open in mid-grab. "Why would he be snooping around here?"

"I don't know. He left as soon as your house lights went out."

"Because he knew we were in for the night," Zach said.

"That's what I'm thinking... Rowan, please...the cactus?"

"Sorry." She yanked out another clump. "It almost sounds like you're saying he leaves once he's sure we're settled down."

"That's exactly what I'm saying. Tomorrow night I'm going to follow him. I would have tonight if I'd had a car."

"What did you do, walk here from the base?" Rowan asked.

"I got Laura to drop me off."

How sweet. Rowan located a needle stuck deep in the firm flesh of Phillip's buttock and yanked as hard as she could.

"Ow!" Phillip rolled around, reaching for the offended spot. Obviously realizing that his movement served to embed more cholla needles deeper into his other flank, he yelped and resumed his original position. Wincing, he reached back to locate the worst of the offending spikes.

She smacked his hand away. "Be still or you'll have it in your hand next." When he rolled back into place, she added, "I don't know why you don't let the authorities handle this."

"Like you did?" he shot back. "Besides, Collins *is* one of the authorities. How far do you think an inquiry will go with him around?"

He was right. If it hadn't been for Phillip's persistence in the first place, Kemp's murder never would have garnered a second look beyond the shoddy evidence Collins had provided.

"Just be careful snooping," Zach told him. "I'm really not in the mood to bury you or defend you for murder. Is there anything you need me to do?"

Phillip propped himself on his elbows. "Yeah, see if you can get some scoop on Collins. Contact someone from our investigative office in Pendleton if you have to."

Rowan yanked the last dozen needles out of Phillip and tossed them into the sack. "That should do it, but you're really going to feel it for a few days. Strip down and I'll throw your clothes in the washer. A long soak in my tub ought to help reduce the stinging and swelling."

"Not if I have to use that flowery soap."

She laughed. "There's a bar of Dove under the bathroom sink."

Phillip peeled off his shirt and took the stairs two at a time. Rowan's stomach did flip-flops at the sight of him. Years of physical training had sculpted his chest and back to perfection. Her fingers itched to caress the angles.

"I'm going to bed," Zach said. "You wanted him cornered. Looks to me like he's not going anywhere."

"I don't think now is the—"

He steered her toward the stairs. "Just get it over with. I doubt you'll get another opportunity as good as this one. The only way he can avoid you now is to jump out of the window."

Rowan waited until she thought she heard Phillip slip into the tub. She gathered his clothes from where he had dropped them outside the bathroom door and moved them as far away as possible. After a deep breath to steel her nerves and her resolve, she walked in.

Phillip snapped a washcloth over his lap. "What the hell are you doing in here?"

"We need to talk. *I* need to talk. And you're going to listen."

He leaned back and closed his eyes with a sigh of resignation. "Fine. Talk. But don't come any closer."

Rowan sank to the floor and braced herself against the wall opposite the tub. "This won't be easy."

"Just spit it out and get it over with."

Harsh. Well, what do I expect? It was about to get worse.

Fighting for the strength to continue, Rowan concentrated on the white scar blazed across his left biceps — the result of his attempt to make love to her in the close confines of a sleeping bag. The confinement had panicked her so much that she had rolled them both onto a tent stake — his first exposure to her intense claustrophobia. Even then, bleeding from the jagged wound, he hadn't been as angry as he was now.

"Could you put aside your anger for a little while?" she asked in a quiet voice.

Silence was his answer. It was better than nothing. She'd take it.

"Why did you file for custody of Ian?"

He was quiet for so long that Rowan was afraid he wouldn't answer. Finally, the tension drained from his shoulders.

"After I saw that truck here again last night, I got scared. I thought it would be a way to protect him if something happened. I wanted our son's safety and security resolved now, just in case."

"I'm not going to fight you on this, Phillip. I'll tell the judge that myself tomorrow morning. Ian is your son. You have a right to be a part of his life. You should have always been a part of his life."

He snorted, shifting slightly in the steaming water. "Strange that you should choose now to remember that."

Rowan flexed her fingers, searching for the right words. She found only the truth.

"I discovered I was pregnant about two weeks after you left on your 'vacation'." She made quote marks in the air with her fingers. "I was a little surprised since we were always so careful about us not getting pregnant. Well, almost always. You don't know how ecstatic I was. All I could think about was telling you we were going to have a baby. But you hadn't told me where you were going or why. You'd kept putting me off, saying you had some things to do and you needed to get away for a while." She could feel herself getting flushed with emotion. "I did call you, Phillip."

He opened his eyes and looked at her. Disbelief shadowed his face.

"I called every day for a week. Your father answered the phone each time. He said he didn't know where you were and to stop calling. I didn't know what to do. I couldn't believe it."

"He didn't know where I was. I didn't tell anyone," Phillip said. "But, Rowan, I didn't stay gone forever."

"Then Daddy had the heart attack. I called again. Nothing from you. Then he died. I called again. Your father said he'd give you the message. I called the next day and the next to see when you'd arrive for the funeral."

She paused then took a deep breath. "I needed you so badly. He said you weren't coming, that you said whatever problems I had were mine to deal with. He said, 'You should realize now, young woman, that you were nothing more than a college fling. Phillip is a

Stuart. Stuarts don't marry people like you. In fact, he hasn't wasted any time finding an appropriate replacement for you. Shall I extend your congratulations on his engagement?'"

"He said *what*?" Phillip came out of the tub so fast that his cloth dropped.

Rowan looked away and motioned him back. "Stay where you are. Please." The pain was fresh again, ripping her heart and dreams in two.

"Rowan, I would never... How could you believe...?"

She swallowed the lump in her throat. "I overheard the argument between you and your father the day before you left me, how he had lied to you all those years when he said he'd been paying your law school tuition, how he'd only been paying a small portion of the money, keeping the school from telling you about your mounting debts and that another payment was due. I heard him tell you that if you didn't go back and work for Big, Red and Thor."

He waved her poor attempt at old humor away as if it were a pesky fly. "Biggs, Reed and Moore."

"Whatever... That you were going to be stuck with that enormous tuition debt. I knew you didn't have that kind of money. I certainly didn't."

"You overheard us arguing?"

She nodded. "I know I shouldn't have eavesdropped, but Claudia was waiting in the car for us and she'd sent me inside to see what was taking you so long to find your keys. The door to the library was open a crack and your voices were so loud, I couldn't help but overhear."

"Why didn't you tell me afterward?" he demanded.

"I was afraid. Afraid that what Donald said was true — that I was holding you back and that your long years of legal education would be wasted in some public school job." She pressed her head against her bent knees.

"So you thought I'd bow to his pressure?" He grabbed a towel from the rack and wrapped it tightly around his waist. Then he sat on the edge of the tub, his elbows braced on his knees. "Rowan, what were the last words I said to you later that same day?"

"That you loved me."

"And I'd find a way to work things out in our lives, that I needed your understanding. I asked you to trust me and give me some time to solve my problems."

"I didn't know it was going to be nine years, Phillip."

"It wasn't supposed to be nine years. It was eight weeks. I joined the Marine Corps. I thought I'd take your father's example, I guess."

"Obviously. Why didn't you tell me then? Didn't you think I would support you?"

He gave a humorless chuckle. "I was afraid I wouldn't be able to support you. It was a shot in the dark. I needed money, security for both of us. Yeah, I could have gotten by working for that law firm, but it would have meant that my father had won and I was another easily-controlled piece in his game. I honestly didn't know if I could make it through Officer Candidate School. I didn't want to get your hopes up only to fail you. I'm not good at failure, Rowan." He paused and shifted on the edge of the tub. "I called you the minute I knew I'd made it."

"And I refused your calls." A tear slipped down her cheek to the point of her chin.

"Why in the name of God did you do that?"

A sob tore from her chest. "I'd love to tell you that I was noble, that I loved you so much all I wanted was your happiness, even if that meant you wanted to be with someone else. But I'm not noble, Phillip. I hated you. I hated the very air you breathed. I hurt so bad for all those weeks you were gone and all I wanted was for you to rot in hell with the bimbo you were engaged to. Then…"

It was too much. She buried her face in her hands and cried. Phillip was instantly by her side, wrapping her in that embrace that was so familiar, so comfortable, so right. Rowan gave in, holding tightly as she had longed to do all these years.

"I didn't get to finish college. The pregnancy was hard on me. I was sick a lot. Daddy's death tore me up. On top of all that, I'd lost you. I honestly thought you had given in to Donald, married some rich socialite to pay off your debts and joined the family law practice."

She took a deep breath. "Mom was in such a state after Daddy died. I didn't know what else to do, so after Ian was born I joined the Marine Corps. It was such a familiar part of my childhood and I knew from Daddy what to expect. One year became two, then three, then eight, then I re-enlisted for four more. It's a good career.

"I swear, Phillip, that I didn't know you were in the Corps until a year ago when I got a promotion and switched to the legal department. It seemed like such a bizarre coincidence. I know I should have told you before now, but I couldn't find a way. I kept putting it off and putting it off."

She pulled her head up to look at him, face wet with tears. "But I'll be honest with you. If none of this other mess had happened, I can't say that I ever would have told you about Ian. No matter how much checking up I did, I couldn't be sure if you were your father's puppet or not. I was frightened, for Ian as well as myself. The last thing I wanted was for Donald Stuart to get his hands on my son. And you know he'd try, Phillip. Out of sheer meanness, he'd try to take Ian and mold that child into his own image."

He cupped her hands in his. "I know. Don't worry. We won't give him the chance. Come on. You've cried enough tears to last a lifetime. You need to get some sleep."

Rowan let him guide her to the bed and tuck her in, even though sleep was the furthest thing from her mind. "I don't expect you to understand and you do have every right to be angry—"

"Oh, you can bet I'm plenty angry but not at you— not any longer. Sleep."

With one long finger, he traced the fading remains of her bruise. The tantalizing sensation of his warm skin on her sensitive cheekbone sent a shiver through her body.

"Phillip?"

He paused at the doorway, a perfectly sculpted statue, beads of moisture glistening on the golden hair dusting his chest. "Yes?"

What good will it do to ask him to stay? I want more than that. "Nothing. Good night."

"Night."

Phillip shut the door behind him and walked slowly down the stairs to the living room. *Nine years wasted. Nine years!* He shook his head in a mixture of anger and regret.

"Beer? Wine? Pants?" Zach's voice emerged from the depths of the overstuffed recliner in the corner. "I thought you'd need something right now." He offered Phillip a beer.

He waved it away. "Rowan told you?"

"Yes, a couple of days ago. I thought you would want to know…after you cooled down enough to listen with both ears open. So, which will it be?" Zach held out a cold beer in one hand and an extra pair of his sweatpants in the other.

Phillip slipped the sweats on then sank into the nearest chair. "Nine years, Zach. We could have been married, raised a couple more kids — all because of a misunderstanding started by my father."

"I know. I'm sorry for both of you, Phillip."

"I thought I'd won. Thought I'd beaten him by leaving and joining the Marine Corps, by making my way without his damned money. And all this time… I've got to call my sister. I left my phone in my shorts upstairs. Can I use yours?"

Zach didn't hesitate to hand it over. "It's after midnight. Do you really want to upset Claudia with this when it's really your father you want to rant and rave at?"

"I can't talk to him, not right now." He punched in the numbers and sat back. Claudia picked up on the first ring, her voice groggy with sleep.

"Hey, it's me."

"Phillip, what's wr —?"

In painstaking detail, he laid out the whole sordid tale. It hurt worse hearing the words the second time. Thankfully, Zach was sensitive enough to leave the room.

Claudia listened in silence, a clue as to how furious she was. He could picture the rage in her blue eyes, her full lips thinned to a line so tight that nothing could part them. She understood the true soul of their father.

There was also not much doubt what she would do after he'd hung up the phone. Her anger on his behalf would be the catalyst between him and his father. There wasn't going to be any need for Phillip to call. He only needed to wait for the mountain to come to him.

Turning, he saw Rowan sitting at the foot of the staircase, hugging her knees. "Claudia?"

"Yeah." He rubbed the ache from his eyes.

"You know she'll call your father."

"And he'll call me."

"You'd better take it to my room. Ian might hear you if it gets ugly."

And it was going to get ugly. "Be right there."

He listened to her soft footsteps retreat. Zach walked in, beer in hand.

"Don't go up there, Phillip. If you do, you know you'll wind up tangled in the sheets." Concern softened Zach's tone.

"Would that be so wrong?" Phillip demanded. "Don't we have the right, after all that's been taken from us?"

"You know the answer as well as I do. Is it worth the risk of losing everything that you and Rowan have worked so hard to achieve?"

A week ago, the answer would have been an unequivocal no. Now, what was life without Rowan and Ian?

But it wasn't his career they were dealing with—it was hers as well. She'd asked for him to help save her and here he was, debating an action that would surely accomplish the opposite. If they had sex, they'd both be in court again, this time for fraternization.

Scuffling in the hallway pulled them around. Ian stumbled toward him, rubbing the sleep from his eyes. Phillip knelt and gave him a hug.

"What's the matter, buddy? Can't sleep?"

He plopped his head against Phillip's shoulder. "Oscar's hogging the bed."

"Make him get down."

"I tried. He won't move."

"Want me to try?"

Ian shook his head. "I want to sleep with Mom."

Phillip pointed him to the staircase and gave him a pat on the bottom. "I'm sure she would like that. Sleep tight."

"Clever," Zach said once Ian was out of earshot. "But he can't sleep with his mother forever. Face it, Phillip. You're a ticking bomb. You can't have both Rowan and your career. You need to do some hard thinking before you walk up those steps. How does she feel? Where does she stand? She is a beautiful woman. Maybe there's already another man in her life."

Jaw set, Phillip whirled around. "Then where the hell is he? Why isn't he here to lend her support? If she were your woman, wouldn't you be here?"

"If she were my woman, I would have never let her out of my life in the first place. She would have been a part of every decision I made, even joining the Marine Corps. Nothing would have kept me from her. If she were my woman, I would have broken down the doors to her home the first time she hung up on me and demanded an explanation." Zach flung the painful words at Phillip with deadly accuracy.

"But you didn't do that, did you? You called her on the carpet for not telling you about Ian, yet you're the one who ran away to join the Corps and let her slip out of your life without a fight. Maybe you should be asking yourself if it was really love you felt for her nine years ago—or maybe your father was right. Maybe she was your flavor of the month."

Phillip cocked a fist and took a step forward. "That's a lie."

Zach held his ground. "If she meant so much to you, if she was the love of your life, why didn't you fight for her then?"

Anguished, Phillip lowered his arm. He stood for a moment, looking at his friend, then clasped Zach's arm, asking for forgiveness.

"Rowan wasn't the only one my father worked on. When she didn't call, didn't come around, didn't write and refused my calls, he started in on me. '*I told you she was no good. She was after the family money. As soon as she found out you were cut off without a cent to your name, she left you.*' Year after year he threw that in my face at every opportunity. What's worse, I actually believed him."

"Yet she didn't hesitate to call you when she really needed help, and you immediately went to her aid. I'd say you've got some serious thinking to do, my friend — about your relationship with Rowan and your continuing job as a judge advocate for the Marine Corps. You can't have it both ways." He yawned. "I'm hitting the rack. If you need me, I'll be in the guest room."

Left alone, Phillip stretched out on the couch and draped his arm over his eyes. Why wasn't life simpler? They had both started out with such grand, youthful plans — to become teachers, to get married. Now this. All because of a malicious, manipulative man.

No, because they had believed in Donald's lies instead of each other. That was the bottom line. Donald had fed the fire that had kept them apart, but they were the ones who'd let the flames burn. Call it youth or inexperience, maybe stupidity.

Zach was right, nothing should have stood between them, but there could be no doubting the love that had existed then. And now?

"Phillip?"

He rose at the sound of Rowan's voice. She leaned over the banister, his cell phone extended down to him.

"It's your father, and you'll be happy to know that he's as endearing as ever."

Even from where he stood, Phillip could hear his father's barking tones echoing from the receiver.

Rowan tossed the phone to him. Phillip caught it neatly in one hand.

"Listen to me when I'm talking, you little bitch!" his father ranted.

Phillip screwed up his face in disgust and pressed the receiver to his ear. "No, Donald, you listen to me. Did you think I would never find out? I don't know who you think you are, messing in my life. All those years, gone. Thanks to you, I have a son I barely know and I've missed almost all his childhood. I don't expect that you would understand the importance of being a father. All you know is manipulation and control. I put up with your authoritarian presence at holidays for Mother's sake, but no longer. As far as I'm concerned, you're dead to me. Stay out of my life. Out of Rowan's life. And you damn well better stay out of my son's life."

He jammed the button down to end the call then turned off the phone with a grunt of satisfaction.

"You're calmer than I would be," Rowan told him.

"You said you hated me before." He looked at her, all too aware that his naked anguish would show on his face. "Do you still hate me?"

Her reply was barely audible. "How can I when every day I see you in our beautiful son?" She pivoted abruptly and started to return upstairs.

"Don't, please." He held out his hand to her. "Don't leave. I need to hold you for a little while, like before. I'm so tired, Rowan. Please, stay with me. I need you beside me."

For a moment, he thought she'd refuse. Then she was before him, folding herself into his embrace.

Bodies cradled together like two spoons, they stretched out on the soft expanse of the couch and drifted off to sleep.

Chapter Twelve

"This has got to be the most unnecessary hearing I've had all year." The judge scribbled his name upon the order regarding custody of Ian and slid the paper to his clerk. "I can't believe the two of you wasted the court's time with a hearing when a stipulation would have freed valuable time for another case. Next time, talk to each other first."

Rowan kept quiet while Phillip apologized to the judge then walked with him out of the courtroom. A lot of problems could have been avoided if they had communicated better. Still more agony would be avoided if they could talk about the one issue they were dancing around now.

Rowan couldn't speak for Phillip, but she ached to renew the physical relationship they had enjoyed so very long ago, no matter how forbidden the military decreed it. Until last night, she'd considered it a moot point. A sensual caress when he was drunk didn't mean he felt the way she did. Then she'd woken with his fingers cupped gently around her breast.

She had tried to put off his action as second-nature, being curled up next to a member of the opposite sex, being groggy from sleep, the memories of their relationship so long ago, but there had been no mistaking the hardness pressed insistently against her, the tingling that had accompanied his caress, the thumb that had dusted along her nipple, his warm breath against her ear. It'd had nothing to do with being asleep. He had been wide awake and wanting her. Sinking backward into his unyielding hardness would have been too easy.

Unfortunately, when she'd opened her eyes, she'd seen Zach sitting across from them in the recliner, frowning like a disapproving guardian angel. She and Phillip had broken apart, embarrassed at having been caught in an intimate moment.

Okay, so it had been wrong. But what could they do? They'd had no control over their actions when they had been asleep, had they? At least that was the excuse she'd use if it came to that.

The returning answer flared inside her. They'd had no business sleeping beside each other in the first place. Yet she hadn't possessed the willpower to say no. Like a flower craving the first warm touches of the springtime sun, Rowan knew she would take any fleeting chance she could to be near the heat of Phillip's passion.

Sunlight blinded them as they stepped from the courthouse. Squinting, Rowan turned in to Phillip to protect her eyes. This, too, seemed natural and right. He had his arm around her and she tucked into the cove of his body. By chance, she looked up. Their simultaneous step faltered. He caught her chin on the crook of his finger, dusting the surface with his thumb. Rowan tilted her face toward him, willing him to close the distance. By slow degrees, he bent to her, his lips parted.

"How'd it go?" Zach strode toward him. Phillip's car now sat beside her van.

Muttering a curse, Phillip set Rowan away from him. "Besides pissing off the judge, it went great. Nothing more than the stroke of a pen. As far as hearings go, it was easy."

"That's good." Zach opened the van door for Rowan. "But it's going to take a lot more effort to get you out of the next one."

They turned puzzled frowns his way.

"I called Mike while you were in court. Rowan's colonel is furious and wants to see all players once we get back. He also has some questions about your current relationship. Considering what I just saw, I can understand that. In any event, for what it's worth, it's probably not going to look good if the two of you drive up in the same vehicle. A little too cozy."

Phillip snatched open the passenger door on the van and guided Rowan to the seat. "We have good reason to be together."

Zach grabbed his arm before he could move any farther. "Sometimes it just doesn't matter. Trust me on this one, please. If you're worried about Rowan's safety, I'll ride back with her."

When Phillip relented, Rowan scooted into the driver's seat. She needed something to occupy her during the awkward silence of driving back with Zach. Silence was the last thing she got.

"You realize, of course, that Phillip will be up here in Twentynine Palms visiting Ian every chance he gets."

Rowan nodded but kept her gaze on the road. "Trying to make up for lost time. I understand that. He wants to be more than just a part-time father. And after all that's happened, he deserves that chance."

"You can bet he'll be an active participant in this parenting thing. I've never known Phillip to do anything halfway, no matter what he tackles. There are a lot of people out there who are saying he could be promoted to colonel if he wanted — maybe even general one day."

"And does he want it?" From the corner of her eye she saw Zach shrug.

"As I said, he never does things by half measures."

"Are you trying to tell me that Ian is a hindrance to him?"

"Not Ian. You."

If she had been walking, Rowan would have stumbled. She didn't know what to say, how to respond. Zach saved her from having to reply.

"You still care for each other. That's more than obvious to anyone who's looking. Even if you can't admit it to one another right now, some day you will. Your actions are already giving you away. And don't try to play games with me by denying it. You could cut the sexual tension between the two of you with a knife."

All right, I won't. But what am I supposed to do? "Zach, I'm not stupid. I know what would happen to us if the military knew we were together."

"But how can you stop it? What would you have done this morning if I hadn't been sitting there when you woke up? What would have happened now if I hadn't busted in just now?"

The thought heated her cheeks and ignited those aching places again.

"I'm not saying the two of you should never be together. That's too cruel to even think about, but you can't do it while you're both in the Marine Corps. One of you will have to resign first."

"And you think it should be me?"

"I think you both need to be realistic."

Tears clouded her eyes. Rowan eased onto the shoulder of the road, put the van into park and clenched her fists on the steering wheel.

"I don't know what to do, Zach. I've worked my ass off these last nine years, trying to get through a pregnancy where I was sick more times than I was well, trying to get over the death of my father, to help my mother through her grief and to survive and support the three of us because the hospital and funeral took all our insurance then some.

"I worked hard in the Marine Corps. Took every opportunity I could to get ahead. Be realistic? I'm always that. It's gotten me through some rough times. But one look at Phillip and I regret all we've missed. I honestly don't know what to do."

"What about when your current tour is over? Would you consider getting out of the Corps?"

"I told you. I don't know what to do. I don't see why I should be the one to make the sacrifice when it's easier for Phillip to resign his commission. If the Marine Corps didn't have its silly rules about officers and enlisted fraternizing, this wouldn't be an issue."

"Please don't cry." He squeezed her shoulder. "I'm sorry I brought it up."

She glanced out of the back window to where Phillip's car idled behind them. "He's going to wonder what's wrong. I don't want him to see me crying."

"I'll take care of that. I'll tell him you threw me out."

The idea was laughable. "He'd never believe it."

"Sure, he will. I can be very convincing. I'm a lawyer. It's what I do for a living. Just drive off and I'll take care of the rest."

Zach popped open the door and jumped out. The instant it was shut, she pulled back onto the road.

Lies. All of it lies. She'd give up everything she'd worked so hard for in a heartbeat if only Phillip would ask.

Phillip stared at Rowan's van as she sped off down the road. "What did you do?"

Zach sank into the seat and looked away. "The wrong thing. Can we leave it at that?"

"Did you have an argument?"

"Something like that. She chewed me out pretty good," his friend muttered.

"Over what?"

"Something stupid. Could we let it go? Let's just say I'm sufficiently chastised and embarrassed."

Phillip pulled into traffic to follow her.

"Have you thought about how you're going to handle this?" Zach stared out the window. "You'll be with them every weekend, every holiday. It's only a matter of time before the inevitable happens. How discreet do you think you can be when both of you glow like supernovas when you're near each other? Phillip, your career will be over."

"Frankly, I'd give it all up in the blink of an eye if I thought we could have a life together." When Zach snorted, Phillip shot him a glance. "You said it yourself. I never should have let her go in the first place. I'm not sure I'm willing to let her go now. I don't think I could stand it if there was another man in her life."

"You might not have a choice."

"Yes, I know that, too. As I said, I would need to know where she stood before I consider resigning from the Corps. Any other suggestions?"

Zach parked his elbow on the door and leaned his head against his hand. "Not this time. I think I need to stop trying to be the voice of reason and butt out. You are on your own from now on, pal."

"That's what I figured."

* * * *

Colonel Scott folded his hands on the desk before him. Rowan couldn't tell if he was getting ready to explode or fighting the urge to do so. They sat in his office — she, Phillip, Zach, Jess and Mike, waiting for the back swing of the pendulum.

"I'm going to make this as quick as possible. I know all of you are working together to find the evidence to clear our staff sergeant here. It's not quick enough. There has been nothing but one disruption after another and I'm running out of patience." He turned to Jess. "I can't speak for your office, Mr. Alderman, but as for the rest of you" — he scanned the room — "this is your priority. Nothing comes before it. Do I make myself clear?"

'Yessir's rumbled through the room.

"Captain Taylor, your command has generously offered your assistance. I'm sure that thrills you to no end."

"To pieces, sir."

The colonel shot him a sharp look. "Good. Dismissed, except for you two." He waved his hand at Rowan and Phillip. Reluctantly they resumed their seats while the others hurried from the room.

Colonel Scott leaned back and steepled his fingers under his chin. "Captain, your colonel and I are wondering if a charge of fraternization needs to be entertained. Convince us otherwise."

It didn't take more than a few words for Rowan to realize how Phillip had gained his reputation as one of the best attorneys in the business. He was confident, eloquent and coherent. Not once did he falter. His argument was convincing, ending with the logic that there would be some degree of fraternization because of the child they had to raise together. Surely the commands would understand and be sympathetic to that. After all, this was not entirely their doing but a mistake wrought years before by his father.

Her colonel nodded slowly. "Very good. I trust you both on this one. Just make sure you leave no stones unturned in her defense. She is a valued member of my staff."

"I'm doing all I can, sir."

Summarily dismissed, they beat a hasty retreat and hurried toward Phillip's small office. Rowan assumed they would probably re-comb through the evidence, searching for clues missed before. Instead, Phillip suddenly excused himself and left her standing outside. He hurried to the parking lot where Laura Cushing was pulling to a stop.

"Nice looking couple," Malcolm Collins said.

He could be no more than five feet behind Rowan, but she didn't bother to turn around and acknowledge him.

"Always on opposite sides of the courtroom, but from what I understand, it makes for a great time making up afterward. They've been hot and heavy for a year now with no signs of slowing down—at least, that's what a friend tells me. They love to argue and patch it up."

He laughed but there was no humor in his tone. In fact, it chilled Rowan.

"Personally, I can't see it. You women are all alike. Always want what someone else has. Never satisfied."

Rowan spun around, prepared to tell Collins to shut up, but he'd already ducked back inside the office. She refused to believe it was true and was afraid that a glance toward the couple would verify all Collins had said. Keeping her chin up and her eyes clear, Rowan walked on to Phillip's office alone.

Laura hauled her briefcase from the backseat. "What do *you* want?"

"I need your car tonight. Let me have the keys." He held out his hand and wriggled his fingers.

Laura slammed the car door shut and knocked his hand aside. "I need. I want. Gimme, gimme, gimme. Who the hell do I look like, your fairy godmother?"

"What's the matter with you?"

She poked a finger into his chest. Phillip winced from the jab and backed away, only to find himself trapped between her piercing nail and the fender.

"You pompous, overbearing, arrogant bastard. Who do you think you are? No one's feelings matter but your own. It's no wonder McKinley ran out on you. I wish I could have had the guts to do it myself instead of letting you drop me first." She shook her head. "Obvious physical attributes aside, I don't know what I ever saw in you in the first place. I'm not an obedient dog you can order around, Phillip. You deliberately humiliated me by dragging me to that autopsy. You didn't have the common decency to let me know I would be prosecuting your old girlfriend *and* the mother of your child."

Phillip held out his arms, pleading. "Laura, I didn't even know about—"

"Don't interrupt me while I'm talking. Then, when I try to discuss a valid trial issue with you, you embarrassed me in front of her, Zach and two strangers"—she rammed her finger into his chest again for emphasis—"by announcing our previous relationship. Now you have the gall to demand my car?"

She drew her shoulders back and took in a deep breath. "I'm not your doormat, Phillip. I'm a living, breathing human being with feelings you can't even begin to comprehend. I deserve a little respect from you as an attorney, a woman, a coworker and a former... God, girlfriend doesn't even fit. How about *liaison*? Because that's all it was to you, wasn't it? Or do I not even rate the respect of that title?"

Phillip stared at her in mute shock. He'd realized the raw deal he'd given Laura days ago. What had happened to his good intentions since then? Had he become so entrenched in his own problems that even the simplest of apologies had slipped his mind? Apparently so. Knowing he had used Laura for his own gain hadn't registered. It was a nasty habit he had continued to nurture, despite the personal and moral revelations of late.

Phillip cupped both of his hands around her rigid fist. "I'm sorry, Laura. You're absolutely right and I'm surprised you didn't let me have it long before now, because I certainly have deserved it. I don't have any excuses for the way I've behaved to you or to anyone over these last several years. All I can say is that it's been like having a stranger living inside me, and I didn't recognize that until recently. With everything that's happened lately, I've come to realize that I need to think about more than myself."

She tucked her arms under her bosom and cocked out a hip. Staring at him, she narrowed her eyes. "Amazing, but I'm not sure I totally believe your sudden move toward morality."

"I'm trying my best."

Laura continued to stare at him, clearly trying to read his face for any deception. Finally, she relaxed.

"Hmmm. For the first time in the year I've known you, I believe I've finally met the human side of Phillip Stuart. He doesn't seem half bad." She smiled.

"Okay enough to at least forge a friendship with?" He smiled and extended his hand.

Laura hesitated, then shook it. "It's worth a try, even if we always do seem to be on opposite sides of the courtroom."

Phillip's smile faded. "There's no way you're going to win this one."

"You never give up, do you?" She rolled her eyes and would have pulled away if he hadn't held her in place.

"Give me a chance to explain"—he motioned to his car—"over lunch at the Officers' Club?"

After giving him an indecisive once-over, she leaned against her car. "There's no one around. I know you have more up your sleeve than you're letting on—evidence, a witness, something. Just tell me here."

Laura listened without interruption and Phillip knew she was evaluating each piece of evidence as he presented it for possible flaws. He even included his suspicions about Collins.

"Why didn't you bring all this up at the Article 32?" she asked.

"We're trying to catch this guy. That's why I was hoping to borrow your car tonight. Mine's a little obvious."

"All right." She pushed away and snatched up her briefcase. "But on one condition. I go with you."

* * * *

Rowan watched the hands of the clock edge closer to ten. She longed to switch off the lights and get this business over with, but nothing unusual could occur that might alert their little spy.

"Now?" she asked Zach and Mike.

They looked at their watches and nodded.

She flicked off the lights one by one…and waited.

Mike peeked through the drapes. "I see headlights. He's leaving. And there goes Phillip."

And Laura. What did it matter? This whole thing was giving her a headache. "I'm not about to sit around in a dark house waiting for news. I'm going to bed. Let me know if anything interesting happens."

* * * *

"A bar. How fun."

Sarcasm dripped from Laura's tongue. Phillip tried not to laugh. She'd been a good sport about lying in wait for Collins to show, then again when they waited for him to leave. But she was more of a morning person than a night owl and it was beginning to show.

Phillip opened the door. "This is where we part company."

"Leave you here alone? In a bar in the middle of nowhere?"

"I'd hardly call the center of town the middle of nowhere. I'll phone a cab to take me back to base. Whatever is going on, I don't want you in danger."

She shoved the car into park and turned off the ignition. "But it's okay for you? Don't you think it's going to seem a little funny, you walking in there by yourself? At least with me along, we can pretend to be a couple."

Phillip paused. Not much argument he could give with that kind of logic. "Let's go. You watch my back and I'll watch yours."

The local bar was crowded for a Tuesday night, but it wasn't hard to pick out their target. Collins sat in a corner booth, his back to the room. The two men with him looked like they had just crawled in from the outback — a week's worth of whiskers, dusty clothing torn here and there, scruffy boots with the soles falling off. A wad of tobacco swelled one man's lip to twice its proportion.

Phillip selected a table across the room and pulled out a chair for Laura. He still had a pretty good view from this angle, then found himself wishing he didn't. With barely a pause in his conversation, one of the desert rats spat tobacco juice into his empty beer glass. Phillip winced.

"Pretty disgusting, isn't it?" The waitress slapped coasters onto the table.

Phillip glanced up, glad for the diversion.

"Too bad we can't restrict the clientele. Those two bums would be the first ones I'd kick out," she said.

"I'm surprised to see a jarhead hanging around with them."

"Who are they?" Phillip asked.

"Junk dealers. Scrap men. And they don't much care where they get it. They did time once for stripping stolen cars. Word has it they were also caught stealing copper wire from the Marine base once, but nothing was ever done." She gave an exaggerated shudder. "They give me the creeps. Plus, they're lousy tippers. So, what'll it be tonight?"

"A couple of beers," Laura replied. When the waitress walked away, she leaned forward. "Collins and two scrap dealers? Looks like your suspicions were right. There's definitely something fishy going on here, don't you think? Phillip? Would you quit staring at them?"

But it wasn't Collins or his cronies who had captured Phillip's attention this time.

He saw her from the back, wearing skin-tight jeans and a tank top that left nothing to anyone's imagination. She captured the attention of every man in the place as she sauntered up to the jukebox. With one flick of her tapered nail, music blared through the bar. She danced up to Collins with a provocative little twitch, inviting him to dance. Phillip never saw her face. He didn't have to.

"What the hell does she think she's doing?" he ground out through bared teeth. Phillip shoved his chair back and stomped across the room. "Rowan!"

He clamped his hand over her wrist and spun her around. A stranger stared back at him.

"Hey, fella, wait your turn. There's plenty of me to go around."

"You tell him, Rusty," one of the scrap men shouted.

Phillip struggled for something to say. "Ma'am, I'm sorry. I thought you were someone else."

She slithered closer and raked her nails down his chest. "I'll be anyone you want me to be, cutie."

Collins smirked and raised one eyebrow.

Laura threaded her arm through Phillip's and pulled him back. "Thanks for the offer, hon, but he's already with me."

Rusty's grin faded. "Doesn't seem like he wants to be." The stranger spun back around to the booth. "Come on, boys. Someone dance with me."

Phillip let Laura lead him away.

"So much for keeping a low profile," she whispered.

By the time they'd returned to their table, Collins and his associates were long gone and so was the element of surprise.

Chapter Thirteen

Rowan rested her head against the tiny sofa in Phillip's office and longed to drown out the crush of emotion around her. She could understand why Phillip hadn't returned to her house the night before. He was under no obligation to do so. She had no claim on him and no right to think he should jeopardize his career by visiting her home any more than professionalism and his duty to Ian dictated. He could go where he wanted and with whomever he pleased, with no fuss from her.

All right, so it *did* bother her. In fact, it enraged her to think he had spent the evening in the company of beautiful, voluptuous Laura, no doubt making love the way they used to.

But nothing goaded her more than his early morning decree for everyone to meet him in his office then for them to be kept waiting. If there had been room, she would have paced the floor.

"Here he comes." Zach shoved open the door wider for Phillip to enter.

A grunt served as his greeting before he sagged into his seat behind the desk.

"You look like you've seen better days," Mike said.

Phillip rubbed his bloodshot eyes. "I was up all night."

"Did you get lucky?" Mike asked.

Rowan resented the hidden implications of the question but she seemed the only one to notice the double entendre.

"You might say that," Phillip muttered. "Collins met with two scrap dealers at a bar last night. The waitress gave me the scoop on them. Then when I got back to my room, I found this note shoved under the door."

He pulled a slip of paper from his pocket and slid it across the desk.

Zach unfolded it. "'Quit snooping or someone's gonna get hurt. This is your last warning.' Obviously, you weren't as discreet as you thought. What happened?"

Phillip squeezed the bridge of his nose. "I did something stupid. Let's leave it at that." His gaze settled on Rowan. "Where's Ian?"

"At day camp."

"I'd rather he were at home with one of us."

That meant her. Rowan shook her head. "He's not going to be happy. The day campers were supposed to go to the water park today."

"Well, then you and Zach can go with him to the water park while Mike and I start checking out scrap dealers on the northern end of the base."

Zach snorted. "No way. I like kids as much as the next guy, but I'm not spending the day with a bunch of wet, screaming rugrats."

Mike shook his head in mock terror. "Don't look at me. I'm not going."

"And neither am I. I've done the chaperone thing more times than I can count. No more." Rowan fished her keys from her purse and tossed them to Phillip. "It was your idea. You go. We'll check out scrap dealers."

Mike and Zach were out of the door before Phillip could protest.

"You don't even know what you're looking for," Phillip called to their backs.

Rowan smirked. "We'll figure it out. Wear lots of sunscreen. Mom will give you the address of the camp."

By the time she reached the parking lot, Mike had their escape vehicle out of its space, ready to go.

Rowan smiled to herself. It was a dirty trick to play on him, but this tiny bit of revenge chased her guilt away.

That'll teach you to stay up all night tumbling around in the sheets.

* * * *

Tired as he was, Phillip had to admit he'd gotten the better part of the deal. First, there had been Ian's obvious delight when he'd discovered his dad was acting as chaperone, then Ian's proud introduction to all his friends. Finally, he'd had a day with a bunch of rambunctious children, playing, wrestling, fussing over minor injuries. A day being a dad—the kind of dad he'd always wanted to be, the kind of dad he'd often longed for.

This was what his life would be like if he gave up his military career, and he hungered for more. Zach had been wrong. It would be worth it. There had to be a way to have the best of both worlds, a way to make the Marine Corps agree.

Ian jumped up as far as the seat belt allowed. "Mom's home."

Rowan waved a greeting from the porch. Oscar wagged his back-end furiously at her side. Phillip was surprised they had beaten him home. Ian was unbuckled and out of the van before it could come to a full stop.

"What's for dinner? I'm starved."

She brushed his hair back with her fingers and smiled. "Steak, baked potatoes and corn on the cob. Zach's cooking on the grill."

"Can I go play?"

"Just don't go out of the yard," Phillip replied.

Ian charged around the side of the house with Oscar in close pursuit.

"You're back earlier than I expected."

Her smile faded as she turned his way. "We found what we were searching for in the first scrap-metal shop, right on the outskirts of Barstow. Jess said he would try to get a photo of your scrap men and take it back to the owner for identification tomorrow. Jess will question him then on his accepting stolen property."

"He'll probably say he didn't know it was stolen. Have I got time for a nap before dinner? After being up all night and chasing kids all day, I'm exhausted."

"Sure." She jerked her thumb toward the house. "Zach's fighting the grill and Mike's in the living room watching a ballgame. The couch is free. I'll wake you in about an hour."

An arctic wind would have had less chill to it.

Mike acknowledged him with a nod when he walked in.

"I understand you had a good trip to Barstow."

His friend's gaze didn't leave the game but he nodded absentmindedly. "Yep. Car ran a little hot on the way back, though. Zach said you're pretty good at fixing cars. Want to take a look at it for me later?"

Phillip stretched out and draped his arm over his eyes. "Sure. After dinner. Has she been like that all day?"

There was a second or two of silence. Mike turned to him. "From the minute she came downstairs this morning. Probably getting a little stir-crazy. I know I am. What went wrong last night?"

"I'd really rather not say."

"Does it have anything to do with Laura?"

Phillip dropped his arm and peered at him. "No. Why?"

"No reason." A hint of a smile lit his face as he kicked back and focused full attention on the television.

Phillip frowned and closed his eyes.

Rowan watched Phillip doze off. How could he act so casually in her home after spending the night with another woman?

She sucked in a breath to calm her nerves. This was how it was going to be forever — Phillip seeing other women, having sex with them, stopping by for an afternoon with Ian and a nap on the couch then leaving, trampling her heart again and again. And one day he would tell her he was getting married. He'd have other children, other ties. They had to salvage a friendship out of this mess somehow or Ian would be the one to suffer.

With her arms wrapped around her midriff, she wandered to the back patio where Zach was adjusting foil-wrapped potatoes, corn and vegetables on the gas grill.

"At the risk of saying the wrong thing, Ro, what's been bugging you all day? As my mother would say, you've been walking around like a bear with a sore ass." He shot her a quick glance. "If it's a female thing, I don't want to know."

Not exactly the confidante she would have normally sought, but something about Zach drew her trust. Rowan settled onto the chaise across from him and popped the top on one of the beers from the nearby cooler.

"How long have Phillip and Laura been seeing each other?"

He spared her a glance, then closed the lid and straddled the end of her chair. "As tempted as I am to lie to you, I won't. They aren't seeing each other. It was a brief relationship that didn't work out."

"But last night—"

"She was helping him investigate. That's all. From what I've seen of him, once Phillip ends a relationship, there's no going back."

Rowan stared at the can in her hand, avoiding Zach's gaze. "Why would you want to lie to me?"

"Because there are times I wonder if either of you is thinking straight where the other is concerned. And you know me, I've always got to put in my two-cents worth." He patted her leg. "I could use a kid fix. Where's that son of yours? Think he'd want to play a little catch?"

Rowan gave a light laugh. "You'd better watch out. He's a ball of energy. He'll wear you out."

"Hey, I've seen the kid sleep. He's got his limits. You watch the grill. I'll see if I can convince him to humor me."

She laughed again. "He's not far. Probably around the other side of the house playing with Oscar. Ian!"

When there was no reply, Zach went to look for him. He returned a few minutes later, alone.

"I can't find him or the dog, inside or out."

Fear shortened her breath. "Phillip specifically told him not to leave the yard." A bad choice of words, especially when translated by the mind of a child. Ian's yard was ten acres, not the area surrounding the house.

"Oh, my God, if something happened to him…"

Zach hauled her to her feet. "We'll split up and search. He's fine. You'll see."

Rowan wanted to believe that, but after fifteen minutes of calling and searching the area, her instincts were telling her to panic. Her heart hammered against her ribs. Something was wrong, she knew it.

The door opened behind her. *Phillip*.

"Where's Ian? I heard you calling him."

In a voice choked with dread, she replied, "I don't know. We can't find him anywhere."

"I thought I told him to stay in the yard."

Rowan waved her arm toward the surrounding landscape. "The desert *is* his yard."

A furrow grew between Phillip's eyebrows. "He knew damn well what I meant. I'm not playing this apples and oranges game with him."

"Here he comes," Zach called.

They saw Oscar leading the way, tongue dragging. Ian lagged behind while he pulled a stick through the sand behind him.

"Where were you?" Zach asked.

Ian skipped along, oblivious to the man's anger. "Playing."

"Why didn't you come home when you were called?"

"I was watching some ants. I wanted to see how long it would take them to fix their hill after I messed it up."

Rowan still shook with fear. "We've been calling you for I don't know how long. Why didn't you at least answer?"

Ian shrugged. "I don't know. I was busy."

"Busy? You were *busy*?" Zach's face turned crimson. "Your mother ought to paddle you good."

The boy looked up, glanced at Rowan then resumed his stick-dragging. "Ooo, like that would really hurt. Mom can't spank very hard. Anyway, I'm too big for a spanking."

Phillip charged past Rowan. "No, but I can, and you're never too big for a spanking, young man."

Ian's eyes widened with a mixture of surprise and fear. He took one step back before his father hovered over him.

"You want to test that information? And as for the effectiveness of any spanking your mother might give, I'll be sure to buy her a paddle so there won't be any question in your mind about how much it'll hurt." Phillip's tone was firm.

Rowan silently commended his action. Ian's quivering chin preceded his wailing then fat tears coursed down his cheeks.

"Go to your room." Phillip pointed to the house. "When you're done crying, you will apologize to Zach for talking back so rudely. You will apologize to your mother for worrying her half to death. And you will apologize to me for disobeying my explicit instructions. Do you understand?"

Ian glared up at him. Rowan knew that expression all too well. She'd been on the receiving end of it many times—defiance coupled with the pain of perceived betrayal.

Tears poured down his face. "Everyone around here hates me!" Ian hiccupped and scrubbed his face with the back of one dirty hand. "I should run away."

Phillip jerked his arm toward the house. "Go to your room. Now!"

Ian stomped his foot. "I hate you. I wish you had never come back." He dashed into the house, slamming his bedroom door for emphasis.

"Man, I never want kids." Zach beat a hasty retreat of his own back to the safety of the grill.

Phillip ran his fingers through his short hair. Uncertainty plagued him, Rowan knew. She'd been down that road before.

"You did the right thing," she said. "If you hadn't spanked him, I would have, for all the good it would have done."

He nodded and walked toward her. "Is that how you feel? Do you hate me, too? Do you wish I'd never come back?" He focused his gaze on hers.

With each step he'd gotten closer, until his body was so near that Rowan could feel the heat radiating from him. She wanted to step back, unsure, but the porch railing blocked her retreat. Hesitantly, she placed her palm against his chest. His heart raced beneath her touch, or was that her pulse straining to be closer?

"I wished for you to come back to me every minute of every day since you left," she whispered. "I don't hate you, Phillip. How could I?" *When I love you so much.*

Their eyes met, a look that said what she could not. Then, slowly, deliciously, his lips covered hers.

There was no time but this. His kiss leaped the span of years, bringing her back to the place where they were as one. Rowan drew in a breath and draped her arm around his neck, pulling him closer.

There was that sound. That special little moan he made whenever he touched her like this. She reveled in it. He still wanted her. He slid his arm around her waist and clutched her to him as he deepened their kiss.

She didn't know how long they stood together, each pressed as close as their clothing would allow. Whatever the time, it wasn't long enough. One kiss followed another, adding fuel to a flame that demanded to be extinguished.

Rowan couldn't breathe. It was too much, too wonderful. Every part of her ached to be with him once more while her conscience nagged at her to stop. She lifted her lips from his and gasped for air.

Phillip danced his tongue down the arch of her throat and brushed feather-light kisses in the hollow above her collarbone. With her contented sigh he dipped lower, tracing the swell of her breast where it peeked above her blouse.

"No, Phillip, we can't." But even as the words left her lips, she was pressing her hips to his.

He caught her leg and drew it around his waist then pushed her against the porch railing.

"Maybe I should turn the hose on you two."

At the sound of Zach's voice, they whirled around.

Zach shook his head. "Could you at least get a room?" After another shake of his head, he left.

Rowan expected Phillip to push her away. Instead, he opened the back door to the house and drew her inside the kitchen, his arm still wrapped possessively around her waist.

"I think we need to talk."

Rowan didn't like the sound of this voice. It carried the tone of this-was-a-mistake. "It's all right. I understand. The excitement of the moment and all."

Phillip released her and took a step back. "Is that what it was to you?"

She wrapped her arms around her midriff to quell the butterflies that suddenly erupted. *Lie to him*, her conscience screamed. Instead, she shook her head. *Tell me you love me, Phillip. Tell me everything is going to be fine, that we'll have a life together.* "Isn't that what it was to you?"

"No, it wasn't," he replied. "If that's all you were to me, I wouldn't have spent the night standing guard over the house."

Standing guard? Rowan cocked her head to one side. Had she heard correctly? "What did you say you did last night?"

He pointed down the road. "After I got that lovely note, Laura and I came back and parked where we could keep a watch on the house."

Giddiness bubbled up inside of her. "You watched over us all night?"

"Well…yes."

"Oh, Phillip, what if the murderer had seen you? You could have been hurt — or worse."

His gaze dusted her face. He traced his fingertips over her cheek. Goose bumps peppered her skin. "I guess I never thought about that. I was too worried about you."

"Oh, Phillip, I —"

His lips swallowed the rest of her sentence, devouring the words as he did her soul. Rowan clung to him, deepening the caress. With a low growl, he wedged her against the sink.

Rowan parted her legs and pulled him closer, arching herself to the hardness that beckoned. He fumbled to breach her shirt, shoving aside the material until he reached her bra strap. With the flick of his wrist, the clasps came free. He swooped his hands forward, capturing her in a gentle hold that shot sparks of fire through her.

There was a sound behind them. They looked up in time to see Mike ducking back into the living room.

Panic paralyzed Rowan. "Oh, no."

Phillip pulled her shirt back into place. "It'll be okay."

She shook her head. "You don't understand. Mike is... Mike's too honest. He'll never keep this to himself."

Phillip took several quick breaths. "Trust me." He turned and shouted in the direction of the living room. "Come on, Mike. Let's see that car of yours."

Rowan sank into the nearest chair. Her knees were shaking too much to hold her anymore. Was that disaster or happiness looming on the horizon? She was no fool. One could not exist without the other, not as far as she and Phillip were concerned.

* * * *

Mike had yet to speak since Phillip had come to the garage. On the surface, he behaved as if nothing was out of order. But every once in a while, Phillip caught a questioning expression in his eyes.

"Here's your problem right here." Phillip pointed to the radiator. "You need a new cap. This one's cracked. See the edge?"

Mike nodded, not looking where Phillip was pointing.

Phillip wiped his hands on a rag and stood back. "All right. Out with it."

"Out with what?" Mike refused to meet his eyes.

"Come on. I know you saw us."

Mike drew in a breath and glanced up. "I didn't see a thing."

"Honestly?"

"That's my story and I'm sticking to it. Off the record, though, I'm going to give you a warning. If you hurt her, I'm bringing you down."

Phillip smiled and shook his head. "I care for her, Mike. I always have. I wouldn't hurt her for the world. You'll see. My word."

"Then that's good enough for me."

"Come on." He gave Mike a heartfelt smile. "We probably have time before dinner to pick up a new cap at the auto parts store."

"Looks like someone else might like to go."

Phillip turned in the direction Mike indicated. Ian was hovering near the corner of the garage, tracing designs in the sand with his foot.

"Have you apologized to everyone?"

Ian nodded, but continued to stare at the ground.

"What about me?"

"I'm sorry," he mumbled.

Phillip squatted down to Ian's level. "Don't I get a hug with that?"

Relief flooded the boy's face. He ran forward and tossed his arms around Phillip's neck. "You mean you still love me?"

"Of course, I do. Come on. Let's change into some clothes so we can go to town."

"Oscar, too?"

Philip glanced over to where Oscar was nosing around the jug of antifreeze. "Get out of there. Are you trying to get yourself killed?" He yanked the container away and put it out of reach on the shelf.

Oscar jumped back and wagged his tail.

"Would that stuff really hurt him?" Ian asked, his eyes wide with worry.

"It could. Dogs love the sweet taste and try to drink it." He shook his head. "It's pure poison but they don't know it."

Ian tugged on the dog's collar. "Come on, Oscar. You don't want that stuff. Let's go for a ride instead."

A jackrabbit darted by the garage and Oscar took off in pursuit.

"Oscar!" Ian yelled.

Phillip chuckled. "He'll be back soon enough. Let's go in and clean up before it gets too late and the stores close."

"I heard that," Zach shouted from the porch. "I've been slaving over this grill all afternoon. No one's going anywhere until after dinner. I'm putting it on the table now."

Phillip scooted Ian toward the house. "You heard the man. Let's eat."

Rowan heard them clatter inside. They were at the table before Zach could put the platter of steaks before them.

Phillip fit too nicely into their lives. She couldn't help but wonder if there was a promise of a future behind that searing kiss of his. It certainly wasn't the kiss of a man preparing to share his life with someone else.

Rowan nearly laughed out loud. He'd be crazy to give up everything for her and she didn't have the option of leaving the Marine Corps for another three years. One thing was certain. She couldn't stay on this emotional seesaw any longer. It *was* time the two of them talked.

The blast from her landline interrupted her thoughts.

Zach plopped a potato onto her plate. "Let the answering machine get it. Food's getting cold. You need to eat."

She laughed at him and stabbed a steak. On the counter behind them, the machine picked up.

"The warnings are over," a man said, his voice muffled and distorted. "Tonight it's your dog. Next time, it's your kid."

The line went dead.

It seemed an eternity before any of them moved, then they jumped for the door. Phillip raced across the yard to the garage, shouting Oscar's name.

The dog lifted his muzzle from a puddle of antifreeze and staggered toward them.

"Oh, no!" Rowan clenched her fist to her mouth in a vain effort to stay calm while Phillip scooped Oscar into his arms. "Take him to the van! We've got to rush him to the vet or he'll die."

Chapter Fourteen

Rowan stretched her arm around Phillip's shoulders. He looked like a grown-up version of Ian, trying his best to keep his emotions in check. Oscar lay unconscious on the stainless steel veterinary table, his tongue protruding. The lab assistants were clearing away the last traces of expelled antifreeze and hooking up an intravenous drip to rehydrate the exhausted pup.

"You're lucky you found the dog when you did," the vet said, checking Oscar's pupils with a quick flick of his thumb.

Phillip cleared his throat. "You'll be able to help him?"

"It was touch and go at first, but we seem to have gotten him cleaned out. For now, it's good. He'll have to stay overnight, of course."

He caught Rowan's fingers and traced each digit. "I'd like to leave him here for a few days, if that's possible."

"I doubt it will be necessary."

"This wasn't an accident. It was intentional. I don't want him hurt again. If you could board him here until I can take him back home, I'd appreciate it. He won't much like it, but I'd rather have him upset than dead."

The vet narrowed his eyes, clearly concerned. "Not a problem. But if I were you, I'd notify the Sheriff's Department."

"We have friends at the house who should have already taken care of that." He scratched Oscar behind the ears then bent and gave him a kiss on the head. "You hang in there, boy."

Rowan wanted to break down and weep. One look at the sheen of unshed tears in Phillip's eyes stopped her. Someone needed to be strong right now. It should be her.

The ride home was quiet except for a sniff from the passenger seat. Rowan half-expected Phillip to brush it off as allergies. He surprised her again.

"Big ole dope of a dog. He's the dumbest animal I've ever met. Has a heart big enough for twenty dogs. It's crazy to love a dog that much." He gave a humorless chuckle. "Zach would say it was crazy to love anyone that much."

"And what would you say?" she asked, her voice barely above a whisper.

"I would say Zach's in for a big surprise when *the* woman walks into his life." Phillip straightened. "We need to get Ian away from here until this is over."

"I don't have any relatives except Mom."

"I was thinking about Claudia. Ian and Emma could go up there. She's living in San Francisco right now. Claudia's job is pretty high-profile. She's an investigative reporter for the local TV station. She lives in a very secure apartment building. My father won't bother them, if that's what you were thinking."

That was exactly what she had been thinking. "Well, if you're sure he would be okay and Claudia wouldn't mind. But how can we make sure they get there safely? Mom refuses to fly. Someone will have to drive them. Any suggestions?"

"Maybe, but before we make too many plans, let's check with your mom first to see if she's going to be able to leave for an extended period of time."

"Call her."

"We were in such a hurry that I left my phone at the house."

"Me, too," she said.

"We'll stop by her place before we go home. I'd rather talk to her without any eavesdroppers. No sense upsetting anyone until we know if this is doable."

"You mean Ian."

"Actually, I was thinking about Zach."

Rowan flashed him a puzzled frown.

Phillip pointed toward the road. "Just drive. I'll explain later."

Light burned behind the drawn curtains of her mother's house — an odd occurrence at dusk since Mom always enjoyed catching the last rays of sunset each day.

"Something's not right. Those curtains should be open. Mom never closes them."

"Jess is with her. I'm sure she's fine."

Rowan pulled into the driveway and jammed the gearshift into park. "Someone tried to kill Oscar and threatened Ian. Why would Mom or Jess be any safer? A bullet can kill from a long distance and I doubt at this point the murderer is real picky about who he shoots."

Phillip conceded the point with a nod. "I'll go in first, just in case."

With her breath held, she watched Phillip approach the house. His stride was poised and calm, never giving away to any sniper that they suspected foul play. A flick of his wrist opened the door. He ducked in then pulled back, his eyes wide with shock.

Rowan wrenched open the van door and dashed up the walk. "Oh, my God, they're dead, aren't they?"

He pulled her back before she could rush inside. "No, no, no. They are *very* much alive. Shh…listen."

She cocked her head to one side. An unmistakable sound reached her ears. Rowan's jaw dropped. "My mother and Jess Alderman are having… They're having… They're doing —"

"Right on the living room couch." He grinned and hooked his arm through her elbow. "Let's go. I've been traumatized enough for one day."

Under Phillip's guidance, Rowan stumbled toward her van.

"Don't look so shocked." Phillip chuckled. "Ian said you thought she had a boyfriend."

"Yes, but I never thought… She's never said anything about this."

"What's she supposed to say? You're her daughter. Shared confidences only go so far. Have you ever talked to her about your sex life?"

What sex life? She shook her head. "I didn't have a clue this was going on. She's been so discreet."

He yanked open the van door. "Then there's hope for us yet."

Rowan spun around, not quite believing her own ears. "What?"

He caught her shoulders in a gentle hold, drawing circles with his thumbs. "You certainly can't mistake the fact that I still want you as much or more than I ever did. If I can't be with you soon, I swear I'll go crazy. I love you, Rowan. You must have realized that by now."

Somehow she had known, but hearing the words and knowing she wasn't mistaken made everything right. She pressed closer, feeling the evidence of his desire and praying he could feel the heat of her response.

"I love you, too, Phillip. I can't say that I've ever stopped loving you. And God knows, I want you so much."

"That settles it then." He jerked his head toward the house. "If they can be discreet, so can we."

"Discreet? We've never been known for our discretion. Look at us now. We can be seen from Mom's house, my house and by anyone watching us."

He dropped his arms and moved away.

"And don't you think Malcolm Collins is going to notice when you rush to the store for condoms? Unless you have some with you."

"I don't. I wasn't expecting—"

"I wasn't, either, and I certainly don't have anything at the house. Collins and whomever else he is working with is not stupid, Phillip. And shopping for birth control isn't discreet. That little news item would get to my colonel's ears in a second and your colonel's a second later." She snapped her fingers. "He'd use it to destroy your career and mine."

"So...what do you want to do?"

"What *can* we do?" The question was meant to prompt discussion, an evaluation of options open to them. "Phillip, I don't have the luxury of having a just-for-the-heck of it relationship. I... *We* have a child to consider. How do we know this isn't sex talking?"

"If it was only sex I wanted, I would have gone to Laura."

Rowan shot him a glare meant to kill. She swung into the van and cranked the engine. "Get in or walk."

"You're blowing this way out of proportion. It was a poor choice of words."

"You got that right." She slammed the door.

Phillip pulled it open. "Don't do this. Don't be this way. You know what I meant. You know the difference between having sex and making love. I was trying to make a point. I simply used the wrong example. You can't hold me to account for what I did or who I was with when we were apart. Surely there has been someone in your life from time to time."

A sigh lifted her shoulders. "All right. You've made your point. If it's love, I'll be in my room waiting for you tonight. If it's lust, don't put one foot on those stairs."

"And what would you suggest I do about the condom issue?"

A half-smile lifted her lips. "If it's more than lust, you'll figure something out. Come on. We'll let the lovers have a little privacy while you call Claudia."

* * * *

Zach splayed his hands across his chest. "The Ice Princess? You expect me to willingly put myself into the frozen path of The Ice Princess?"

It would have been comical had the situation not been so dire.

"I heard that," Claudia shouted from the other end of the line. "You tell that self-indulgent—"

"Stop it, both of you." Rowan grabbed the phone from Phillip. "Claudia, my son's life is in danger. I need your help, please."

"I'm sorry. You know I'll help. It's just that Zach Taylor is the most—"

"I know, but aren't they all to some degree or another? We'll call you back when we make a decision on when they'll be leaving."

Phillip expected her to launch into Zach next and from the way Zach fidgeted, it looked like he expected it, too. Ian's arrival defused the situation.

"Is Oscar going to be all right?" His bottom lip quivered with every word and tears filled his eyes.

To Phillip's surprise, Zach pulled him to his lap. For someone who had sworn not to have children a few hours ago, he fit the father role well. "The doctor is doing all he can."

"Can I see him?"

Phillip pulled up a chair. "He's at the vet resting so he can get better. He'll be home before you know it, ready to play, chase rabbits and begging for something to eat."

Rowan tsked. "Oh, Zach, your dinner. I'm sorry."

"I kept it warm for you in the oven."

"Thank you." She touched his arm. "I'll get something in a minute. I want to make sure Mom can do this, unless I shouldn't bother to try."

"Go ahead. I'll watch the tadpole for you, even if it does mean getting frostbite." He leveled his gaze to Phillip's. "And no lectures about getting along. I'll behave if she does."

He laughed. "No lectures. I promise."

Ian hopped down from Zach's lap. "Dad, the sheriff was here after you left."

He lifted a questioning brow to the other two men.

"It looks like the guy may have gotten sloppy," Mike said. "The sheriff took the jug of antifreeze for fingerprints." A triumphant grin spread across his face. "There are boot prints in the sand."

"How do we know they aren't from one of us?"

The grin widened. "Because the deputy sheriff tracked the prints to the road."

"Hot damn." Phillip smiled. "Now all we need to do is tie them to our suspect. We have to find some way to trip him up."

Rowan poked her head into the room. "You can work that out with Jess. He and Mom are on their way over. I'm going to take a long soak in the tub. Ian, bath time for you, too."

"Aw, Mom."

Phillip scooped Ian up and held him upside down until he started to giggle. "Come on. I'll let you beat me at computer games once you're done."

* * * *

Rowan slid into a sea of bubbles. Maybe the warmth would ease her tension away. The last of the bruises from her various adventures, even the scratches from Kemp's wife, were beginning to fade. She sighed. So much for her body, but would there ever be a day when her life would return to normal?

All she had wanted to do was get to the bottom of the flurry of accidents centered on the Lava training area. She had been doing her part—being a Marine, protecting her own. What had it gotten her? Threats, agony, turmoil…and Phillip back in her life. *The one plus or another minus?*

The bath pillow cushioned her as she leaned back. Forgetfulness would be nice, if only for a moment.

Dreams pulled her in. Rowan let them. Sleep would be a welcome escape. She didn't know how long she lay there — minutes, hours? It didn't matter. It wasn't long enough. She cursed the fact that it was time to summon her energy and get tucked into bed.

With a cat-like stretch she opened her eyes then started when she saw Phillip sitting next to her on the edge of the tub. He was naked, muscles shifting under taut skin. The heat of the bathroom had already slicked his body with a thin sheen of moisture.

"What —"

"Ian's in bed fast asleep. You said to come up if it was love."

"Then I presume you somehow managed to discreetly find a condom?"

"This is love, remember? That would be lust." He brushed his hand through the sudsy water and caressed the long length of her leg, sliding slowly up the sensitive skin to her inner thigh.

"Don't get me wrong. I want you so much that I feel as if I'll explode any minute. But I asked myself, if something happened and for some reason you and I could never make love again, would I still love you and stand by you? The answer was yes. I'd love you no matter what.

"So…" He swung himself into the other end of the garden tub and lowered his body into the swirling water. "I'm going to sit over here and simply be with you, no matter how much it kills me."

"Oh, Phillip, I..." She slid toward him, gliding her body against his, a silken caress.

Phillip sucked in a breath as her belly brushed against him. He cupped her buttocks and nestled her closer. With a feathery touch of her tongue, she kissed him, inhaling the very essence of his being.

"Over my dead body. I love you no matter what," she said, "but I'm afraid I can't be as noble as you right now." She straddled his hips and rubbed herself along his length.

Phillip shuddered. "If you keep that up..."

She pulled up and stroked him again, smiling when a soft groan left his throat.

"Rowan, we can't—"

"We can, this way. We have before. Remember? That hot tub in the Poconos?"

"How could I forget? But I'm not going to last very long if you keep doing that."

Rowan caught his hand and guided it to where their bodies touched. "Neither will I if you do this."

He dipped his hand between them, parting her with a flick of his fingers before probing deep inside her. She moved against him, urging him on with each caress he gave.

Agony, pleasure, that white-hot rush she loved and tried so hard to forget... It burst upon her with little warning, engulfing her with its power, paralyzing her. She tensed with the spasms, then felt him shudder with the force of his own release.

Chapter Fifteen

Lightning backlit the gathering clouds. It was bad enough to have her family leave after nightfall, but with the storm closing in, it was all Rowan could do to keep her anxiety hidden.

Ian's unhappiness about the long road trip to Claudia's house didn't help matters, either. He fretted over Oscar and worried about leaving her and Phillip. She was at a loss as to how to explain things in terms he would understand. Phillip handled the situation with patience and love.

She didn't know what he'd said in the hour he and Ian were sequestered in Ian's bedroom. All she could hear through the doors was the low, rumbling conversation. But when they walked out, Ian was more accepting. Too bad Rowan wasn't.

Not that she didn't trust Claudia or Zach with her family. They would protect the people she loved best. She wished she could go with them. Everything was spiraling out of control and all she wanted to do was hide away until the whole mess was over.

Phillip shut the trunk on her mother's car. "That's it. Time to hit the road."

Her mother heaved a sigh and stuck out her hand to Jess. "I want to thank you for all you've done, Mr. Alderman." Her eyes were shining with unshed tears.

He shook her hand while his gaze traveled the curve of her face. "My pleasure, Mrs. McKinley. My services are always available to you."

Rowan rolled her eyes heavenward. "Mom?"

"Yes, dear?" She forced her gaze away from Jess.

Rowan shook her head. "Just give me a hug." She wrapped her arms around her and whispered, "Cut the melodramatics, Mom. We know. You really need to keep your doors locked. Now give this poor guy a good-bye kiss. He looks like he can hardly stand to let you go."

Her mother pulled back, showing a mixture of astonishment and embarrassment. "You understand? I mean...you don't mind?"

Rowan laughed. "Of course I don't mind. You're a beautiful woman. You deserve to be happy, to have a life of your own, the love of a good man."

Joy covered her mother's face. In one fluid motion, she turned and flung her arms around Jess' neck. He hauled her close, plastering a kiss on her that could have steamed rice.

Zach coughed into his hand. "It's getting late. We've got a long drive ahead of us."

Rowan hugged and kissed Ian. He was so sleepy that she doubted he'd even remember. After fastening his seat belt, he toppled to one side and nestled his head into a pile of travel pillows.

Zach started the car. "Should take about ten hours. I'll call the minute we get into San Francisco."

The rain started with their departure. A perfect backdrop to the mood surrounding Rowan — Jess, too, judging from his hang-dog look.

"Sorry, Jess." Phillip clapped him on the back. "Zach was the only one of us not directly involved with this case. There wasn't much choice."

"I know." He glanced toward Rowan. "I want to thank you for what you just did. Your mother and I have been seeing each other for about six months. When you were arrested..." Suddenly looking weary, he closed his eyes. "I didn't know what to do. It's hell to be torn between the woman you love and your job. You don't know how grateful I was to discover you were innocent. I love your mother, Rowan. I want to marry her. She's always been afraid of how you would take it. You were so close to your father."

On impulse, Rowan gave the man a bear hug. "Marry her. Make each other happy. Don't let anyone or anything stand in your way."

Not like I did. She wagged a finger at him and smiled. "In fact, I expect you to make an honest woman of her."

He tossed back a laugh. "You have my —"

A thunderous boom drowned out the rest of his words. The house went dark.

"And when do I get to make an honest woman of you?" Phillip whispered against her ear. He slipped his strong hands around her waist. "Let's watch the storm from your room. Zach left us a little present — a box of little presents."

Rowan glanced around to see if Mike and Jess had overheard, but the storm had already driven them inside. She knew that the two would be staying downstairs in Ian's room and the spare bedroom. Blessed privacy for her and Phillip.

"Are you asking for a commitment from me, Phillip?"

He dusted his fingers along her neck. "I'm giving you one from me."

"Phillip, don't—"

Her protest was swallowed by his kiss. With lips still sealed, he scooped her into his arms and carried her upstairs.

So much for discretion.

Rowan didn't care. Phillip could haul her to hell and back right now as long as it meant being with him. Mike and Jess would have to be trusted to keep their mouths shut.

Phillip kicked the bedroom door closed the instant they crossed the threshold. He broke off their kiss long enough to place her in the center of her bed and kick off his shoes, then he stretched out beside her and found her mouth once more.

With shaking hands, Rowan caught the edges of his shirt and tugged it up. He stripped the garment over his head, then did the same to hers. Her bra was quickly added to the pile, exposing her aching breasts to his questing fingers. A flash of lightning highlighted the passion in his eyes, turning them to liquid silver. Still shaking, Rowan furrowed her fingers through his short hair and pulled his head to her breast, gasping when he sucked her nipple deep into his mouth.

With a flick of his wrist, he released the snap on her shorts. Phillip swooped his hand inside, cupping her buttocks before sliding the material down and off her legs, then he brushed his hand back up, coaxing her to open for him.

Rowan bit back a cry as he stroked his fingers against her heat. He traced his thumb over those places only he knew how to bring to life, igniting a fire only he could quench. Time was endless, frozen, as he tantalized her with his long fingers. She rode the waves of pleasure, her low cries punctuated by the flashing of the desert storm.

She tensed as the pleasure engulfed her, quivered in his arms as it overcame her, then held him close in that final fulfillment as it subsided.

With lazy satisfaction, she beckoned him close, stripped his shorts away and reached out to cup him in her hands. The vein on the underside of his cock pulsed as she stroked his erection with one hand and kneaded his balls with the other. Phillip moaned softly, head tilted back, eyes half closed with ecstasy. Flicking her tongue over her lips, she bent and took him into her mouth — deep.

"My God, Rowan," he gasped and cupped her head. The flex of his fingers and the subtle thrust of his hips begged for more.

She swirled her tongue from base to tip, delving into the slit for a moment before starting back down again. Phillip splayed his legs wider, opening himself as far as his stance at the edge of the bed allowed. Rowan squeezed his sac and sucked him hard. Tension shuddered through his body. She matched his groan with one of her own — her way of telling him to come.

He froze, no doubt weighing his choices in his lust-fogged brain — come or pull free and fuck her? She decided for him, drawing away by slow degrees until she could look up at him. His body glistened with sweat. Hard breaths trembled his shoulders. Rowan raised to her knees and nestled his cock between her breasts.

"Fuck me," she whispered, then crawled backward on the bed.

His gaze tracked the glide of her fingers up her inner thighs. His breath caught when she spread her labia for him. She writhed into a caress over her clit. Phillip groaned and fumbled to seat a condom. She reached for him the second his knee hit the bed, pulling him close as he covered her body with his.

Their tongue met on ragged gasps as she wrapped her legs around his waist and he slid home.

Oh, God. She had forgotten how deliciously overwhelming he could be. They deepened their kiss, writhing their bodies in time with the dance of their tongues.

He pulled back, then pressed forward, harder. Rowan dug her heels into his buttocks, demanding more.

Phillip smothered a groan into her neck. He grabbed her bottom in one hand and tilted her hips up.

Together they moved, clinging tighter with every rock of their bodies. His heat bathed her from head to toe. Her climax built—her clit rigid against his hard cock. She craved the relief orgasm would bring but fought the mounting wave, wanting them to come at the same time.

Phillip broke the kiss. "Come with me, baby."

"Now?" she asked.

"Oh yeah."

She took his mouth in a frenzied kiss, hoping it would be enough to muffle their groans. Mother Nature blessed them with a flash of lightning. Thunder rumbled over the house, masking all sound right when they needed it most. As they slid down the other side of bliss, she wished the storm would stay with them a little while longer so they could do it all over again.

* * * *

Phillip fumbled for the bedside phone. A glance at the clock showed it was eleven-thirty. They'd just drifted off to sleep. No good-news calls happened at this time of night.

"Hello?"

"Is this the McKinley residence?" a man asked.

"Who wants to know?" Phillip barked. If this was another threat...

"California Highway Patrol."

Adrenaline raced through his heart. He snapped upright. "What's wrong? What's happened?"

Rowan pushed herself to one elbow and swung toward him. He didn't want to look at her face, didn't want to see the panic there that mirrored his. He swung from the bed.

"There's been an accident," the officer said. "A car driven by Captain Zachary Taylor was run off the road east of Joshua Tree."

Phillip grabbed his clothes. "Joshua Tree? Why did it take so long to call us?"

Rowan jumped to her knees. "What? What is it?"

He waved her down.

"The storm kept us from reaching him. The road was flooded. The vehicle rolled. They missed the wash, but—"

"Are they hurt? Where are they?" Was he shouting? It seemed so.

Rowan leaped from bed and scrambled for her clothes.

"All three occupants were unconscious when we reached them. Weather conditions and flooded roads wouldn't allow any other option. The Naval Hospital is handling emergencies for now."

"How are they? What's wrong? Are they all right?" Phillip told himself to shut up so the man could answer.

"I can't say. I also can't be sure how long they'll remain here. Soon as things clear, patients will most likely be moved to area hospitals."

"We're on our way." Phillip slammed the receiver down and hauled on his jeans while he told Rowan. He didn't need light to know she was terrified. He was scared to death.

She wrenched open the bedroom door and shouted downstairs for Mike and Jess. Panic made her voice shrill. While she hurried to dress, he raced downstairs to break the news to the other two men. Only afterward did he realize how abruptly he'd presented the information, considering Jess' intimate involvement with Emma.

But there was no taking it back. He'd make up for it later — if any of them had a later.

* * * *

Rowan sat statue-like on the drive to the hospital. She would not give in to hysterics. Nothing could be accomplished by it. Strength was needed — for Ian, her mother, Phillip, even Jess. She had to hang in there. Yet it took every ounce of willpower to adhere to that decree, especially when they walked into the hospital.

The mud-splattered highway patrolman stopped in mid-pace when they rushed in. His partner stood nearby, head bent in deep conversation with the Navy emergency room doctor.

Noticing their arrival, the doctor cut him off. "You're the family?"

"Yes," they answered in unison.

"How is Ian? Where is our son?" Phillip's tone was strained, but at least it had come out with some semblance of calm. If Rowan had been the one doing the talking, she would have shrieked.

"We're getting him settled in intensive care," the doctor replied.

Rowan bit her knuckle to keep from sobbing aloud. Phillip didn't do as well. She watched him blanch, saw panic racing over his face and she wrapped her arms firmly around his waist. He hugged her as if she were a lifeline, his arms shaking.

"He took quite a whack on the head," the doctor told them. "He's been out cold since they were found."

"You mean he's in a coma?" Phillip choked out.

The doctor shook his head. "No. He's got one heck of a concussion and is unconscious. The next twenty-four hours are going to be critical. Once the weather clears, we'll determine if he needs to be taken to Loma Linda or Desert Regional. By then he might be well enough to go home."

With a choking gasp, Jess pushed forward. "Emma? How's my Emma?" His deep voice was painfully tight.

"Resting comfortably and awake. She's got a broken arm, scrapes and plenty of bruises, but otherwise she's going to be fine. Because she also suffered a concussion and was unconscious when she was brought in, I'd like her to stay overnight. You can go see her."

Jess rushed off to the hospital ward upstairs.

"Zach Taylor?" Mike asked.

For the first time, the doctor refused to meet anyone's eyes. "As I was telling the patrolman, the surgeon pulled a nine-millimeter bullet out of his shoulder."

Rowan gasped. "He was shot?"

The doctor nodded. "His health and age are in his favor, but we can't give you a prognosis yet. Last report is that his blood pressure is low, he has a severe concussion and his leg was badly fractured in two places. As I said before, if he hadn't been in such good health, he'd be dead by now. You might want to notify his relatives."

Rowan's stomach knotted and she hugged Phillip tighter.

"When can we see our son? And Zach?" he asked.

"We will let you know as soon as your son is settled in his room. Captain Taylor is still in recovery, but I understand he'll be moved to a room soon."

"Dear God." Phillip pinched the bridge of his nose, closed his eyes and tightened the grip he held around her shoulders. She gave in to the need to wrap him to her and swung fully against him. He put his other arm around her. Anyone who didn't like it could go to hell.

The doctor's pager beeped. He unclipped it with a motion born of years of practice then checked the readout.

"I'm sorry I can't tell you more at the moment, but as soon as there is any news about your son or Captain Taylor, someone will let you know."

A Navy corpsman handed the doctor a clipboard, whispered another patient's name and returned to his corner desk station.

The doctor, looking harried and tired, murmured, "Excuse me. I'm needed in the emergency room," and left Phillip and Rowan to make their way upstairs.

"Go see your mom," he said when they reached the ward waiting room. "I'll wait here and come get you the second we're able to see Ian."

Rowan nodded and walked to her mother's room. The sight of her lying in the bed stopped Rowan short. Her skin was barely a shade darker than the stark white of the sheets. Blue veins showed clearly at her temples and throat. Both eyes were darkened with bruises and her arm lay in a rigid cast suspended across her chest.

Jess held her free hand, slowly rubbing his thumb over her knuckles. Her mom's eyes were closed. Jess' sniffle indicated tears. She'd done this, risked her entire family on some crazy quest for answers. Tears streamed down her cheeks. She took a step back, not wanting to intrude.

Jess lifted his head and turned her way. His blue eyes shone with unshed tears. "I know what you're thinking. It's not your fault."

He relinquished her mom's hand gently as he stood and came her way.

Rowan shook her head. "I started all of this."

He wrapped his arm around her shoulders then pulled her into a hug. "And you're going to help finish this, honey. You need to stay strong, stay focused and remember that you aren't at fault. Collins is, and we are going to prove that."

"Oh, for heaven's sake, can't a girl get some sleep around here without you two getting all noble on me?" Emma's voice was weak and scratchy but steady.

"Mom." Rowan crouched at her mother's side.

"Jess told me about Ian and Zach," Her mom said. "I'm doing fine, darling. I just need some rest." She grasped Rowan's hand. "Go to Phillip, honey. He needs you now. Jess will stay with me."

Rowan scrubbed the tears from her cheeks.

"I'll let you know as soon as I hear something about Ian. I love you."

She turned to leave then paused and gave Jess a quick kiss on the cheek. "Thank you."

She returned to the waiting room and tried to sit while Phillip paced. Time passed with agonizing slowness. *How long does it take to get one little boy settled? Has something else gone wrong?* She launched to her feet to pace in the opposite direction as Phillip and nearly smacked into two deputy sheriffs walking through the door.

"Excuse me, Captain Stuart? Staff Sergeant McKinley? We need to ask you a few questions."

Phillip pressed his hand against her back. "We've already given statements to the officer who called us from the hospital."

"Yes, sir." The taller deputy nodded. "But we have some questions about the passengers of the other car — the one that rammed your friend's vehicle. You did know, didn't you, that one of the two passengers was involved in the accident as well and brought in for treatment?"

Rowan scowled. "What other man?"

"Witnesses say two grizzled-looking men in a beat-up truck plowed into the car Captain Taylor was driving. The driver lost control of their vehicle afterward and skidded off the road. One got away. The other one was hurt too badly to escape. He was still out cold. His ribs are smashed. One leg is badly broken," the shorter deputy replied.

A nurse poked her head into the room. "You can see your son now," she said, beckoning them to follow.

The deputy stepped into their path before they could do so. "Do you have any idea why this happened?"

"Yes." Phillip pushed by, taking Rowan with him. "But we need to see our son first."

She leaned into the comfort of his hand at her back as they followed the nurse down the corridor to Ian's room. Knowing he was hurt still didn't prepare her for the sight of him in that huge bed.

He was a healthy boy, tall for his age, yet now dwarfed by the machinery, tubes and wires attached to his body. An ugly purple bump dominated his forehead. There were cuts along his arms and cheeks.

As if sensing her thoughts, Phillip said, "Glass from the rollover."

"He looks so little, so vulnerable. I wish I could hold him."

He pulled the single chair in the room to the bedside. "Sit down, honey. Talk to him. Maybe he'll hear us."

She longed to comb her fingers through Ian's hair and cuddle him on her lap. She settled for holding the one hand not hooked up to an IV.

Phillip did most of the talking. Any words that came to her mind lodged in her throat while she forced the tremors from her voice.

"We love you."

"You're going to be fine."

"Rest and get better."

"Hang in there."

Upbeat and positive, nothing to let Ian know how serious his condition was. Rowan kept praying Ian would open his eyes and give them his sweet smile, but he lay there, his small hand limp in hers.

This is a nightmare. It has to be. Life wouldn't be so cruel as to take their son away when they were finally a family. She didn't know how in the world Phillip managed to stay so calm, but she blessed him for it.

She wanted to scream at the injustice, to collapse on the bed and cry.

"Phillip?" Mike's voice at the door brought their heads around. "Zach's awake. He's asking for you. The deputies are on their way to talk to him. The nurse isn't happy about it but they insisted. I don't know how much they're going to get out of him in his condition."

Phillip curled his fingers over Rowan's shoulder. "I'll be back in a little while. Will you be okay?"

She gave him a quick nod, then covered his hand with hers. "I love you," she whispered.

"I love you, too." He said it in full voice, not caring who heard or knew. "Ian's going to be fine and we're going to be a family."

Rowan's stomach roiled. If only it were as easy as it sounded.

* * * *

Phillip had seen Zach after dusk-till-dawn parties and all-night stretches of duty. Even then he had looked better than he did now. Normally robust and in good humor, now Zach was deathly white and could barely summon the energy to move. Tubes entered his nose and arms, pulsing with fluids and oxygen. Phillip's heart twisted at the thought of losing his best friend.

"How is he?" Phillip asked the attending nurse in a voice meant only for his ears.

"Starting to become feverish and he's weak from the loss of blood, but he's got enough morphine in him to keep the pain away. He's also not going to be as coherent as you'd like. It would be best if you got this visit over with quickly. He's still in critical condition. If he didn't seem so distressed with the need to talk with you, I would have sedated him immediately."

Phillip glanced over his shoulder. The deputies were keeping a respectful distance but that wouldn't last long. They had a job to do. He motioned them in. Mike followed.

Zach regarded them through dazed, half-lidded eyes and tried to extend his uninjured arm to Phillip, who reached forward and clasped it gently between his hands.

"Ian...Emma?" It was barely a croak.

Still grasping his hand, Phillip sat on the edge of the bed. "Resting." That was all he needed to know.

Zach closed his eyes and swallowed hard. "It happened so fast. He came up behind me from nowhere. I wasn't even away from the house ten minutes and there he was. He had his brights on, and for a minute, I thought he was going to plow into the rear of the car. The rain was the worst I've ever seen. I could barely see the road as it was, then those damn bright lights."

Zach paused to take several shuddering breaths. "Finally, he passed. Glass exploded beside me." He closed his eyes, then opened them once more as if struggling to stay awake.

"We can finish this later. You need to rest."

Zach squeezed Phillip's hand feebly. "I'm okay. It's funny. I didn't realize I'd been shot at first. All I remember thinking was that Ian never made a sound and Emma didn't scream. I fought the wheel, trying to keep on the road. I was afraid to stop because I didn't know what might happen. Then he swerved into us over and over again. I hit a patch of water and he rammed us again. We rolled. Next thing I knew, I woke up here."

"They caught one of the guys, Zach. He's right down the hall. The other one got away. There were witnesses. Once the bastard comes to, we'll be able to nail this case shut."

Zach nodded. "I'm sorry, Phillip. I was supposed to protect—" His face turned an alarming shade of gray. Beads of sweat gathered at his temples and along his upper lip.

"Don't even start that. If it weren't for you, Emma and Ian might not be alive right now."

"Brave kid," Zach murmured. "Not a peep. Not a complaint."

Phillip didn't have the heart to tell him it was because Ian had been knocked out cold. Zach's grip slackened and he started to drift off to sleep. A piercing tone from the corridor flashed his eyes open.

Zach struggled to right himself. "What—?"

Phillip gently pushed him down. "It's nothing. Rest." He walked over to the deputies. "What is that sound?"

"Code Blue," the tall one whispered. "Someone's died."

God, no! Please, no! Phillip tore from the room as if the devil was on his heels.

He jerked to a stop shy of entering Ian's room. A Navy corpsman and doctor stood over his bed. Rowan was at the foot, hands folded in prayer beneath her chin. He was afraid to cross the threshold.

Rowan looked up, tears shimmering in her eyes. She held her hand to him. "Come see."

Somehow, he forced himself to move. He caught Rowan's fingers—his lifeline to reality.

"Look." She motioned to the bed.

He pivoted that way and was greeted by Ian's groggy gaze.

"Hey, Dad," he croaked.

Phillip didn't know whether to laugh or cry. He compromised with a little of both.

"He started to come around a few minutes ago," the doctor said with a smile. "Some trouper you've got here. Quite a little fighter."

"That's our boy," Phillip said, still dazed from his fright.

"You're shaking," Rowan whispered. "What's wrong?"

He shook his head. "There was a Code Blue. I thought…" The words were best left unspoken. "I should let Zach know everything's okay here. I left him in kind of a hurry. I won't be long."

Mike and Jess intercepted him two feet from Zach's room. "The guy who ran Zach off the road is dead. Looks like someone walked right in and smothered him."

"Since I doubt his partner could walk in here without being seen or smelled, I'll give you ten guesses who killed him." Phillip massaged the ache between his eyes. "Now what?"

Jess gnawed on his toothpick. "He'll go after the other desert rat…wherever he is."

"Well, I don't know where he is, but I have a pretty good idea how to find him." Phillip laid out his plan.

* * * *

"I don't know why I let you talk me into this." Laura fidgeted with her seat belt as if trying to decide if she was really going to follow Phillip into the bar.

"We're both wired. The place is surrounded. There's no danger to either of us."

"It's one in the morning. The bars will close in an hour. Are you sure this woman will still be around?"

"Right now, I'm not sure of anything except that I want to get this done." Before someone else died, someone he loved.

She flicked open her seat belt then flung open the door. Stomping ahead of him as they had planned, she marched into the bar.

Phillip chased after her and spoke in an over-loud voice. "Will you wait up?"

Laura flopped behind the nearest table and whispered under her breath. "She's in the corner booth."

He dared a glance up. Rusty sat facing them, her short skirt hiked up to her rear end.

"I thought I told you to wait," he snapped at Laura.

"I'm sick of you ordering me around." She shoved herself to her feet, drawing the room's attention and toppling the chair to the floor.

"We're finished. I thought I made that clear. If you follow me again, I'll have you arrested." Slinging her purse over her shoulder, she stormed back out of the bar.

The room was silent for a few seconds then everyone turned back to their business. It took half as much time for Rusty to saunter his way.

"Have a fight with your girl?"

He forced his gaze to travel the length of her body. "Not my girl anymore. She caught me with someone else. Don't understand why she's so hot about it. She doesn't own me. Cold fish in bed. She doesn't understand what I need. Know what I mean?"

She slithered closer. "Yeah. I know all about a man's appetites. So, are you hungry now?"

Chuckling, he caught her around the waist and pulled her onto his lap. "Starving. Got any *food*?"

"I might know where we can get some. What's your budget?"

"Rusty, the sky's the limit tonight."

"Well, then"—she hopped to her feet—"I know a cozy little place real close."

"I hope so." He jerked his thumb toward the door. "She left me stranded."

"Just a few blocks away. You know, you've got to be the yummiest lookin' thing I've seen in a long time. I'm real glad you're back in the neighborhood."

Phillip laughed and hooked her arm through his. "Sounds like you're the one who's starving."

"I might be, as long as the sky's the limit." She leaned close and dropped her voice to a whisper. "And speaking of limits, I'll have to see some cash before we mosey on over to my place."

Phillip stood and smiled. "Of course." He pulled Rusty close, bent as if to give her a kiss and passed her a one-hundred-dollar bill. "That's for starters."

Rusty's avarice shone across her thin face. "C'mon."

They made it as far as the parking lot before the deputy sheriffs closed in. "You're under arrest for prostitution, Rusty."

She sputtered obscenities at the deputies and Phillip as they cuffed her then shoved her into the patrol car beside Jess.

The toothpick danced from one side of Jess' mouth to the other. "If you quit your blabbering long enough, we might be able to make a deal."

Chest heaving with indignation, she glared at him. "What kind of deal?"

"You were seen dancing with a couple of men the other night."

"I dance with a lot of men every night."

"No games," he barked.

She drew back.

"Two desert rats and a man with dark thinning hair, a Marine high-and-tight haircut, ferret face. Sat in the corner booth. They seemed to be on pretty good terms with you."

Rusty shrugged. "Okay, so I know 'em. What's it to you?"

"One's dead. We want to talk to the other one before he winds up dead, too."

Her bravado faded. "That's all? And you'll let me go?"

Jess twirled the toothpick. "Free and clear."

"All right, I'll tell you. No skin off my nose. I don't owe those two a damn thing."

The deputy scribbled the information on a notepad and shoved it to his partner.

Jess unfolded himself from the car. "Okay, gents, let the lady go. Let's get a team over to this guy's house and take him into custody."

Rusty was out of the car the second the cuffs came off. "Wait a minute. You can't leave me here. What if this maniac comes after me?"

Phillip leaned close, pinning her to the vehicle. "Now why would he do a thing like that? Is there something you know that you should be sharing?"

She sputtered for a response, searching each face for answers. Finally, she drew up her shoulders. "All right.

I'll tell you everything I know if you promise to protect me until Malcolm is locked up."

After Jess nodded, she crawled in the backseat once more and, after having been read her rights, Rusty made her preliminary statement. It verified everything they already suspected. Now all they had to do was catch Collins, and the net was tightening fast. At least, he hoped so.

Standing with Jess, they watched the patrol car drive off with Rusty in the deputy's care.

"I just got word," Jess said as he pulled open the door on his car. "Collins was watching when you pulled up to the bar. He followed Laura back to the base. She's been notified and is moving to the next part of the plan. The MPs aren't far behind. They're keeping a close eye on her and her shadow. She's going to drive around a bit and give us a chance to get into position before she goes to the legal offices."

Phillip nodded and prayed this was going to be the end of it.

* * * *

Cramped in an unmarked van across the street, Phillip, Jess and the MP chief watched Collins edge toward the legal office. Looking in all directions, he lifted his fist and beat at the door. Laura waited a few minutes then opened it a crack.

Stick to the script, Laura. Don't let him in.

Voices came over the wire Laura wore. It sounded as if she and Malcolm were standing no more than five feet away. Her voice shook. Who could blame her? She was facing a murderer. If Collins took a notion, she'd be dead in seconds and there would be nothing Jess or Phillip could do to save her.

Phillip didn't have a problem with her helping earlier, but this was going too far. Yet she had insisted. Rather than argue, he'd relented. Now he wished he'd argued harder. He pulled up the night-vision binoculars for a closer look.

Malcolm leaned against the wall. "Didn't mean to bust in on you, but I saw you at the bar with Stuart and thought you might need a little cheering up. You two have a tiff? Thought you might want someone to talk to."

"I appreciate your concern, but I really don't feel like talking about it, Mr. Collins. With all due respect, I don't discuss my personal life with my friends. I certainly don't feel comfortable talking about it to someone I barely know."

"I understand completely. Been down the breakup road myself because of someone else. It's been pretty clear where Stuart's interest has been since he arrived. It's enough to—"

"Mr. Collins, please."

"Sorry." His gaze wandered for a moment before returning to her. "A little late for you to be working, isn't it, Captain Cushing? Or are you burying yourself in your work to ease the pain of Stuart's betrayal?"

She shrugged. "Call it whatever you'd like. Not much else for me to do now. Besides, I can't sleep when I'm working on a big case. I get too wrapped up in it all. Trying to pull all the evidence together to nail the accused."

"So, the evidence is pretty well stacked up against Staff Sergeant McKinley? After that pathetic attempt at a defense by Captain Stuart, I'll be surprised if she doesn't get life in prison. Just goes to show what happens when you let your personal life interfere with business, something my wife never understood."

"It does seem that the evidence weighs heavily against her. I should know more by Monday morning, unless something delays the lab report. Oh, that reminds me. Tell me, Mr. Collins, did NCIS identify that new set of fingerprints that were found at the murder scene?"

"Fingerprints?"

"Yes, the ones found on the floor next to the deceased. A fingerprint expert retained by Jess Alderman located them this morning — faint, but there. I'm not surprised your team missed them. It took a specialist to lift those prints. They didn't belong to the accused or the deceased. Anyone who has been in the building since has had gloves on."

Malcolm caught a moth in his fist and squeezed, then tossed it to the ground. "First I've heard of it. Wonder why I wasn't notified?"

Laura hiked a shoulder. "It wouldn't surprise me if Alderman was trying to hog the glory for himself, just like Phillip. Two peas in a pod. Well, I've got to get back to work. Thanks for checking up on me."

With a casual wave, Malcolm walked away. Once the door was shut, he picked up his pace.

"And there he goes," Jess mumbled. "How much do you want to bet he heads straight for the NCIS office to snag those prints?"

"Just like a rat to peanut butter," Phillip said as they watched Malcolm's truck tear out of the parking lot.

"My men are waiting for him," the military police chief said. "We also have a team watching the hospital. Wherever he goes, we've got him."

Phillip had his doubts. Collins wasn't stupid. This man watched and waited. With Rusty's statement, they had enough to haul him in. Why they were playing this game now Phillip didn't know. Still, he sat in the cramped confines of the surveillance van, mouth shut, heart pounding, waiting for word.

The police radio crackled to life. Someone had set off the armory alarms, mobilizing a base-wide shut down and the force. *Not hard to figure out who.*

Phillip grabbed the chief's arm. "It's a trick. He's used it before. Tell your men not to leave the NCIS building or the hospital."

"Calm down, Captain. My men know their job. All Collins succeeded in doing is shutting any escape route for himself."

Phillip snorted. "The man and his cohorts have been sneaking on and off base for months without being detected. He knows a hundred ways off this base. What he *succeeded* in doing is tying *your* hands."

The chief stared at him for what seemed an eternity then pulled the van onto the road. They eased to a stop around the corner well within sight and a short jog from the NCIS building.

"Let's go." The chief opened his door and jumped out. "Captain Stuart, please stay behind."

He snorted. "I'll stay out of the way but not behind. I've come this far with you. Taking it to the finish isn't going to hurt."

"Remember that if you get caught in cross fire."

With no further discussion, they trotted into position behind the two young MPs. Collins hadn't bothered to hide his presence. His vehicle sat in the parking lot fully illuminated under the streetlights.

Weapons drawn, they overtook the building. Phillip hugged the rear, but even from that vantage point, he saw the light from Collins' office. A paper shredder hummed. Every few seconds, another piece of evidence buzzed through its blades.

Jess nodded and the team advanced.

"Halt!"

Startled, Collins jumped back and flung his hands in the air. Pages of the investigation report scattered across the floor.

Collins laughed off their presence and dropped his arms. "You scared the daylights out of me. What did you think I was, a burglar?"

Phillip squatted to pick up the papers. Each one was labeled as the investigation into the death of Charles Kemp. "Why don't you tell us, Mr. Collins?"

Jess holstered his weapon and straightened his suit jacket. "You've got some explaining to do, Malcolm."

He had the nerve to laugh. "I don't know what you're talking about."

Phillip waved his hand over the scattered pages. "Oh, I think you do."

With a slow shake of his head, Jess motioned to the MPs. "Take him out front."

Each grabbed one of Collins' arms and escorted him to the waiting room.

"I never thought I'd be interrogating one of my own," Jess said, a hint of sadness in his voice.

"Better yours than mine," the MP chief said. "For a while, I was beginning to wonder." He scratched his head and avoided Phillip's gaze. "Sir, all I can do is apologize. Those who treated Staff Sergeant McKinley less than honorably will be formally counseled. If I can prove any other charges, they'll be dealt with appropriately."

Phillip nodded. "I appreciate that. Had I been in your situation, I can't say I wouldn't have felt the same way."

Jess heaved a breath. "Yeah, well, I guess I'd better get this over with." He dug a toothpick out of his pocket, shoved it between his teeth and strode forward. "Malcolm, as I said, you've got a lot of explaining to do."

A smirk cut Collins's features. "I still don't know what you're talking about."

"Don't play games. By now, the police will have picked up your scrap-selling partner. I'm sure he's not going to hesitate to spill his guts, especially when he discovers his friend is dead. I'm not getting any younger, Malcolm. Do me a favor and make it easy on us both."

Collins smirked and kept his mouth shut.

Jess dropped his head in a slow shake. "Cuff him."

The younger of the two MPs approached Collins, handcuffs open for his wrists.

Collins lunged for him and snapped a chokehold around his neck. With his free hand, he plucked the pistol from the lance corporal's holster.

"Everyone back off," he snarled, pointing the 9mm pistol at the young Marine's head.

No one moved in the shocked silence that followed.

The MP chief eased forward, slowly fanning the air. "Just calm down. See? We're all moving off."

Phillip and Jess backed away with him, never once losing sight of that pistol cocked to the lance corporal's head.

"Don't do this, Malcolm. You know it's over. Shooting him won't make things easier on you." Jess' voice was firm and unwavering. "There's nowhere for you to go from here. You know that. You saw to that yourself. Think of your family, your children. Drop the gun."

Collins's eyes were wide, glassy, his high forehead shiny with beads of sweat. With the mention of his family, his chin quivered. His hostage remained frozen. The young Marine at least had sense enough not to startle his captor into pulling the trigger.

Jess held out his hand. "Give me the gun, Malcolm. It's over. If you shoot, you know you'll never make it out the front door. You don't want to risk that. You don't want your daughters—"

"Enough with my daughters!" He tightened his grip on the Marine and jammed the barrel deeper into his temple. "You don't know how it is. You don't know how hard it is. Everything was fine until that McKinley bitch started poking her nose into my business. Now it's all ruined."

Phillip took one step forward, spreading his hands wide. "Wait."

Jess sucked in a breath.

Phillip kept going. "This Marine isn't part of this. He's done nothing to you. You want revenge? Take me instead. You don't want to hurt this kid."

Collins's eyes glittered at the thought. "Ah, Stuart. Always the martyr. The hero." He cocked his head to one side to consider the offer. "All right, Captain. You *are* the cause of my troubles at the moment, you and that bitch McKinley. If I have to put a bullet into someone to get out of here alive, it might as well be you.

I have nothing to lose at this point, anyway. And I would enjoy seeing you fall before me."

Shoving the Marine aside, Collins motioned Phillip closer with a jerk of the weapon.

"On your knees, Stuart. Let's see how brave you are when death is seconds away. You beg me enough, I'll let you go—maybe."

Phillip eased forward and sank to his knees. Pleasure gleamed in Collins's beady eyes. A maniacal grin slashed across his face. Laughing, he leveled the pistol at the space on Phillip's forehead above his nose.

In that split second where Collins' attention focused on Phillip, the young MP pounced, hitting Collins sharply on the elbow. The pistol skittered across the floor.

Collins stumbled to the side, arms windmilling as he fought for balance.

Phillip turned his crouch into a forward lunge, driving his shoulder into Collins' stomach. They hit the floor hard, toppling chairs in their wake.

Fist doubled, Collins swung, clipping Phillip's chin. He ducked the next blow, seizing Collins' wrist in a grip that threatened to snap bone. He drew back and smashed a fist against Collins' jaw. The man cried out and swung with his free arm. Phillip caught it, twisted and drove him to the ground.

Anger boiled within him, a rage greater than any he had ever known. Fury at the person who had caused his family and his friend such harm. Collins thrashed beneath him, bucking under Phillip's weight, kicking out for freedom.

Phillip jerked his arm higher, dislocating his shoulder blade. Still Collins fought, his rage making his strength superhuman. Phillip held on, letting him wear himself out, then jammed his knee into the small of his back.

Collins cried out and collapsed, sobbing at his defeat. The MPs jumped in and snapped the cuffs in place. Phillip rolled away and let them have him. It was over.

Jess gave him a hand up. "Nice job. I can't say I wouldn't have been tempted to beat the hell out of him if I'd had him down."

"I'm no saint." Phillip hauled himself to his feet and dusted off his clothes. "Trust me. It was tempting."

He listened to the litany of rights being read. Even someone like Collins had the right to a fair trial. Hopefully, the evidence would put him away for a long time.

Spitting blood, Malcolm shot hate-filled glares toward first the MPs standing guard over him then to Phillip. "Know any good lawyers?" he asked with a smirk.

Phillip stared back, his eyes cold and emotionless. "Not a one."

"Well, I'm not talking until I have one."

"No surprise there."

The MP chief clicked off his radio and trotted toward them. "They've got your partner and he's spilling his guts. About you, your theft ring, Sergeant Kemp's murder and your attempts to frame Staff Sergeant McKinley. Maybe you want to think twice about talking."

Collins clamped his lips tight and stared into the distance. Phillip wasn't sure, but he thought he saw a tear slip down the man's cheek. He shook his head over the irony. Collins had justified his actions for the sake of his children. It was doubtful he'd see much of them anymore.

Chapter Sixteen

The sound of footsteps pulled Rowan to the hallway for what was probably the hundredth time. A nurse zipped by, flashing a smile as an afterthought.

With each minute since their departure, Rowan had run through the list of everything that could go wrong until worry had gnawed a hole in her stomach.

"I do wish you'd quit pacing." Mike tossed down the last of his coffee and crumbled the paper cup. He'd had so much caffeine tonight that his hands shook.

"Why? Not leaving you enough room to do your own?" Her intended humor sounded snappy and irritable, matching her disposition. She hoped he wouldn't call her on it. He was still her superior officer and once this was over with they would slip back into those roles. After all that had happened, that might not be so easy. Rowan relied on professionalism to see them through the transition.

He tossed his cup into the trash can. "Nope. I'm getting exhausted from watching you."

Rowan forced a smile. *One worry off my mind.* Hugging herself, she tried to quell the jitters. "Why is it taking so long? You don't suppose something's happened, do you?"

"I hope not." Mike glanced over her shoulder and down the hall. "Here comes Laura. Maybe she's got some news."

Rowan turned slowly. Not her first choice of visitors, but if she had some word, good or bad, Rowan would take her.

"Any news?" Laura asked as she neared. "Did they catch him?"

"We were hoping you could tell us," Mike said.

She shrugged one shoulder and lifted her palms. "I have no idea. He followed me to base from the bar, so we took the plan to the next level. He showed up at legal like Jess thought he would. That's the last I saw of him. I haven't seen Phillip since I left him at the bar."

"Could you use a cup of coffee?"

Laura gave Mike a half-hearted laugh. "I could use a stiff drink, but I'll settle for coffee. Do you know where there's a machine?"

"I'll get it for you."

Mike hurried off before Rowan could offer to go in his place.

Nothing like being stuck in an awkward situation.

She pivoted on the ball of her foot to resume pacing. Laura stepped into her path.

"I'm glad he's gone. It'll give us a chance to talk."

"I don't think there's really anything we need to talk about, Captain Cushing." Rowan tried to sidestep the woman. Again, Laura stood in her way.

"I disagree. We need to talk about Phillip. He's not the man you used to know." She gave a humorless chuckle. "Oddly enough, he's not the man I thought I knew, either."

Rowan raised her hand. "Please save the lecture about me standing between him and his career. I've heard it before. Phillip's decisions are his to make and I doubt very seriously if he would be willing to risk everything just for me."

"Then you must be blind."

Rowan stared at her, mouth agape.

"That man loves you. He *loves* you. He's one hell of an attorney, but if you think he normally goes to this much trouble to clear his clients, you're wrong. He leaves the grunt work to someone else." Laura drew in a breath before she continued. "There's no reason to keep up a facade with you. We've both slept with the man and we both know it. But in the year I've known Phillip, I've never once seen him look at a woman the way he looks at you. He'd give it up for you — all of it and not because of your son, either. Because of *you*. Just make sure it's what you both want first. I'd hate to see either of you regret it down the line."

Rowan lifted her chin, trying to be stalwart when all she wanted to do was cry. "You're wrong."

Laura shrugged. "We'll see. Whatever the two of you decide, I wish you the best of luck and happiness."

She brightened with Mike's return and held out her hand for the coffee. "You're a lifesaver."

Rowan sank into the nearest chair and covered her weary eyes with her hand. She longed to believe what Laura said, but it seemed too perfect. *Isn't that what I always I told herself? If it seems too good to be true, then it is?*

"Here they come."

With Mike's words, she glanced up, heart pounding. Phillip and Jess strode toward them, broad smiles cutting across their faces.

"You were perfect." Phillip laughed and swung Laura into his arms, spilling her precious coffee to the floor.

"Put me down, you big ox. I was petrified. Did you catch him?"

He set her on her feet. "Right in the trap. He finally gave a full confession." He plopped into the chair beside Rowan, nudged her leg and gave her a wink.

She leaned as close as propriety allowed, longing to drop her head to his shoulder, to wrap her arms around him in an embrace so tight he could never break free.

Her gaze fell to the bruise marring his cheek. By instinct she reached for it then pulled her hand down.

"Looks like he didn't give up without a fight."

He dabbed at his chin. "Let's just say he didn't give up easily."

Jess snorted. "Don't let him pass this off as nothing, Rowan. If it weren't for Phillip's help, there's no telling what might have happened tonight."

She glanced at the bruise once more. Whatever had happened, she didn't want to know—at least not right now.

"So…why did he do it?" she asked.

Phillip shook his head. "Apparently his divorce left him financially strapped, mentally unbalanced and desperate. Not a good combination. When he caught the scrap dealers stealing copper and aluminum from the training areas, he realized a potential source of income, so he cut a deal with them."

Jess settled into one of the chairs with a sigh. "They expanded their operation to include just about anything they could get their hands on. According to Collins, the money was too good to pass up. Each time there was the potential for getting caught, they caused an accident."

"Which is where I bumbled in," Rowan said.

Jess nodded. "He said he never meant to kill Kemp. He wanted to get out of there without getting caught. When the two of you showed up, he knocked you out. Kemp didn't fall as easily when Collins hit him. In fact, he fought back. They fell together. The gun went off, shooting Kemp in the head. Collins knew he had to cover his tracks, so he dragged you over to where the body was, put the gun in your hand and fired a shot into Kemp's thigh."

"End of story," Mike said.

Rowan scowled. "It might not have been intentional, but he can forget about getting any sympathy from me. I still hope he rots in jail for killing Charlie and putting my family through hell."

"He'll be doing hard time in a federal penitentiary for the rest of his life, Rowan. I promise." The set to Jess' jaw affirmed his words.

Phillip laced his fingers together then cracked his knuckles. "All we need now is the dismissal of charges against you from the Commanding General. With luck and good timing, we should have that on Monday morning."

"Good. That gives me all day tomorrow to catch up on my sleep," Laura said. "I'm going back to the BOQ. Does anyone need a ride?"

Mike stood and stretched the kinks from his back. "Can you drop me off at my place? I'm looking forward to a night back in my own bed. See the rest of you Monday."

Rowan watched the two walk away. With each step, they got closer until their hands interlaced. She smiled. They'd make a cute couple.

"How are our patients?" Phillip's whisper tickled her ear.

"Sound asleep, resting comfortably and on the mend. Mom and Ian can go home on Monday. Zach will need to stay at least until the end of the week. His fever needs to come down and the doctors are monitoring him for infection from the gunshot or the broken leg. I spoke to one of his brothers and let him know what happened. He's on his way here, even though I told him Zach was going to be fine. I also called Claudia. She's worried sick."

He patted her knee. "I'll call her when we get home. It's been a long night, but it was worth it to get this over with. We should be getting some rest ourselves."

Resting his hand at the small of her back, Phillip led her to the van. Rowan watched for some indication that Laura was right—or wrong, for that matter. Phillip drove them to her house in silence. It was just as well. Rowan didn't feel like talking things out. She didn't want to hash out the demise of a relationship that shouldn't exist, to be the catalyst that took away what fleeting moments of pleasure remained between them.

They walked into the house arm in arm. Phillip flicked on the light and tossed the keys to the kitchen counter.

"Sure is quiet here without Ian and Oscar."

Rowan wrapped her arms around his waist and hugged him tight. He covered her lips with a deep kiss then set her back.

"I need to shower. Join me?"

Smiling, she slipped her hand in his and led him up the stairs. They took their time massaging tense muscles under mountains of soapsuds and rediscovering all those sensual places she'd memorized years ago. They loved until she ached then loved some more. Wrapped in each other's arms, the bedroom drapes open to the dawn, she watched the sunrise over the horizon with Phillip and another precious day of togetherness begin.

Rowan forced away all logic and the need to rationalize every action. Hope for a future? She didn't care. This was now and now was damn good. If it were destined that she only had him for brief moments of time, she'd take it.

With a sigh, she curled her body next to his and fell asleep, only to wake when he nudged her to get ready for visiting hours at the hospital. Their day ended as it had begun, together. Then Monday morning arrived and with it, old doubts returned to nag.

They dressed in their respective uniforms — the captain and the staff sergeant — and drove to the office in separate vehicles — the attorney and the client. Knowing looks, sweet smiles, gentle touches, even so much as that tender hand against her back as he opened the door for her lay hidden away. Rowan hated the deception and the rules that made it imperative.

They sat in the courtroom, side by side — prim, proper, model Marines. The wait was agonizing as Colonel Scott gathered his troops.

He'd always had a flair for the dramatic. This time, Rowan didn't care. If he wanted to drag the entire office into the courtroom to announce her charges were dismissed, that was fine with her. Anything to get this over with.

Until she heard the words, she feared it might not be true. Then that little phrase she'd been waiting for came.

"The charges against Staff Sergeant Rowan A. McKinley are hereby dismissed."

Rowan sagged with relief. A cheer erupted with the announcement. Ellen reached from behind and hugged her tightly.

"Good work, Captain." The colonel shook Phillip's hand and turned to Jess, Laura, Mike and Rowan. "All of you."

He personally congratulated each one in turn until he came to Rowan, then clutched her by the upper arms before hugging her.

"You've been through quite a lot. You take the rest of the week off. Make sure that boy of yours and your mother are up and running."

"Thank you, sir. And thank you for standing by me."

He held her at arm's length. "That's what we do for our Marines."

His business look fell into place, but his regard for her still twinkled in his eyes as he addressed Phillip, Mike, Jess and Laura. "I'm going to see that each of you is given a letter of commendation. Now…everyone back to work."

Her coworkers rushed up, full of congratulations and demands for a party to celebrate her return.

"Why does it always have to be at my house? Okay, I give up," she said, laughing. "This Friday night. But I'm not forking over the money for this, and you bring your own booze, as well as help clean up."

Everyone filtered down the hall from the courtroom back to their offices until Rowan was standing outside alone with Phillip. Separate once more — still.

His voice was low, gentle. "I'm going to follow Laura back to Camp Pendleton, but I'll be back Friday after work. Do you need any help with Ian before I leave?"

Avoiding his gaze, Rowan shook her head. "Jess will be watching Mom. Ian will be fine. He's really a pathetic little sweetie when he's not feeling well, not any trouble at all."

Phillip glanced at his watch. "I've got time to pick up Oscar from the vet before I go."

"I'll take care of it. He can stay with us until you come back up. Ian will like it and Oscar will give him some company while he recovers. Besides, it'll give you a little more riding room."

How much longer are we going to stand here talking like polite strangers?

"You don't know how hard it is to stand here and not kiss you good-bye." His voice was the barest of whispers, meant for her alone. "I love you, Rowan. I'll find a way to work things out. Trust me."

Then he caught her elbow and guided her back to his office, where he shut the door and kissed her hard. All Rowan wanted to do was cry. It was nine years ago all over again. Rowan didn't think she could take it a second time. Yet, she hadn't trusted him that first time and look how things turned out. The power, it seemed, was in her hands. He was offering her hope, a chance to be together, if only behind closed doors.

Fleeting moments of pleasure. She'd take them and deal with the pain, if it was to come, later. Trust him? Yes, this time she would.

Rowan forced a smile. "I'll see you Friday night then. Drive carefully."

Walking away was one of the hardest things Phillip had ever had to do. With each step, he forced his gaze forward. Nothing could jeopardize his plans. Not now. Not when they were so close to realization.

Propped against her car, Laura waited for him in the parking lot, her foot resting on the bumper of his Mustang. A month ago, that sight would have been enough to set his teeth grinding. Now he just stepped over her leg and opened the door.

"You're going to resign, aren't you?" she asked.

"I've already talked to our colonel. Faxed my resignation to him this morning. He's calling Headquarters Marine Corps personally to see if it can be expedited. Colonel Scott is backing him up."

"Did you tell her?"

Phillip shook his head. "I didn't want to get her hopes up — or mine, either, for that matter. They may not release me from my commitment."

"That's a mighty big risk to take without talking to her. How do you know she even wants you in her life permanently?"

Phillip stared ahead. "I don't, but it's a chance I'm willing to take. This time, I'm not letting her go."

He slipped behind the wheel and started the engine. "Last one home's a rotten egg."

Smiling, she jumped into her car.

It was the longest drive of his life, followed by the loneliest night. Anxiety roosted in his stomach. Work the next morning was impossible to concentrate on. By noon, he got the official word. Still it took four more agonizingly long days before the approval for his resignation was in his hands. He stared at it, then with a smile, he pulled a last cigar from his desk drawer and went to the back step. The door behind him opened the minute he lit up.

"I'm glad someone around here can celebrate," Laura told him. "Have you heard who received new orders? Zach Taylor is being reassigned to Twentynine Palms."

Eyes dancing with mischief, Phillip glanced at her over his shoulder. "Oh, he's going to love that. I can't wait to get back up there and be the first to tell him."

"It's always about you, isn't it?"

Phillip laughed. "Not so much anymore."

"I've got orders there, too."

"Somehow, I don't think you'll mind so much." Grinning, he gave her a wink.

Laura blushed and slugged him.

"I've got a lot to do, but I'll be heading up to Twentynine Palms tonight. I still have to clean out my office and load everything from my house, so I'll be coming back Sunday night if you want to tag along."

"No, thanks. Mike's coming down here for the weekend." Laura leaned forward and brushed a brief kiss across his cheek. "You're doing the right thing, Phillip. Now put out that stinky cigar and get moving. You do have a lot to get done."

Indeed, he did, and there really seemed like no time better than now to get started. One more victory puff and he ground out the cigar. He hardly knew where to begin. Anticipation made him as giddy as a teenager on his first date.

Packing up his house was first on the list, but it would be hours before he could leave. He didn't think he could stand to wait around in the nearly empty cottage filled with boxes that long. Without Rowan, Ian and Oscar, it was worse than a tomb, lonely and depressing, no longer a home.

A smile curved his lips. Home was where Rowan and Ian were. And tonight, he was going home. There was one more piece of business he had to finish.

He'd spent the better part of the week trying to decide if he should even attempt to talk to Sally Kemp. A check of the psychiatric ward showed her grief had put her over the edge. Her children remained in foster care. She was beyond reason.

Phillip tried to tell himself that it wasn't his place to interfere with the woman's life or her treatment, but the thought of those children in a foster home tore at his conscience. They had lost their father and now their mother. He'd never be able to live with himself if he didn't at least try to see the woman. Her doctor agreed it wouldn't hurt.

She was waiting by the barred window when Phillip arrived. Her face was red and swollen from tears. According to her doctor, she spent the better part of each day crying. Her hospital gown engulfed her. Hard to believe that a person could go so far downhill so quickly.

"Mrs. Kemp?"

She forced her head in his direction. "Do I know you?"

"I'm Phillip Stuart." He extended his hand. Sally never saw it.

He pulled up a chair and sat across from her. "I know things are difficult for you, but I thought you would like to know that we caught the man who killed your husband. He'll be going to jail for a long, long time."

"The man? Rowan McKinley killed my husband."

Her voice was bitter, angry. Where grief shadowed her face before, rage now existed.

Phillip covered her hands with his. "No, Sally. She didn't."

In detail, he explained it all. With each word, the tears returned in a constant flow down her cheeks. Afterward, her lips formed the words 'thank you' but no sound came out.

"I loved him so much," she finally managed to say.

"I know. I understand. But now you have to pull yourself together for the children that love gave to you."

Sally pulled in a breath and gave a single nod.

* * * *

Phillip forced the lid closed on his fourth suitcase. All that remained were his uniforms. Zach could have those. Phillip knew he'd never need them again.

A car pulled up outside. It was probably his landlord coming by to drop off his rental closure papers. He opened the door to set his suitcase outside. It wasn't his landlord.

Phillip pulled himself to his full height and stared at his father. It took more nerve than he could imagine for the man to show up now. His very presence screamed interference and intrusion.

"What do you want, Donald?" As if he couldn't guess.

His father stalked toward him, nostrils of his hawk-like nose flaring. "I thought it necessary to pay you a personal visit." His calm tone belied the squall on his face.

Phillip tensed. "And I thought I made myself clear when we spoke the last time. I have no desire to see you — ever."

His father waved the words away as if they were inconsequential. For him they were because they were not what he wanted to hear. "I put that down to the heat of the moment, forgotten by now."

Phillip snorted. "You have a convenient memory when it suits you. What do you want? I'm a little busy."

"You could at least extend me the courtesy of inviting me in."

"Courtesy is the last thing I owe you. Now...you claim your visit has a purpose?"

Donald propped himself against a porch post and studied his nails. "Associates of mine indicate you're thinking of resigning your commission."

"Correction. I *have* resigned my commission."

"It can be easily reversed." He looked up. "I'll admit I was against you joining the Marine Corps, but when I saw the political advantages it gave you—"

Phillip tossed out a laugh. "You're the one with political aspirations, not me. But since no one seems to want to elect you, even for the position of dog catcher, you seem to be ill-suited for politics."

"Why close the door on a great opportunity?"

"For who? You?" *The man is priceless.* In Donald Stuart's eyes, life was supposed to revolve around him.

Phillip picked up his bags and walked to his car. His father followed.

"Everything I've done in my life has been for your—"

Phillip whirled around. "Don't start with that crap. Nothing you did was for my benefit. It was for yours— your image, your goals. The great Donald Stuart. My God, when I was ten years old, you took me aside and told me not to call you Dad anymore because it didn't look professional, not that you were much of a father before then. You never bothered with Claudia or me until you realized our possible advantage to you, then you insinuated yourself into every aspect of our lives."

Donald's lips thinned. "It's that woman talking, isn't it?"

"What woman? Rowan?" Phillip opened the trunk and stuffed one suitcase inside. "Leave Rowan out of this. You know very well that all of your issues are with Claudia and me, now that we've taken great pains to distance ourselves from you."

"How can I leave trash like Rowan McKinley out of this? She's been nothing but trouble for us since the minute you met her. You don't even know if this brat is really yours. Her type will sleep with anybody."

Never in his life had Phillip wanted to hit someone as much as he did now. He settled for a steady glare he hoped conveyed his contempt for the man. "I'm not going to dignify that with an answer."

He tossed another suitcase into the trunk.

Donald caught the handle. "Don't you see how she's turned us against each other? First you, then your sister and now your mother."

Phillip straightened. "Mom?"

His father adopted that haughty air of superiority. "She's got some feminist notion in her head about striking out on her own. She actually intends to divorce me over this incident with your little friend. The woman needs psychiatric help."

"Personally, I think she deserves a medal for putting up with you all these years."

Phillip snatched the last bag from his father's grasp and tossed it into the trunk with the others. "I'm glad to see she's finally wised up. I'll have to call her with congratulations when I get home. As for you" — he slammed the trunk closed — "let me make myself perfectly clear. I *never* want to see or hear from you again. You are to stay away from Rowan, my child and me."

"Aren't you going to include your sister and mother in your cozy little group?"

Phillip grinned. "Sounds like they're pretty good at taking care of themselves." His humor faded. "Stay away. If you don't, I'll slap a restraining order on you so fast it will boggle your mind."

He swung into the Mustang, gunned the powerful engine then drove away, leaving Donald staring after him in a cloud of dust.

* * * *

Butterflies did somersaults in Rowan's stomach. Phillip would be here any minute. She prayed for the composure to greet him with casual indifference, lest those crowded into her party see the true extent of her feelings. Yet she couldn't keep her gaze from wandering down the road for that first glimpse of his Mustang. With its appearance, her heart raced into double-time.

"Dad's here!" Ian sprinted for the driveway with Oscar close behind. "And Mom, look who's with him!"

Phillip swooped the boy into his arms. Rowan felt a catch in her breath. What would she do on that horrible day when and if he came to tell her that he was marrying someone else? How could she hold her head high when her heart would be shattered into a thousand pieces?

Zach crawled from the car, dragging a set of crutches. "I'm out, I'm free and I'm starved." He gave Rowan a quick hug. "Hospital food is terrible. I still can't believe you refused to sneak in any good food for me. What's to eat?"

"Hamburgers, hot dogs, steak, chicken… You name it and we've got it," Rowan said with a smile.

"Great. Then next week you can help me find a place to live. I've got orders to this godforsaken place."

"I see." She tucked her arms over her chest. "Maybe we can enlist Claudia's help in your quest for accommodations."

"Claudia?" His dumbstruck look gave the impression he didn't have a clue who Claudia could be. Rowan knew better.

"She'll be here any minute to meet Ian."

Zach sagged under the weight of her announcement. "Ian, show me the way to the food. I need to fortify myself."

Ian giggled. "You know the way."

"I'm so faint from hunger that I can barely stand." Zach rolled his eyes theatrically and faked a wobble.

Laughing, Ian grabbed Zach's arm and guided him toward the picnic table, Oscar galloping ahead of them.

Phillip chuckled. "I see they've been having a great time."

"They sure have. Ian loves that crazy dog and I'm almost certain the feeling is mutual. Although Oscar's loyalties switch when food's involved. I was wondering, Phillip. I know I should have asked this before now, but each night you called this week, I didn't think it was something to discuss over the phone. Could Oscar stay with us?"

"I have a better question." He took a step forward. "Can I?" Reaching around, he pulled a paper from his back pocket and placed it in her hands.

"What is it?"

"Marine Corps Headquarters approved my resignation."

Rowan could scarcely breathe. "Why?"

He slid his arms around her waist and pulled her close. "Why do you think? Rowan, I love you. I've always loved you. My heart has always been faithful to you. Marry me."

"Oh, Phillip, yes," she replied.

When he tilted his head to kiss her, she pulled back. "Phillip, someone might see."

He grinned and looked over her shoulder. "Somehow, I don't think they'll mind."

She turned around. Silence descended as each guest held up a toast in their honor. With a smile, she draped her arms around Phillip's neck.

"Mom and Jess are going to Vegas tomorrow to get married. Want to make it a double wedding?"

Phillip's kiss was his reply.

Epilogue

"How do I look? Do I look okay?"

Rowan shoved herself out of the chair stomach first and readjusted Laura's veil. "For the millionth time, you look beautiful."

"And Mike's here? Right?"

Stretching the kinks from her aching back, Rowan laughed. "Of course he's here."

"Yes, but..."

Rowan placed her hands over Laura's lips. "Enough already. He loves you and it's time to get you married."

It was a wonder she wasn't more nervous. Laura had certainly had more than her share of roadblocks since Mike's proposal six months ago. A recent court-martial case that had placed bride and groom on opposite sides had not only threatened to run over into the honeymoon but had also put the two at such odds that it had almost ruined the wedding.

At one point, the groom had even moved in with Phillip and Rowan when the bride had accused him of spying on her case notes. Thankfully, that little incident had blown over in less time than it had taken for Mike to pack his bags.

Two days ago, one bridesmaid had broken an ankle playing flag football. Another was battling the flu. The ring bearer hadn't stopped crying during rehearsal.

Then there was the shortage of hotel rooms for the out-of-town guests. That meant borrowing space at the homes of friends. Ten of Mike's relatives were camping out at Phillip and Rowan's house, adding to Rowan's tension and shortening her temper. If it weren't for the help that Claudia, Emma and Phillip's mother had given these last few days, she might have exploded from the constant crush of people in her space.

Now all that was behind Laura and Mike. The sun beamed a blessing through the high church windows. Everything was finally going smoothly. Even the ring bearer was all smiles as he played tag with the flower girl.

Laura hugged her as close as Rowan's belly would allow. "You've been a godsend these last six months. I swear you've missed your calling. When you leave the Marine Corps, you should become a professional wedding planner. With your organizational skills—"

"Stop it. You'll have my head as big as my belly." She clapped her hands. "Okay, everyone line up. You know your cues. I'm going to take my seat. You're on your own from here."

Rowan tucked the bridal bouquet into Laura's shaking fingers, pulled the veil over her face then slipped into the church.

As promised, Claudia and Ellen had saved her a seat near the front. It was going to be a relief to finally sit down. She was glad she and Phillip had married quickly in Las Vegas. Big weddings were not for her. Her pregnancy, combined with helping Laura plan this wedding, had exhausted her more than she'd anticipated. Thankfully, Phillip had been there to lean on when she'd needed it.

It seemed they had been blessed the last year. Phillip'd had no difficulty finding a job as a teacher at the local high school. In the evenings, he taught law courses at the community college and extension university. He spent his spare time with the scouts or coaching Ian's sports teams. Then there was his dedication to her.

He never hesitated to lend a hand, but the instant he'd discovered she was carrying their second child, she'd become a pampered princess. When morning sickness had overwhelmed her, Phillip had been there to hold her head and mop the sweat from her brow. Heavy work was forbidden. Back massages and tummy rubs had become a daily event as she'd grown Through appointments, ultrasounds and during all facets of the pregnancy, Phillip had stayed by her side.

She couldn't function without him and didn't know how she'd managed all these years without him. She never wanted to find out if she could again.

The music began, chasing away Rowan's thoughts. Mike and Phillip filed in and took their places. As he caught her eye, Phillip gave a wink. Rowan blushed.

To hide her smile, she turned with the guests to watch her handiwork unfold. The bridesmaids and groomsmen were all smiles. Zach supported his partner on his arm so skillfully that only those closest to Laura knew the bridesmaid had a broken ankle. Still, the best man stood out handsomely among the rest of the party.

Then the wedding march began. Rowan's smile faltered as a contraction took her breath away.

Oh, no. Not now.

Her back had been aching for more than a week, plus she had been having tiny twinges of pain for the last several days but nothing consistent. In fact, she had put it down to the stress of last-minute wedding preparations. Now, at the worst possible time, they hit her full force.

She gripped the back of the pew in front of her and focused her gaze on the bride, avoiding Phillip's gaze. It was a futile attempt at deception. Once Laura walked by, Rowan chanced a look at the head of the aisle.

Concern creased Phillip's forehead. He knew her better than she knew herself, often anticipating her needs before she could voice them. There was simply no keeping secrets from the man.

She gave a quick shake of her head. His frown grew. The ceremony drew his faltering attention back to the bride and groom. As Mike took Laura's hand, the contraction passed.

Thank goodness. Nothing should spoil this day for Laura. Rowan refused to let the arrival of one tiny baby set the couple back. In a few hours, everything would return to normal. Mike and Laura would be married. Her house would be her own.

Another contraction seized her.

Rowan tensed and sucked in a breath through clenched teeth.

On either side of her, Ellen and Claudia leaned in close. "Are you all right?" they whispered in unison.

Rowan forced a nod but the smile refused to come.

"I know I said I wanted to be with you when the baby came, but I didn't mean literally. If I had known you were going to pull a stunt like this, I would have stayed at Emma's with Ian and the grandmothers," Claudia said. Her normally cool voice bordered on panic. "Please, don't have it here."

Rowan could hear the hidden plea. "I can't help it," she whispered back. "He's not due for another week."

Ellen raised her eyebrows. "You must have had a back-up plan, just in case—"

"No, I don't have a back-up plan, just in case," Rowan snapped.

"Testy, too," Ellen tsked.

"She's been that way for a week," Claudia added.

"Baby must be coming quick."

Rowan prayed that wasn't so. It couldn't be. Her labor with Ian had lasted a good twelve hours. But with the priest's first reading, her water broke.

Mortification paralyzed her as the puddle beneath her grew. She wanted to burst into tears and would have if she wasn't afraid doing so would draw attention her way.

The pain intensified with each minute that passed. Only through sheer will did she manage to get through the too-long mass. The wedding was beautiful, but she saw it all through a haze of pain.

She waited, avoiding Phillip's questioning gaze, until Mike and Laura walked back down the aisle. Once they'd passed, she clutched Ellen's arm.

"Phone nine-one-one. The baby's coming. Now!"

What came out as a whisper rippled through the guests like wildfire, reaching Phillip before he arrived at the receiving area outside the church.

A crowd swarmed around Rowan. She saw Phillip pushing his way back up the aisle, but the exiting guests were blocking his way.

She was conscious of the priest plucking at her sleeve, urging her to a side room while Ellen begged her to lie down on the pew. It was a tug-of-war, with Rowan as the rope and the guests as spectators. Madness. Insanity. All she wanted was Phillip.

She heard his barked command. A path cleared and he slipped those strong arms around her.

"It's okay, honey. I'm here now."

With a nod, she relaxed against him. Yes, all was right with her world. Phillip was with her just as he had been since the day they'd been married—her partner, her love, her life.

He wrapped his fingers around hers. "Hold on, sweetheart. The paramedics are on the way."

"Tell that to your son."

Phillip placed his hand on her belly. Tears glistened unshed in his silver eyes. "Patience, little guy. Your mom and I would like a doctor present."

Sirens blared from outside. Seconds later, a paramedic rushed in.

"Give her room! Everyone back!" He skidded to his knees beside Rowan. "How close, ma'am?"

"Real close," she said in a rush of breath.

"Think you can make it to the hospital?"

Rowan nodded, despite her misgivings.

Phillip smiled and brushed a kiss against her temple. "Then let's go bring James into the world."

They made it as far as the ambulance.

She grabbed Phillip's hand and yanked the gurney to a stop. "I can't. Not in there. It's too closed in."

"It's no different than getting in your van." He motioned the paramedics on, gripping her fingers tight as they lifted her into the ambulance. "Look at me, honey. Just look at me and everything will be all right. Remember, I'm your coach. I'm supposed be the boss."

"Not on your best day." Any further remarks or claustrophobic fears were wiped away by the force of the next contraction. Following his lead, Rowan breathed. Five minutes later, James McKinley Stuart slipped into the world, red-faced and squalling.

Exhausted yet elated, Rowan let the paramedic tuck her newborn son into her arms. One look at the shock on Phillip's face forced a giggle from her throat.

"What's the matter, sweetheart?"

"He's so tiny." Phillip's eyes were riveted upon the squalling red bundle.

"And already stubborn. I imagine we'll have our hands full with this one."

Phillip relaxed. "Maybe… You know that was easier than I expected."

Rowan rolled her eyes, and gave an exhausted sigh. "Then next time you can give birth."

He smiled and dropped a kiss to James's head, then hers. "Anything for you, love. Anything."

Tears overwhelmed her. "Then I'd like a little girl next time. Okay?"

"My pleasure."

"I love you, Phillip." Her answer was choked but she couldn't tell if it was from the tears of joy or the loving kiss he pressed to her lips. *Always faithful. No doubt about it.*

Want to see more from this author? Here's a taster for you to enjoy!

Rules of Engagement: Ice Princess
Caitlyn Willows

Excerpt

Sharp, painful jabs of sunlight forced open Claudia Stuart's eyelids. She squinted against her pillow, trying to focus on her surroundings through bleary eyes. *Why the hell did I leave the drapes open?* She closed them every night, her protection against the world.

"Oh my God."

Her soft mewl of agony felt like a shout. Wincing, she fought against the pounding beat of a headache reverberating throughout her aching body. She tried to center herself by focusing on any one part of her anatomy that wasn't sore. None existed.

A faint, persistent sound filtered through her pain. The foghorns from San Francisco Bay had never seemed this close before. Her senses slowly emerged from the blanketing haze. She wasn't in San Francisco. She was in Las Vegas. And there was an odd noise coming from the far side of the king-size bed.

Stretching out a shaky hand to balance herself against the spinning room, Claudia brushed against something warm, solid and most definitely male. She held her breath and twisted around to see a dark head partially buried in a mass of tangled covers. Horror clenched her gut.

Franklin?

The very idea churned her stomach. Franklin had made his intentions clear. She'd made hers even clearer — *no*. If he'd slipped something in her drink and taken advantage, she'd see him behind bars.

Claudia shook her head. *Not possible.* Franklin was in San Francisco. He had no idea she'd gone to Vegas. He thought she was on vacation, visiting her brother in Twentynine Palms, California.

So, who am *I in bed with and why the hell can't I remember how I wound up like this?*

She squinted at the waves of dark hair.

Wavy? With growing horror, she realized that the hair was clipped military-style — sides cut tight and the top allowed to grow a little longer, permitting the errant waves.

"Oh my God!"

The loud croak of disbelief aggravated her headache. Claudia didn't care. This was too horrible to believe. *It can't be. It just can't. Of all the men in the world, why this one?* The one who did things to her insides she would deny to her last breath. The one who made her want what she refused to allow again...ever.

She lashed out under the covers with her foot, whacking Zach Taylor squarely in the ass. "Get out! What are you doing in my bed?"

A muffled 'oomph' and a string of curses emerged from the pile of bedding. "What the hell?"

Zach bolted upright, clutching the edge of the sheet to his chest like a maiden bride. It did little to cover his naked body.

Make that gorgeously naked body.

Claudia shut down the fuzzy image of running her fingers over his carved chest. *What is he doing here – in my hotel room, in my bed? More to the point, why is he naked?* And she, too, for that matter. But if the tingle between her legs was any indication, she already knew the answer.

What have I done?

Scowling, Zach pushed himself upright.

Nothing made sense and all her thoughts were a jumble. She dredged up her only defense – the one that had failed her last night – control.

"I said get out."

She reared her foot for another attack against his oh-so-fine ass. With a lithe twist, Zach avoided the kick and pinioned her leg under his arm. Electricity zinged up her thigh, aiming to roost in the warmth at the top.

His quick jerk pulled her off-balance. She flopped back down onto the bed. The sudden movement brought waves of nausea.

Her distress must have been plainly written on her face. He jackknifed over the edge of the bed, scooped up a nearby trashcan and shoved it under her nose. Two used condoms stared back at her. It was all her stomach needed to tip it over the edge. Ignoring the trashcan, she dashed to the bathroom, trying and failing to drag a blanket with her.

She fell to her knees before the toilet with images of those condoms etched in her brain and threw up, naked and puking in a hotel toilet, fighting her hair. Humiliation overwhelmed her. Zach would never let her live down this moment.

Kill me now.

"Here… I got you."

Zach wrapped the blanket around her then pulled back her hair.

Claudia clutched the edges of the soft cover in one hand as another wave overcame her.

"Why are you being so nice to me?" she asked when she recovered.

"I'm thinking I might have a masochistic streak in me," he replied.

After what seemed like hours of wrenching heaves, she levered herself upright, still shaking.

"Do you want to go lie down or stay here for a while?" He combed his finger through her hair — petting her, soothing her, breaking down her defenses.

She shrugged his hand away. "Bed."

He helped her stand. "Rinse and spit first. You'll feel better." He ran a glass of water for her then held it to her mouth. She complied with his suggestion, ignoring their reflections in the wall-sized mirror. Zach cupped her elbow and helped her back to the other room. Once she caught sight of it, Claudia wished she'd remained in the bathroom.

The room was an unholy mess. Clothes — hers *and* his — were strewn from one corner to the other. A pair of panty hose was draped over the lampshade. A bottle of champagne was upside down in the ice bucket. Another rested unopened on the desk. Room service trays were piled with dirty dishes. Money in denominations ranging from twenty to one-hundred-dollar bills lay scattered over the bed and on the floor.

She sank to the edge of the bed and buried her head in her hands. Zach left her, only to return and press a cool, damp washcloth into her hand. She ran the cloth over her face and tried to gather her wits.

"Here." He held out a glass of water and a handful of aspirin. "I think you could use these."

She glanced up. He'd pulled on a pair of white boxers but hadn't bothered with a shirt or shoes. His muscular chest was bare. A sprinkling of hair that narrowed to a distracting line leading down into his waistband grabbed her attention. More hazy images intruded — wandering her tongue down the bunny trail while she divested him of his boxers. At least she'd maintained some measure of power and control last night, but how much had she lost?

Claudia accepted the glass and the pills with shaking hands. She drank, darting surreptitious glances toward her unwanted companion.

Captain Zach Taylor, attorney and United States Marine, epitomized everything she distrusted in a man. Darkly handsome with full, sensuous lips and a flashing dimple, he represented to her the typical carefree philanderer — the kind of man who could break a woman's heart and never think twice about it. She'd already had her heart broken once and that was enough to last a lifetime. Her older brother Phillip had introduced them years ago, and ever since, the antagonism had been mutual.

Yet that was nothing compared to the lust-filled fantasies of him dancing through her head every time she made herself come. Her first glance at the man had sent her heart and stomach somersaulting with glee. All her hard-won control had sifted away. Zach was the one in charge and she'd done everything in her power to keep him from realizing that.

'You need to loosen up, Claudia Stuart, and stop being such a prude.'

Zach's teasing remark had been made in front of a crowd of friends at a Christmas party in Phillip's home — mostly fellow attorneys from the Judge Advocate's Office at Camp Pendleton. The jibe had drawn a big laugh from the Marines. Zach had been one of them, and his personality was in a league of its own.

She recalled that he had wanted her to give him a simple kiss under the mistletoe. Cold rejection had been her answer, delivered publicly to humiliate and discourage further interest. In retaliation, he'd dubbed her Ice Princess. The nickname had stuck — and so had the animosity and that damnable unrelenting want for him.

She'd let him egg her on at that party. There'd been a stupid bet. She'd lost. The price? That blasted mistletoe kiss. But there hadn't been anything simple about it. Claudia would never forget the fire, the raw sensuality that had engulfed her, threatening her carefully erected defenses. She swore the heat from his erection that had been wedged between them had branded her. There were times she could still feel it throbbing against her. She'd done her best to avoid a repeat incident. The only time Zach had ever been in her bed was in her fantasies. Until now…

Claudia put down the glass, forcing a calmness she didn't feel. "It looks like we robbed a bank."

"Hit the jackpot, as I recall."

"I remember something like that, but it's about all." She rubbed at the ache in her head. "God, this is my worst nightmare."

Zach leaned against the dresser and stared at his toes. "I've never had a woman complain before, but in this case, I'd have to agree."

Claudia soaked in the sight of him, standing there unguarded. Her focus wandered to the scar on his left biceps from a bullet wound. Old fear gripped her heart. He'd been injured trying to protect Phillip and Rowan's son the previous year. The news had brought her to her knees. She cared for him more than she'd ever admit, making her more determined than ever to never let him near her heart.

He lifted his gaze to hers, nailing her in place with its dark brown intensity. "We're married."

Claudia's jaw worked, but it seemed an eternity before she could push out the single word. "Impossible."

"But true," he replied.

He shoved away from his perch and walked to the desk. With a flick of his wrist, he dragged out a paper from underneath the champagne bottle. Thrusting it at her, he said, "I found this when I got the aspirin from my ditty bag."

Claudia craned her neck at the paper but refused to touch it. A different wave of nausea engulfed her.

United this day in Holy Matrimony, Zachary Stephen Taylor and Claudia Marie Stuart…

Their signatures were sprawled with untidy abandon at the bottom of the document. Two of the people who had accompanied them to Vegas had signed as witnesses.

"This has to be a joke," she muttered, although the document and the evidence throughout the room left no doubt.

"Oh, how I wish that were so."

A little melodramatic, but it certainly echoed her feelings.

"Listen—" he began.

Claudia held up her hand. "Put on a shirt or something. I don't need you walking around here half naked."

"What's wrong? Too tempting for you?"

There it was, that killer smile guaranteed to make a woman's heart stutter and her lady parts stand up and take notice—Claudia's included. She narrowed her eyes. "Why, you self-serving—"

"You're pretty tempting yourself." He waved a finger at her.

Claudia glanced down. She'd let the blanket fall, exposing her nudity. Nothing was left to the imagination. Embarrassment burned her from head to toe. With as much nonchalance as she could muster, she tugged up the blanket.

Zach half-grinned. "Pity. I was rather enjoying the view."

"Shut up."

His grin widened. "That's a fine way to speak to your new husband."

She rubbed her forehead and tried to control the laughter that was threatening to turn hysterical. "You would be the last person I'd consider marrying."

"But, to put it bluntly, that's what we did. We're husband and wife." He waved the certificate once more then tossed it to the rumpled bed. "Legally married by Reverend Thompson at the Vegas Chapel, wherever the hell that is." Any humor his voice had held was gone.

Claudia tugged the edges of the blanket closer. "I didn't think they were allowed to marry people who were drunk."

"Maybe they didn't realize how far gone we were" — he clutched his hands to his heart — "or maybe our boundless love and devotion for each other was too much to deny and they married us without delay."

"Cut the melodrama," she snapped. "In any event, it's something I plan to rectify at the earliest opportunity. I'm sure I won't hurt your feelings when I tell you I'll be filing for divorce as soon as possible."

"Summary dissolution," he corrected.

Here they were in this lousy predicament and he wanted to debate technicalities. "I need a lawyer."

"You just married one, remember?"

Claudia wanted to screech at him. Instead, she kept her voice level, maintaining her control, speaking in cold, clear tones that even a moron would have no trouble understanding. "I don't care what you call it or how it's done. I want out of this alcohol-induced nightmare. Do you understand me?"

"Loud and clear." The ice in his voice matched her own.

Good. At least there's something we agree on. Although, from the looks of the room, they'd found other mutually agreeable matters during the night.

Zach sighed. "Despite us being drunk, it appears we were careful. There are two condoms in this trash can, two more in the bathroom. I know you think I'm a sex-starved animal, but believe me, I have my limits. Frankly, I'm surprised to find more than two. But on the off chance we weren't and you discover you're—"

"I'm on the pill." Her body, her rules. She trusted no man—and certainly not a flimsy piece of rubber.

"Okay...good."

He sounded disappointed.

Trying to ignore her aching stomach and pounding head, she wrapped her blanket around her rigid body and headed for the bathroom to change. His silence followed her

Shutting the door, she caught a glimpse of herself in the mirror. Her platinum-blonde hair was flying out in all directions and her skin had a tinge best described as pasty in the overhead lighting. Her blue eyes were almost black in her pinched face. They were bloodshot, as well.

A stunning sight. She dropped the blanket and stepped into the shower.

"If you can't remember it then it never happened," she whispered into the biting chill of the spray.

But it *had* happened. If she wanted to deny the evidence around her, that was one thing, but her aching muscles and soreness were quite another.

Was it as wonderful as I'd fantasized? Damn, I wish I remembered.

Claudia laughed at the contradiction. She didn't want him, yet she wanted it to have been a night she'd remember forever? More input for those fantasies.

She warmed up the spray and let the water beat life into her system. Sinking into the bottom of the tub, she hugged her knees to her chest. She tried to focus on the last twenty-four hours and figure out where she'd faltered, where her defenses had been breached.

Her sister-in-law Rowan had talked her into going to a wedding. Phillip had been the best man. Zach had been a groomsman. Immediately following the ceremony, Rowan delivered a son, after successfully hiding the fact she was in labor *during* the ceremony.

Then there had been the wedding reception. Drink had flowed. Claudia had abstained. At some point, the wedding party had decided to take a road trip to Vegas. They'd wanted to borrow Phillip's brand-new minivan. He'd agreed, on one condition—Claudia must drive. She'd been the only sober one. She'd agreed as a favor for her brother.

They'd arrived at midnight with Zach and six other people. All Claudia had wanted to do was find a room and go to sleep. But, as usual, she'd allowed Zach to bait her.

'Just one slot. Play just one. I'll even give you the dollar.'

Anything to shut him up and put much-needed distance between them so the buzz he always gave her would die. She'd fed the dollar in...and had gotten a thousand back. The cocktail waitress had brought one drink after another. She and Zach had gambled and kept winning. Champagne, wine and beer had mixed with lethal intensity.

She dropped her head to her knees. A vague memory of one hell of a kiss with both of them plastered against the slot machine drifted into her foggy senses. A glint of gold and diamonds caught her eye. He'd even bought her a beautiful ring. None of it made any sense.

They didn't get along. Their constant sniping at each other proved that. Hell, she'd fueled it to save her heart. *How in the world could we have gotten married?*

A knocking at the bathroom door startled her from her thoughts. She tensed, afraid he might barge in.

"What do you want?" she shouted.

"I have to pee," he snapped back.

"Can't you wait?"

"You've been in here for half an hour already. I can't wait much longer. If you don't come out, I'm coming in whether you like it or not. I'm giving you another five minutes."

Claudia balled her hands into fists and stood. It was going to be a long drive back to Twentynine Palms.

Home of Erotic Romance

Sign up for our newsletter and find out about all our romance book releases, eBook sales and promotions, sneak peeks and FREE romance books!

About the Author

Blessed (or cursed) with a vivid imagination, award-winning author Caitlyn Willows eventually learned to turn that talent inward. Readers will find deep emotions and sizzling sensuality seamlessly woven into her action-filled stories. Believing life is to be lived and felt, not merely watched, Caitlyn delivers real-to-life characters in unforgettable tales of love, adventure, and always steamy passion. No one is more surprised than she at the direction life has taken her. She is also a mosaic artist and an avid crafter with a passion for cross-stitch. Caitlyn lives in the beautiful desert of Southern California with her husband (a genealogist). She is always on the lookout for the next interesting tidbit that will help fill her writing well.

Caitlyn loves to hear from readers. You can find her contact information, website details and author profile page at https://www.totallybound.com